Cool air dri
the scent o

Music floated through the corridor, the seductive undertone hauntingly familiar. The music was hypnotic, mesmerizing. Tess could barely think over the loud beat of her heart.

Every sense screamed to beware. She was about to come face-to-face with her stalker, her biggest fan. But over the hammering of her heart and accelerated senses, her will to put an end to this deadly game prevailed. She had to face him, find out who was behind this bizarre masquerade. Anticipation mounting, she made the turn at the end of the corridor and came to a riveting halt.

A female wax gargoyle stood in the doorway, long blonde hair billowing in the breeze. Her glass eyes shimmered with madness, an eerie smile on her face. In one hand, she held a mission bell, the other reaching out for a candle.

Music played from the old phonograph, the plucking of guitar strings laced with seduction. A breeze blew in through open terrace doors, stirring the sweet scent of jasmine from the candelabras.

Two wax nymphs stood at the bar, glass eyes shining bright in the candlelight, pliable fingers wrapped around flutes of pink champagne. Lit cigarettes burned in ashtrays. From behind the bar, a winged monster served drinks.

In the center of the ballroom, two gargoyles held a pose as if they were dancing, their waxy bodies closely pressed together, their reflections glowing in the mirrored ceiling. From the old phonograph in the corner, the hypnotic music played.

Tess gasped, her hand clasping her mouth. “Oh, my God!”

Mike raised his gun, circled the room. “Come out with your hands up. Hancock County Sheriff. Put your hands where I can see them.”

Her Biggest Fan

by

Sharon A. Donovan

Dear Aunt Nickey.

Thank you For being
one of my biggest fans.
Love,
Sharon

Her Biggest Fan

Contact Information: info@thewildrosepress.com

Cover Art by *Nicola Martinez*

The Wild Rose Press
PO Box 708
Adams Basin, NY 14410-0706
Visit us at www.thewildrosepress.com

Publishing History
First Crimson Rose Edition, 2010
Print ISBN 1-60154-813-3

Published in the United States of America

Dedication

To my mother, for inspiring me to write this book, based on the mysterious light of Shamrock.

Special thanks to my editor, Lori Graham, for all the hard work and dedication that went into the writing of this book.

Chapter One

From the sidelines, The Master snapped photos, his breathing raspy, excited. He licked his lips, anticipating the things he had planned for her. Contessa Kincaid, his princess. So beautiful, her face all aglow with fame. Pretty little princess for a day.

Strike a pose and smile for the camera. It's your moment in the sun.

Snap snap. Capture the moment.

That's it, princess, gotcha.

His hungry eyes took a slow, sensual journey up and down her incredible body, devouring every inch. Such a lovely face, green eyes sparkling like emeralds. Pure perfection. Hourglass figure, oh so voluptuous. Looking so hot in that slinky red dress, snug as a bug in a rug. Hold it, strike a pose. Princess in a centerfold.

He pictured all that lush mahogany hair tickling his skin, brushing his chest as it fanned out in wild disarray. Oh yeah. And her legs, oh so long and shapely. The things he had in mind to do to that body were downright sinful.

Snap snap.

That's it, princess. Give us a sultry come hither.

Snap, snap.

Time to go and set up my special surprise for you, princess.

****

Seated with her editor in the ballroom of the Waldorf-Astoria, New York Times best-selling author Tess Kincaid held her breath. This was it, the big moment. The presenter was about to announce the winner of the RITA award for best romantic suspense. Silence hummed off the cavernous walls.

"And the winner is…Tess Kincaid."

Thunderous applause exploded through the ballroom. Tess couldn't believe her ears. She sat there, dumbfounded, unable to catch her breath.

"You won!" Her editor elbowed her. "Congratulations, Tess. It's your turn to shine. Go on up there and accept your award. Go!"

Tess sprang to her feet, lighter than air, floating to the stage with the greatest of ease. She passed world-renowned authors who were seated along with editors and agents from some of the biggest publishing houses in New York. Her heart swelled with pride as she accepted the golden statuette.

"Thank you." She graced the audience with her most dazzling smile. "There simply are no words to describe how I feel at this moment. This is such an honor, a dream come true. I am truly humbled and will cherish this award for the rest of my life. Thank you from the bottom of my heart."

It took everything Tess had to control her trembling legs as she returned to her table and took her seat.

"To Tess Kincaid!" Champagne flutes touched, the tinkling of cut glass ringing across the room. "Here, here!"

Tess raised the glass to her lips, basking in the rapture of her first RITA. "And who says thirteen's unlucky? After twelve years of being nominated for best romantic suspense, I finally won. And it feels wonderful."

"Well, it's about time," her editor said. "Your thrillers are all best sellers. I'm willing to bet it was the hot-looking detective in your latest book who earned you the RITA. Do you know people are blogging about him? His midnight blue eyes; his full, sensual lips; his killer body? Even the beer he drinks. I hear sales of Argyle socks have skyrocketed since he wears them. Mega kudos, Tess."

"My head's still spinning." Tess finished her champagne on a wistful sigh. "What a grand finale for my time in New York. I sure will miss the Big Apple. As much as I adore the plays, Broadway, and the theater, not to mention all the major publishing houses, I left my heart in Bar Harbor. With inheriting Daddy's seaside home after his death…there's no time like the present."

"I'll miss you, my friend, especially all those power lunches at the Four Seasons. Are you sure this is what you want?"

Tess's eyes glistened. "Absolutely. I don't think my writing will suffer—in fact, just the opposite. The view overlooking Frenchman Bay is breathtaking, all those waves crashing over the bluffs. Oh, Edith, I'm telling you, the view is simply spectacular. If all that rugged beauty doesn't stir my creative muse, nothing will. There's just something so alluring about the sea, all the forbidden secrets the waves carry when they crest and fall. Watching them has a hypnotic effect on me, a writer's dream. I could stare out to sea for hours and come up with a dozen different storylines. You'll see."

"Well, good luck to you, my dear. Just a word of caution…while you do all this soul searching, don't wait too long before starting your next novel. You know what they say—use it or lose it."

Tess laughed, feeling incredibly giddy and lightheaded. She grabbed her beaded bag from the table and stood. "With all the excitement and not eating all day, this bubbly is going straight to my head. If I don't leave now, I'll get all weepy and make a fool of myself. I'd better go flag down a taxi. I was going to book a room for tonight, but since I live so close and have so much last minute packing to do,

I'd better hit the road. I'll be in touch when I get settled in Maine."

"Best of luck, Tess. Let me know if you need anything. I'm just a call away."

"Thanks for everything, Edith." Tess hugged her, a flutter of emotions swirling through her. "Where would I be without you? You made my writing shine right from the very first manuscript. I'll sure miss you, my friend, but once I get settled in Bar Harbor, promise me you'll come out for a visit. The kids would love playing on the beach and whale watching, just the way I did when I was a little girl. You have an open invitation any time."

****

Tess got out of the taxi when it came to a halt in front of her Park Place condo, paid the driver and scurried under the gold leaf canopy. Rain pounded on the awning like hailstones, the beat fast and furious. The doorman greeted Tess with a curt nod. "Good evening, Ms. Kincaid."

"Hello, Ralph," she beamed. "Yes, it's been a very good evening indeed."

Shaking the rain from her long mahogany hair, Tess sashayed through the glass entryway, her elegant heels clicking on the marble corridor. As she crossed the threshold to the plush rose carpeting, she got a little thrill, thinking of the RITA in her purse. Remembering her mail when she got to the bank of glass elevators, she turned to the adjacent wall.

Nothing but bills, she mused, until she noticed something written on a plain white envelope. One word was scribbled in crimson ink, in big sprawling letters, as if written by a child.

Contessa.

A chill skittered down her spine. Other than her father, the late Jake Kincaid, nobody knew her by that name. The elevator doors parted with a gentle swoosh, snapping her back to the present.

Stepping aboard, she jabbed the button, watching the numbers as the elevator made its silent flight to the thirteenth floor. Curious, she ripped open the letter, goosebumps prickling her flesh. One sentence stood out like a neon light. In the same blood-red ink, the same squiggly handwriting. One sentence glared at her.

I'm your biggest fan.

Chapter Two

The minute Tess crossed the threshold of her condo, she came to a dead halt. Lace curtains billowed in the breeze, with rain blowing in through open windows. Every window in the living room was wide open. The haunting melody of "Moonlight Sonata" drifted through the room, its eerie undertone daunting.

She dropped the letter she had been clutching between clenched fingers, her heart racing. Was he in here, her biggest fan? The door swooshed shut behind her, the automatic closing making her feel trapped. Panic raced through her, her heart thumping with an overload of adrenaline. Just then, the Beethoven classic reached its eerie crescendo, the tinkering of piano keys splintering her nerves.

Turning on her heels, she bolted for the door, her skin drenched with perspiration. Fumbling for the brass doorknob, she grabbed it, her hand slick with sweat. Flinging the door open, she tore down the corridor, glancing over her shoulder. Her gaze swept the hallway, searching dark corners. No one in sight. She poked the elevator button, her frightened green eyes mirrored in the glass doors.

Come on, hurry up. She was all alone on the thirteenth floor. Her nerve endings twitched. Her biggest fan could be silhouetted in the shadows, waiting to pounce on her like some wild predator.

Where's that elevator?

No time to wait.

Reaching the stairway, she fled down the steps,

her stiletto heels tapping on the marble floor. She scurried past a bank of empty leather sofas. The funereal smell of mums in tall vases permeated the lobby. Reaching the reception desk, she rang the bell repeatedly.

"May I help you, Ms. Kincaid?" The manager silently slipped through the massive arched doorway in his prim black uniform, his waxy face as sober as a funeral director's. "Is there a problem?"

"Yeah," Tess said, gulping in air. "Someone was in my condo while I was out. All the windows are open and a CD is playing. Call the police, please. Whoever it was could still be up there."

"Get a hold of yourself, Ms. Kincaid." The manager glanced around as a few onlookers stared. He lowered his voice to barely more than a whisper. "I can assure you no one broke into your condo. We have one of the best security systems in Manhattan. Believe me, nobody got past the camera. Perhaps you left in a hurry and simply forgot about the windows and stereo. If you will just settle down and take a deep breath…I really must insist you keep your voice down. You're creating quite a stir."

"Didn't you hear a word I said?" Tess's jaw dropped. "Someone was in my condo. Call the police right this minute or I will."

Two security guards materialized at Tess's side. "Right this way, Ms. Kincaid."

Before she could stop them, they hustled her out of the lobby and into the office, the heavy wooden door clicking as it closed. A guard with salt and pepper hair eased her down into a plush leather chair. He poured water from a cut glass carafe, ice cubes tinkling. "Drink this and tell me what happened."

Sputtering, Tess tripped over her words. "He…she…someone was in my condo tonight while I was out. And…just before I went up…I checked my mail. There was a letter, from someone claiming to be my biggest fan, scribbled in red ink, real creepy, like blood."

The security guards exchanged a glance. "And where is this letter?"

"Up in my condo. I dropped it when I realized someone had been in there. Please, believe me. Call the police."

"Let's go have a look," the older guard said. "I've been on duty all night long, and don't believe anybody got past me. But to ease your mind, we'll be happy to check it out for you. We want our residents to feel safe while residing in our building."

Tess placed the glass on the table, her hands quivering so much water sloshed back and forth, teetering just below the rim. She stood on shaky legs, knees rattling together, and sucked in her breath. "You'll see. Someone was in there."

After arriving at her condo again, Tess unlocked her door, security a step behind. A sick feeling washed over her. No music played and every window was tightly closed. Yet the thick gold carpeting beneath them was saturated. She looked around and blinked.

"But..." she stammered, her mind racing. "How?"

The security guards checked every room, looking in closets and behind the shower curtain. "No sign of disturbance or forced entry, Ms. Kincaid. Nobody hiding in the closet or beneath the bed. The only thing out of sorts is some drenched curtains and wet rugs where you left the windows open."

"But," Tess protested, her voice fading. "The windows were definitely closed when I left this afternoon. With the storm threatening all day, I never would have left them open. When I returned this evening, they were all wide open and 'Moonlight Sonata' was playing on my stereo. Come on, I'll show you." She hustled to the entertainment center, her soaked nylons squishing in her shoes. When she popped the lid of the CD player, it was empty. Her heart thumping, she sunk to her knees, flipping through her collection of music. Beethoven's Greatest Hits was neatly stacked with the rest of the CDs.

"How in the world?" Tess rose to her feet, spun on her heels, her eyes searching. "But 'Moonlight Sonata' was playing when I came in earlier...I know it."

"You mentioned a fan letter?" The guard with the salt and pepper hair eyed Tess suspiciously. "Can I see it?"

"It was right there." Tess pointed to the spot just inside the foyer. Nothing was there. Her voice broke. "It was right there, honest."

"Ah...look, Ms. Kincaid..." The guard placed a hand on her shoulder. "You probably just left in a hurry and forgot about the stereo and windows, no big deal. Been known to do it myself. Rest assured, no one's in here. This building's got state-of-the-art security. After a good night's rest, you'll feel better in the morning."

Tess double bolted the door behind them, turmoil swirling in the pit of her stomach. An uneasiness washed over her, unnerving her. Despite what security thought, she knew better. Someone had been in her home, opening and closing windows like some enigma, vanishing into thin air without a trace.

Who was her biggest fan? With so many crackpots in New York City, it was hard to know.

Good riddance. The peaceful serenity of Bar Harbor beckoned her—the sooner, the better. With the excitement of winning her first RITA, finding the peculiar fan letter in her mailbox and coming back to the bizarre happening in her condo, her left eye began to twitch. Within seconds, her temple throbbed with pain. Using her thumbs and fingers, she gently massaged tiny circles on her head. Just what she needed, one of her migraines.

After taking some prescription pain medication, Tess tossed and turned, her black cat curled across her feet at the foot of the bed. Just as her migraine began to dwindle, her phone rang. Groaning, she squinted at the glowing red numbers on her digital clock. Midnight. She reached for the receiver.

"Hello?"

"Did I wake you, Contessa?" he whispered.

"Who is this?" Tess bolted upright, her heart racing. "Who are you and what do you want?"

Dark laughter echoed through the phone. "Well now, princess. That's easy. I'm your biggest fan...and I'm coming for you. And when I getcha, wear something real sexy for me, like that black lace thong. I just loved running my fingers through it earlier tonight when I went through your panties."

Chapter Three

Driving along the rocky coastline of Maine, Tess drove her sleek black SUV along a stunning landscape of maturing red oaks, birch and sugar maples. The trees were a fiery shade of liquid crimson and gold, the amber leaves of autumn spreading through the hills like wildfire.

Being so close to nature and so far from New York, her biggest fan seemed like a distant memory. Her blood turned icy, recalling his raspy whisper, his dark laughter, his threats. If he'd gotten past the security cameras and into her condo once, she wasn't about to stick around and give him an opportunity for an encore. The minute she slammed down the receiver, she packed a bag, grabbed her cat and was out the door to the airport. Viva Bar Harbor.

After years of traveling by taxi, Tess's driving skills were rusty at best. Weaving in and out of the gently sloping hills bordering the rocky coastline, she bit her lip, wondering what had possessed her to get off the plane and go straight to a car dealer, purchase a new vehicle and drive it out of the parking lot.

Utter insanity.

She took the bend in the road a little too sharply, just missing the guard rail. Her tires squealed and her heartbeat tripled. She searched for the exit, perspiration beading her forehead. Dusk was closing in over the harbor, and so was a storm. According to her map, she was very close. A low rumble of thunder rolled across the murky skies.

The last thing she needed was to be skidding along sloping cliffs above the ocean in the middle of a downpour.

Hunger pains gnawed deep in her gut, just as things began looking familiar. Relief soared through her. With those dark thunder clouds looming, it wouldn't be long before the skies opened up in a torrential downpour. Following the sign to Acadia National Park, she made a left and followed it to her hometown. Anticipation mounted in her chest just as another clap of thunder rumbled a low but distinct warning of the coming storm.

As she weaved her SUV along the stretch of road overlooking Frenchman Bay, the sweet smell of clover and the salty sea air blew in her open window, filling her with a sense of nostalgia. In the distance, the squabbling of seagulls echoed over the clanking of harbor bells as trolleys lifted for boats. Reaching the end of the winding road, she made a sharp left. At the top of the hillside, keeping vigil on a stunning rock formation jutting over the crashing waves of the Atlantic, the stately manor she'd inherited loomed above the powerful surf.

As the sound and smell of the sea awakened her senses, memories of her childhood surfaced. Building sand castles on the beach, hunting for sunken treasures in the caves, the sharp bite of the waves smacking against her skin. As the salty sea air invaded her senses, she could hear the echoing peels of laughter and feel the warm sand between her toes as she and her friends raced along the beach, footloose and fancy free.

Lost in fond memories, she careened through the wrought iron gate and up the driveway. Old ghosts from her past drifted out of thin air, haunting her. She envisioned her dad standing in the courtyard, dressed in his chef hat, grilling burgers after a day at the beach. When she and her parents were a family, they often went to the headlands to whale watch and search the bluffs for puffins and sea ducks.

Reaching the top of the drive, she put the SUV in park and gazed at the land.

An overgrown lawn fanned out in front of the seaside estate. What once stood as an elegant manor surrounded by several acres of manicured vineyards now resembled a sloping dell of overhung trees, vines and neglected foliage. A velvety blanket of glossy green ivy covered the west wall of the manor, while draping vines of bougainvillea climbed the east like a stairway to heaven.

Just as Tess turned off the ignition, a streak of lightning splintered the sky with forks of brilliant white light. Within seconds, the clouds opened, sending pellets of rain toward earth. Grabbing her purse, overnight bag and cat caddy, she made a run for it, stomping through tall blades of slick grass and thorny vines, wincing when the unruly branches slapped across her legs. As she raced up the stone steps to the wrap-around veranda, bullets of cold, hard rain pounded her head and body, drenching her to the bone.

As she entered the foyer of the century-old estate, the echoing sound of silence vibrated off the cavernous walls. A lion-head fountain was mounted on the brick facade, its unplugged lifeline an eerie reminder of the emptiness that lurked within.

Tess wiped her feet on the weather-beaten mat, rain plopping as it puddled on the marble tile. Tossing her purse and bag beneath the old tree stand, she unleashed her cat from his caddy. Freddy scampered off, his claws clicking on the marble floor.

The mansion smelled musty from being closed up for so long. Spider webs draped over stained glass windows and picture frames like looping veils of Spanish moss. The staircase, with its richly carved mahogany balustrade, bore off to the right. Tess reached out, tracing the smooth newel post, smiling at a distant memory of herself bounding down the steps, pigtails flapping, eager to get to the beach. Then her dad's voice exploded in her head, scolding her for running down the stairs, the memory so palpable she felt his booming voice vibrate off the stucco walls. Tess's hand quivered as she withdrew it. Peering down the barrel-shaped corridor, she felt the life being sucked out of her, as if invisible fingers were coiling around her throat.

The roiling presence of her dad made her nerve endings jump. The minute she'd set foot in the foyer, she'd returned to her childhood, to a home that bustled with vitality. Now it was as hollow and empty as a mausoleum. She jingled some loose change in the pocket of her hoodie, just to generate some life.

She stood still for a moment before proceeding, emotions wedged in her chest. The spirit of her father was so real she could almost reach out and touch him. As she ventured down the corridor, childhood memories erupted from every corner, stirring feelings that had been tucked away in the deepest recesses of her mind. All those good times, better times. The echo of her footsteps spooked her, as if her past was chasing her present.

Pictures of Jake Kincaid in his glory days hung between burnished copper lanterns, his searing gaze penetrating, almost as if he was watching her from the grave. She shuddered, goose bumps prickling her flesh. The dreariness of the manor unnerved her.

She flicked on a few lights, glad she'd had the power turned on. The rain beat on the stained glass windows, wild and primitive. A streak of lightning flashed, illuminating the dimly-lit corridor, shrouding her father's portraits in an other-worldly glow.

The foyer forked off toward doors leading to strolling gardens connected by a stone bridge. Like the surrounding acres, the flora was withered and dead, weeds and dry earth the only remnant of the once-thriving English gardens that had graced the twenty-four room mansion.

As Tess ventured a bit deeper, the hair on the nape of her neck stood straight up. It was so faint she could barely hear it over the thunder, but as she crept down the corridor, haunted by old ghosts, her flesh crawled. She stopped, listened, certain she'd been mistaken. As she took a few steps, straining to hear. The chilling melody of "Moonlight Sonata" floated down the hall. Her heartbeat tripled. From the grand ballroom, the soft sound of piano keys drifted, louder and louder, faster and faster, reaching a spiking crescendo.

Then all was quiet as the manor settled from the riveting climax.

An eerie twine hummed through the corridor, ringing in her ears. Shocked by the scaling spike of piano keys, her knees buckled. She leaned against the wall for support, her breathing ragged.

In barely more than a whisper, she called out, "Daddy?"

Her mind raced. Could her dad be alive? Was this all a joke, one of his notorious pranks? Had he staged his own death? Tears stung her eyes. She had to find out, but still, she proceeded with caution. She sensed evil from deep in her soul.

Camouflaged in the dim lighting, Tess scaled along the walls of the corridor, blending into the dark wood paneling. Inching her way a bit deeper, back against the wall, she crept, her heart pounding. Beads of sweat trickled down her spine. A door banged, sounding like shutters smacking the house in a storm. Then she felt a rush of cool air coming from the grand ballroom, dank with the smell of rain and something else. Burning candles.

Fear clutched her from deep within, squeezing her gut. As she got closer, the scent of jasmine grew stronger. The sweet smell permeated the air. It felt as if her father was still alive, entertaining in the grand ballroom. Just as Tess reached the arched column to the massive hall, lightning illuminated the sky, followed by the sound of thunder exploding. Then all went dark as the power went dead.

Tess stood at the entrance, polarized. When the icy instrumental of "Moonlight Sonata" started all over again, she took a step back and gasped. Peering into the massive hall, she stared in disbelief.

On either side of the mahogany bar, candelabras gleamed, long white tapers flickering in the dark. Open terrace doors banged in the wind. The hissing rain blew in, stirring the scent of jasmine and stale tobacco. Pleated silk drapes rippled, chrome tassels clinking as they swung back and forth like pendulums.

Rain puddled on the cherry wood floor that once sparkled beneath the mirrored ceiling and crystal chandelier. The music came from the old Victrola. What totally floored her, though, was that in the center of the room, looking for all the world like guests of honor at a grand masquerade, were two wax gargoyles dancing cheek to cheek, costumed in feather masks as bizarre as the setting.

Gasping, Tess backed into a spider web, its willowy mesh veiling her head and face. Shuddering, she thrashed about, shrieking when a hairy spider crawled down her nose. Still screaming, she tore through the hallway, heart thumping, bumping into walls, feeling her way. Where was her purse? She needed her keys. She tripped on something. Her cat hissed and ran for cover, his claws tapping on the floor. Tess barged into something big and hard. Her heart in her throat, she screeched and came to a dead halt, expecting steely arms to coil around her any second. But nothing happened.

Reaching out with her hands, her heart racing, she realized it was the tree stand in the foyer. Relief stormed through her as she recalled she'd thrown her purse at the base. Stooping down, she snatched it up and fled through the door.

Once she was outside, a streak of lightning lit up the sky, shedding enough light to see the steps and her SUV. Making a wild dash for it, she flung the door open, hopped in, jabbed the key into the ignition and gunned it. Nothing. Damn.

Locking the doors, she reached for her purse, fishing through it until she located her cell phone. Praying the battery wasn't dead, she flipped back the lid.

Thank God.

Punching in 9-1-1, she waited for someone to answer.

"Hurry," she screamed into the phone.

When the dispatcher finally came on the other end, Tess rushed to get the words out, her voice cracking. "Someone is in my house. My name is Tess Kincaid and my address is 1300 Mockingbird Lane. Please hurry."

Chapter Four

Tess heard the rumble of an engine as it climbed the winding road to her estate. Wet tires zinged on slick pavements. Twin beams glared as the vehicle took the bend and tore up her driveway, brakes squealing to a jarring halt.

A county sheriff leapt out, slamming the door. Lightning and thunder clashed with a dramatic boom. Still trembling, Tess stared in awe. The sheriff strutted toward her, his muscular physique silhouetted against the dark, stormy night. Darker still were his brooding eyes, hard and unyielding as they seared into hers. His blond, shaggy hair rippled in the wind, his crisp white shirt billowing against his broad shoulders. A crack of lightning unleashed, splitting the sky into an explosion of light. The stallion tattooed on his arm bucked beneath his bulging biceps, looking every bit as wild and untamed as the battle raging through the sky.

Tess hopped from her SUV, looking up into a face so ruggedly handsome it stole her breath. An erotically-charged bolt of electricity surged through her system. Her voice caught. "Ah...I'm Tess Kincaid. I inherited my father's estate after his death. When I arrived here tonight, the terrace doors were open in the ballroom...and there...well, you'll see."

"Mike Andretti." He extended his hand. "Hancock County Sheriff. I'm well acquainted with the Kincaid estate. In fact, I'm your neighbor, living in the ranch down the road a piece, the old Wexler estate. Get in out of the rain and lock the doors; I'll be back as soon as I've checked the place out. Did you notice any sign of disturbance?" He turned to her, gently nudging her into the SUV. He drew his Glock, cocked the hammer. The click was followed by an encore of thunder.

"It's ah..." Tess felt stupid, realizing how it would sound. "You'd better see for yourself...in the ballroom. It's a scene straight out of a horror show."

The sheriff cast a sidelong glance before dashing across the courtyard.

With the lightning casting him in partial light, Tess watched his moves, long legs eating up the pavement. Momentarily forgetting what she'd witnessed in the ballroom, she watched him barrel up the steps and through the door.

Then with the same swiftness as when it had been snuffed, the power returned, showcasing the entire mansion in brightness. Flaming copper finials bordered the entrance gate to the courtyard, its regal appeal inviting. Standing tall and mighty against the dark stormy night, the fiery torches gave the illusion of shooting stars with tails.

A warm sensation spread through Tess as another childhood memory surfaced, and once more, the booming voice of her dad exploded in her head. While standing out in the courtyard, he'd point to a shooting star and tell her to make a wish, then he'd kiss the tip of her nose and tell her all her dreams would come true. Tess stared at the torch-lit finials in the courtyard and felt her dad's presence. "Oh, Daddy."

Before she knew it, she was out of the SUV, racing through the wind and rain, up the stone steps to the mansion. Adrenaline pumped through her veins, pushing her. What if her dad was still alive? She had to find out. Hope soared as she barged through the door, but she didn't get far when she collided with a six-foot roadblock of pure steel.

"Thought I told you to stay put." Sparks of liquid gold flickered in his broody brown eyes. "Don't listen too well, do you?"

A muscle twitched in Tess's jaw. "Ah...did you find anyone? Is Daddy..."

"No. Believe me, no one's in here. Now what's all this about the ballroom lookin' like a scene out of some old horror flick?"

Tess couldn't believe her ears. Was he nuts? He had to ask? What kind of an officer would find such a bizarre setting anything but what it was—creepy?

She stared at him, her eyes questioning. "Didn't you see the gargoyles? And what about the music playing on the old Victrola? Then, what about the terrace doors all ajar? The burning candelabras? You didn't find that strange, a bit out of the ordinary?"

He stared at her, his jaw rigid. Faint lines etched the corners of his tightly drawn mouth. "What are you talking about, Ms. Kincaid?"

A feeling of déjà vu washed over Tess. The memory of her New York condo rushed in.

No, not again.

She swiped at a wet strand of hair, absently slicking it behind her ear. "Ah..." She blinked. "Come on, I'll show you."

As she led the way down the corridor, the walls seemed to vibrate with the essence of her dad, his deep belly laugh so palpable she swore she heard it. He had been blessed with a wicked sense of humor. It was as if he was still in this house, playing one of his legendary pranks from the grave.

Reaching the grand ballroom, Tess stood there, too baffled to speak. "But it wasn't like this forty-five minutes ago, really. See those gargoyles over there?"

She gestured toward the mythical gods keeping vigil on either side of the bar. Their sinister smiles taunted her, as if daring her to tell their dirty little secret. Tess tripped over her words. "But they were...they were out there, costumed in feather masks, dancing, their arms around each other. 'Moonlight Sonata' played on the old phonograph, just the way it did when Daddy hosted glamorous balls for his Hollywood friends. The candelabras were burning and all the windows and balcony doors were open, just the way they were back then." Tess felt tears threaten. "I'm not crazy, really. I know what I saw and it wasn't like this. Please believe me."

The sheriff scratched the bristly stubble on his chin as rain water dripped from his hair and shirt. He cleared his throat. "Look, Ms. Kincaid. Nobody's sayin' you're crazy. Not only was I your dad's neighbor, but we were good friends. His vineyards border my land, and one day we got to talkin' about the old days when he was a Hollywood legend. It didn't take long before he started braggin' about his daughter, Tess Kincaid, best sellin' author. When your name appeared on the New York Times best-seller list, you made your dad real proud."

Emotions lodged in Tess's throat. "Really? I never knew. If only I'd visited more, spent more time with Daddy. I had no idea he was so depressed..." Some tears spilled down her cheek. She swiped at them with the back of her hand and sucked in her breath. "I still can't believe it. What in the world would make Daddy take his own life? Can you answer that, Sheriff?"

"Call me Mike," he said, yanking a hanky from his back pocket. He handed it to her, his jaw rigid. He puckered his lips. "Never saw it comin'. If I had, I woulda moved heaven and earth to prevent it. Took me and everyone else in the harbor by surprise, but I'll tell ya' somethin'. About a week or so before his death, he dug out some old photos of you growing up, told me stories of when y'all lived here as a family.

Those were the best years of his life. He regretted his marriage breakin' up, especially losin' you in the custody battle."

He stopped, his gaze sweeping the ballroom. "When you and your mom moved to New York, I guess his spirit died. It broke him, gnawed at his gut. Losin' his family, on the tail of the loss of the career he loved so much, left scars that never healed. Much as I hate to admit it, your dad was every bit as emotionally crippled as he was physically. Only thing that got him fired up was relivin' the glory days when he starred on the big screen in those old Westerns."

"I know," Tess agreed, thinking back to the rise and fall of the great Jake Kincaid. She peeled off her drenched hoodie, hanging it on the back of the bar stool to dry. "Daddy was never the same after the car accident that injured his leg. It left him so gnarled up and crippled; he was in constant pain. When he could no longer mount a horse or handle the stunts, it destroyed him and his marriage. Then he started drinking..."

"I know. Your dad was fine when he drank some wine from his own vineyards, but when he hit the hard stuff, man, look out. Things got *real* ugly. Your dad was mean as a snake when he drank whiskey."

Tess felt a pang in her heart. If only things had been different, maybe her father wouldn't have become such a lonely old man.

"Daddy was so different back then, the life of the party. Everyone loved him. The accident changed him, hardened him." She looked at Mike. "No one can take my childhood memories away, the sweetest days of my life. I'm sorry you didn't know him then. After the accident, my father alienated himself from most people, like a recluse. I'm sure he treasured your friendship and knowing you filled some of the emptiness in his life gives me comfort. The fact he let you in says a lot about your character. Thank you."

Silence hovered between them as they both indulged in private memories of Jake Kincaid. Mike broke the barrier. "So how about tellin' me what ya' saw earlier in here."

Tess sighed, wondering if her mind was playing tricks on her. Maybe she was just so overcome with emotion and memories that she imagined seeing her mom and dad dance, the way they did in the early days of their marriage. She walked across the scarred, cherry wood floor to the gargoyles, the soles of her drenched sandals sticking to the floor like suction cups. She stared at the wax figures.

"Daddy loved collecting, almost as much as he did acting. He had a real fetish for frightening people, doing the most bizarre things at his masquerades. Do you remember that old thriller, The Wax Museum? It was his favorite. He watched it over and over again, to the point of obsession. When he was in California on a shoot, he was always looking for gimmicks for his parties. When he discovered an antique shop on Venice Beach that sold wax gargoyles, he had them shipped here so he could use them as props. I'll never forget the masquerade he hosted on April Fool's Day."

She smiled as she looked around the room. "As fate would have it, the afternoon of the party was when he stumbled upon these mystical gods. He propped Zeus and Mnemosyne at the bar. Their bodies are so pliable he wrapped their fingers around cocktail glasses and turned their heads toward one another as if in deep conversation. At first glance, they looked real. Guests figured they were portraying the Greek god and goddess for the masquerade. When they didn't respond, the guests would poke them and then freak. Daddy would buckle over with gales of laughter. I can still hear it as I look around this ballroom."

"I see his collection grew." Mike gestured to several winged creatures, including Pegasus, the Nine Muses, and gods of fire. "You mentioned that when you first looked in the ballroom, the gargoyles were dancing in the middle of the floor in costume. Show me which masks."

Wordlessly, caught up in memories, Tess walked to a glass-encased curio filled with a handsome collection of fans and feather masks. She went to open the door, but Mike's long fingers snaked around her wrist.

"Don't touch anything, just in case." His gaze met hers, holding it for a second. "We'll wanna dust for prints. Now show me which ones."

Tess pointed to the lady-of-the-evening feather mask. "Mnemosyne was wearing that one and Zeus was donned in the Venetian, black velvet, devil mask."

She watched Mike study them, somber eyes searching. Then he turned to her. "Should I decide there's reason, one of the deputies will run a check on the masks. Here's what I think, though, Tess. Your dad's suicide was a brutal shock to your system. The minute you walked through the doors after so many years, memories were bound to haunt your subconscious, play tricks on your eyes. To top it off, the entire island suffered a blackout. You probably lit the candles, the only source of light in the mansion, and then maybe you were so caught up in the memory of one of your dad's masquerades, you visualized the way things used to be, instead of the way they are. Who knows what the mind will do under stress. Coulda easily imagined hearin' music playin' and opened the terrace doors out of habit. Make sense? Comin' into a room which left such a jarring impact on your childhood is bound to conjure up some strong images. Now let's go see if your dad left any coffee in this old house. I could use a cup, and by the look of things, so could you."

Tess sighed, debating whether or not to say anything. Since it was all she could think about, she huffed and looked the sheriff straight in the eye. "You know, Mike, I gotta be honest with you. When I first heard the music playing and smelled the candles burning, I was out in the corridor and got spooked. I kept thinking Daddy had to be alive...I just thought...are you sure he..."

"Tess." Mike put his hand on her shoulder. "Believe me, your dad's gone. Take my word for it."

Tess walked along in silence, haunted by old ghosts. Too much too soon. She bit down hard on her lip, tasting blood. She felt confused and vulnerable. Could she have imagined the ballroom as it used to look?

She shook her head, trying to clear the cobwebs. It was true; she'd been under a terrific strain, emotionally. She was trying to adjust to her father's suicide, as well as a move, at the same time she was trying to finish her book in order to meet the deadline. Maybe walking into the ballroom where her dad's spirit was so palpable had made her mind temporarily snap.

She hadn't yet mourned her father, bid him a proper farewell. She'd come to the funeral, paid her respects, and flew back to New York, all in one day. It had been too much for her to bear.

Now it was too late, too late to stroll with him through the vineyards one more time, or to hear the robust laughter that had filled her childhood days with sunshine. Her heart wept.

"Tess," Mike broke into her thoughts. "You okay?"

"Just letting it all sink in, trying to accept the fact I'll never see Daddy again. We were so close once and a part of me longs for the good old days. If only I could…" She choked back the tears. "Maybe I could have done something, prevented him from—"

"Hush, now, darlin'; what's done is done. Believe me, there was nothin' you coulda' done. When someone makes the decision to end their life, that's it. The mind snaps, shuts down. Apparently, your dad decided enough was enough."

"But why? Why wait twenty years? Usually, if someone is going to commit suicide after a trauma or life-altering event, it's within the first year, don't you agree? Daddy coped with his accident and the destruction of his family for the last two decades. Things just don't add up. And…what about a note? If he talked about me as much as you say he did, wouldn't it stand to reason he'd leave a letter to say goodbye?"

Mike shook his head, his golden brown eyes troubled. "Don't know; wish I had those answers. But there's no use dwellin' on somethin' we just can't change. I'm sorry, Tess, real sorry."

Tess looked around the kitchen, half expecting her father to strut through the door, script in hand, ten gallon hat perched on his head. Overwhelmed, she slumped into the breakfast nook, emotions clouding her brain. She missed him, the one and only Jake Kincaid.

"Your dad was a force to be reckoned with." Mike's slow smile broke into a wide grin. A deep dimple glinted in the cleft of his chin. He opened the cupboard to retrieve the coffee canister. Tess watched him scoop some beans, grind them, fill the basket, pour water through the machine and turn it on. Within a few minutes, the fresh aroma of hazelnut wafted through the room. While the coffeemaker hissed and spewed, Tess couldn't help notice the ease in which the sheriff moved about in the Kincaid kitchen.

Propping her chin between cupped hands, her

gaze swept the room. Wooden appliqués and wrought-iron accents enhanced the French Quarter theme. Copper pots and pans hung on a brick façade above the oven. To the left of the breakfast nook, a torch-lit lantern gave way to a regal courtyard surrounding a fountain of Aphrodite. At the top of the adjoining hill, the bell tower loomed.

"Here's your coffee." Mike set a steaming mug on the breakfast table. "It'll take the chill out of your bones."

Tess inhaled the aromatic fragrance, remembering her father sitting at the booth, drinking coffee and reading his reviews. She looked at Mike. "Don't you need to get back to work? Surely, I'm not the only woman in crisis on the entire island?"

He winked. "Only one tonight, darlin'. Just about to leave when your call came in. Like I said, Jake and I were friends, and I know he'd want me looking after his daughter."

Tess nodded, then raised an eyebrow. "You just said you were on your way home. If someone was in here, they're long gone. You don't have to feel obligated to sit with me just because of Daddy. Go on, the night's still young. You probably have plans. Are you dating?"

The minute the words were out of her mouth, Tess wished she could take them back. "Ah…that just rolled out. I'm sorry. It's none of my business. I don't know why I…"

Mike's laughter filled the room. "Truth be told, I did have a date, but your call came in the nick of time. I've been dating this woman for a few weeks, but we don't really have all that much in common. I wasn't looking forward to the show or the company."

Tess felt a little thrill. He was single. Then glancing toward the back stairs leading to her father's wing, her mood darkened. She sipped her coffee, choosing her words carefully. "Mike, please don't take this the wrong way, but I need to know. Since you and Daddy were so close, you're probably the last person he talked to. If there's anything you can think of that might shed some light on his suicide, please don't hold back. It's eating me up inside, not knowing why he did it."

Mike finished his coffee and walked over to the sink, his boot heels clicking on the tile floor. He rinsed out the mug. Water sputtered from the rusty taps. He walked back toward Tess, his easy swagger stirring the musky scent of his aftershave. He stood so close to her the air bristled. Body heat radiated from his chest and arms. He pinned her with his penetrating gaze. "When I didn't see your dad in his yard for a few days, I got worried and came out to check on him. Called out his name a few times, no response. Something about the house seemed all wrong. One of his movies was playin' in the home theater, but outside of that, no sign of life. I'm the one who found your dad's body, Tess."

"You?" Tess stared, her lips unable to form her thoughts into words. Tears pooled in her eyes. She felt as if someone had punched her in the gut, knocking the wind out of her. Then she blinked, licking her parched lips. Her heart went out to Mike as she tried to put herself in his shoes. What a horrible thing to see, sheriff or not. He'd been good friends with her dad and finding his body would have been a living nightmare.

She blinked back a tear. "That must have been so hard on you, Mike. I'm sorry; I can't even imagine what that must have been like. When the police called that morning, they said a neighbor reported it, but I was too shocked to ask any questions."

Mike's broad shoulders slumped. He looked out the window, into the courtyard and surrounding woods. Lightning streaked, showcasing a gnarled red oak deep in the thicket. Clearing his throat, he turned to her. "I'll never forget that day as long as I live. Findin' your dad like that had to be the most gruesome thing I've witnessed in ten years as an officer. It's still the last thing I see before I close my eyes at night."

"I'm so sorry." Tess's eyes grew misty with tears. There simply were no words. She reached over and touched his arm. "I'll pray for you, pray it gets easier."

Mike's chest rose and fell. He held her gaze for a second, then looked away. "Best be on my way. By the look of that storm, it's here for the night and I need to check on my horses. They get real antsy when it thunders. I'll come by in the morning to check on you. Get some rest."

"I'll walk you to the door; it's the least I can do."

****

From deep in the woods, The Master kept vigil from the watch tower, peering into the mansion. He clapped with delight. *Bravo!* Hats off to his production. What a stellar performance by an all-star cast. His gargoyles with their waxy bodies, oh so pliable. And the look on Contessa's face...well worth the price of admission. Pretty little princess stunned speechless.

The Master's heart swelled with satisfaction. Ghost haunts seaside manor. Dear old Daddy lives on. His manic laughter rolled into the forest and into the deepest part of the thicket.

Thunder claps boomed through the night wind, fierce warriors slashing swords, crashing and colliding. Lightning danced across the sky in a devil-may-care flirtation, swooning and swaying, teasing and taunting. It was all so magnificent.

The Master reigned, ruled the elements of earth, wind and fire in all their glory. Such perfect theatrics for his drama. What a thrill.

Lights...camera...action.

The Master beamed, snaking the tip of his tongue into the hole where his front tooth was missing. The salty breeze rippled through his long red hair and beard, the silver hoop earring in his left ear shimmering in the moonlight. He was god of Thunder, god of Lightning. He was Thor. He created fire in the heavens with a thrust of his hand. He stood tall and mighty, back arched, clenched fist thrust high in the air. The beat of the rain on the tower echoed the accelerated beat of his heart.

The Master spied on Tess and Mike, using his nighttime binoculars. He snickered to himself as he observed. White Knight charges to the rescue, gun cocked and ready. Princess bats her bewitching green eyes, pouts her pretty little lips—oh so inviting. Princess shows White Knight the feathered masks. Princess and White Knight deep in conversation. White Knight makes his exit, pretty little princess hot on his heels.

The Master groaned, recalling the taste of her sweet, sweet lips, the scent of her skin—oh so arousing. He remembered the feel of her hair brushing his chest as he carried her, his Princess Contessa, to their castle of love. Adrenaline and testosterone pumped through his veins like wildfire, the memories oh so erotic.

The pretty little princess betrayed him. She would suffer for her sin. Before the final curtain, she'd be begging to die. And he'd be happy to oblige.

During the last scene, he'd thrust his hand to the heavens and demand a command performance of thunder and lightning. It would be the show to end all shows, the grand finale. Oh, the drama he had planned.

The Master watched the sheriff race down the stone steps and across the courtyard through the pouring rain. He hopped in his vehicle, the door slamming. He gunned the engine and shifted gears into first. Gleaming headlights glowed in the misty night as he backed down the driveway, tires singing on wet pavement. Turning around in the fork of the road, he drove down the steep hill, the growl of the engine reverberating through the scrub pine and oak forest.

Picturing the things he had planned, the Master tossed back his head and cackled like a hyena. Adrenaline and testosterone surged through his veins. Leaping high in the air, he howled at the moon.

The Master preened.

Oh yes, princess. I'm coming.

Just like predators stalking the woods for prey, he'd hunt her down, and when he caught her, he'd pounce on her like the big bad wolf. The things he'd do to her were downright chilling. She'd have her starring role, queen for a day.

After all, I'm her biggest fan.

Chapter Five

The following morning, Tess stood on the veranda sipping a cup of coffee. It was amazing what a good night's sleep could do for the body and soul. It was nearly noon and she felt wonderful. Not a cloud in the sky. The fall foliage spreading through Acadia Park was breathtaking. Chickadees chirped from woodland pines. The sun blazed through a maturing red spruce forest of scrub pines and birch, the rich saturation of colors reflecting on the water. The air smelled so fresh and clean after the rain, giving birth to the rambling roses growing wild on the hillside.

Setting her mug on the railing, she leaned over to pet her cat. Freddy rubbed her leg, meowing for attention. Tess looked down into where her blue garden used to be, her childhood sanctuary. She and her dad had planted it the first summer she visited after her parents' divorce. What once graced the manor, a beautiful royal flush of pure blue spires, was now as dead and overgrown as the surrounding vineyards. Her heart sank. Her favorite flower, the forget-me-not, was buried beneath all the rubble of the blue border. With a renewed spirit and a place to start, Tess drained her coffee and started for her garden.

Crushing twigs and pinecones beneath her sandaled feet, she opened the gate to the white stone arbor, its rusty hinges creaking with age. A discarded wheelbarrow slumped on a broken wheel, adding to the dishevelment. All the overkill made her cringe. Seeing the mess in the harsh light of day saddened her, tweaked something deep in her very soul. Looking around, she got busy, yanking the dead foliage from the sodden earth.

Spotting a pair of weathered clippers beneath the thorny vines, she snipped and pruned the thick snarl of weeds. From the ocean, the harbor bell clanked, echoing across the dock. A gaggle of seagulls squawked in the bluffs, frothy waves crashing into shore. The warm sun felt good, bathing her back and arms. She felt some of the tension ease from her taut muscles. Rolling her head from shoulder to shoulder, she smiled. So her sand castle on the sea wasn't exactly a castle in a fairy tale, not by a long shot, but whatever the case, it felt good to be home.

Weeding the garden was just what she needed to put her back in touch with nature after living in the city for so many years. Wiping the sweat from her brow, she snipped away with her clippers, shocked how fast the sun dried the damp earth. A warm feeling washed over her when the first forget-me-not popped its head out after being freed from the vines, its delicate scent wafting through the air.

Satisfied when a few more were uncovered, she stepped back to observe. Spying a broken flower, she plucked it up, bringing it up to her nose. Inhaling the sweet fragrance, she could almost hear the laughter in the garden the day she and her dad planted the wild flowers. Twirling the petal between her fingers, she squinted up at the brilliant ball of gold glinting through the sugar maples. The sun had turned her arms a healthy shade of pink, and she'd bet her last dollar a dusting of freckles peppered her nose.

Feeling as dried from the sun as the earth around her, she gazed across the land to the rustic bridge overlooking a cascading waterfall. At the crest of the hill, a water pump sprouted amidst a patch of wild blueberries.

"Come on, Freddy," she called out to her cat. "Let's go cool off and get some water."

Walking through a grove of maturing red oaks, Tess thought it a crying shame how the once lush grounds had been neglected and were now mostly rotted with fungal decay. She remembered a time when apples, oranges and strawberries bordered the landscape, along with blueberry bushes and cherry groves. Her father's vineyards had thrived in the rich soil, growing succulent grapes the color of rubies. Come harvest, he'd produce a full-bodied wine, rich and robust, bottled and labeled under the Kincaid private collection. But he'd let it all go—his gardens, his vineyards, his family, his life.

Frustrated, Tess snatched a handful of grapes from the vine, pitched them down and stomped on them. Red juice squirted between her toes and all over her white sandals. Anger fueling her, she snagged another handful and thrust her fist high in the air. Her voice rang through the vineyard.

"Damn you for letting it all go! Damn you for being so selfish! Damn you for taking the easy way out!"

Tess's eyes filled with tears. She felt a swirl of emotions churning in her gut, the feelings that had been balled up in her chest since her father's suicide. She hadn't let them out, keeping her grief neatly tucked away for fear of losing control, but being in the vineyards where her dad's spirit lived on was more than she could take.

She swore she could hear his bellowing voice echoing through the vineyards. Mostly, she remembered the feel of his strong arms when he'd embrace her in one of his fierce bear hugs, lift her high in the air and twirl her around, telling her she was the prettiest little girl God had ever created. All of those memories were almost too much to bear, and like the proverbial flood gates, Tess let herself go, freeing the tears she'd been harboring for the past six months.

"Oh, Daddy, I miss you. Why? Didn't you know how much this would hurt me? What could have been so bad you took your own life? I want you back. I need you, miss you so. If only I could hear your laughter one more time. If only we could take one more walk through these vineyards and you could tell me one of your favorite tales about starring in your beloved Westerns. I see you everywhere, strutting around in your ten gallon hat, a smile on your face as big as the bay. The happiest days of my life were when we lived here as a family. Remember how we'd go down to the beach to whale watch? Or how about the time we found that baby seagull, hurt and abandoned on the bluffs? You picked it up and brought him home; we nursed him back to health. When he was strong enough, you said we had to let him go. Saying goodbye was so hard. Now I'm saying goodbye to you. Daddy, it's the hardest thing I've ever done. I'll never forget you. I hope you found peace. I love you."

Tess fell to her knees and wept her heart out. After exhausting herself, she heaved a heavy sigh and slid to the sodden earth, the dank smell filling her senses.

From deep in the thicket, a falcon screeched; its shrill cry sliced through the silence. Hearing a slight rustle in the leaves, Tess didn't budge. When she felt a presence looming over her, the hair on the nape of her neck stood straight up.

From the corner of her eye, she caught a glimpse of a cowhide leather boot. Icy fingers of fear skittered down her spine, chilling her to the bone. She went to scream, but nothing came out.

Tess stood, a bit flustered. She must look a

fright, red puffy eyes, cheeks drenched with tears.

"Didn't mean to disturb ya', Tess." Mike tipped his cowboy hat. "But I've been watchin' ya' for a while now and wanted to make sure you're okay. Besides, since I know your cupboards are empty, I brought breakfast. Now ya' can't tell me the smell of these oven-fresh muffins don't tempt your tastebuds." He rustled a bag in front of her. "Straight from the Seaside Bakery."

When she got a whiff of the rich buttery pastries, all thoughts of vanity disappeared. First things first. She hadn't realized how hungry she was. After the bizarre happening in the ballroom, she'd lost her appetite; now, with her stomach rumbling deep in her gut, she realized she hadn't eaten since the measly ham and cheese sandwich in the airport before her flight.

Seduced by the savory aroma wafting from the bag, she closed her eyes and inhaled. "It's been years since I've had this kind of treat. I can't believe they're still around. Their pastries were always so good; you could smell them baking all over the harbor. When I'd come back here in the summer, Daddy always made sure he had plenty of their muffins and donuts, just for me. Don't keep me in suspense, Sheriff. What's in the bag?"

"Only the best, darlin'." He opened the bag and allowed her a little peek. "Best Bar Harbor has to offer. Chocolate chip and blueberry muffins, fresh baked this morning, big as your fist."

Totally unabashed, Tess sniffed the air, the rich chocolatey aroma taking her to another place and time. She was a child again, racing down the steps in her bare feet, straight for the kitchen where she knew she'd find a bag of goodies. Her dad would pour her a tall glass of milk and tell her to drink it so her bones would get strong. The memory comforted her. An easy smile teased her lips, changing her mood to one of complete lightheartedness. "One of those muffins would sure hit the spot. Come on, I'll put on a fresh pot of coffee."

Mike grabbed her arm when she tripped over the gnarled root of a white oak. "Easy does it. This land needs a major makeover. If you're interested, a real good buddy of mine owns a landscaping business. This is his slow season, so he could probably start right away and give ya' a good deal. It's up to you, but I gotta be honest. This place is an eyesore, a downright disgrace. It'll do my heart good to see these grounds resurrected, thrive with life the way they did before your dad let it all go south."

Just then, a crisp autumn breeze rustled through the vineyards, stirring the air with the scent of the earth. Tess felt her Dad's presence more than ever, his lingering spirit palpable. She sighed wistfully. "Saying goodbye is really hard; knowing I'll never see Daddy again, hear his rich laugh roll across the land. He loved toiling with his grapes, making his wine. I like to think his spirit roams these grounds, the vineyards he once took such pride in. It gives me comfort, closure."

"But wanna know something? I feel better now, less burdened. Daddy was a tortured soul after his accident. I guess there are a lot of things I just didn't realize. He was in horrible pain, physically and emotionally. Most of that pain stayed with him for the rest of his life. He's out of misery now, God rest his soul. There was nothing I could have done to protect him from all of this so it's time to let go and place it in God's hands."

"That's where it should stay." Mike scooped up a copper penny from the ground and handed it to Tess. "Here ya' go; make a wish and pitch it over your shoulder. Then your wish'll come true."

Tess stopped walking and stared, an odd sensation creeping through her. "Daddy used to tell me to wish on a star and all my dreams would come true." She held the penny, rubbing it between her fingers. It felt warm from the sun beating down on it. Her gaze raked the grounds. Then she laughed, a melodious lilt that echoed across the vineyards. "If I were to make a wish, it would be to have a Fairy Godmother wave her magic wand over this land and turn it into the manicured grounds it once was."

A woodpecker drilled into the bark of a pine, its vivid red crown gleaming in the sun. "Well, darlin'," Mike grinned, "I can't promise ya' a Fairy Godmother, but like I said, my buddy's landscaping business has been known to perform small miracles in these parts. He just might be the Fairy Godfather you're wishin' for."

Tess tossed her head back and laughed. "As long as he has lots of elves to help him. I've inherited the Kincaid estate, so it's my responsibility to take charge; after all, I'm mistress of the manor."

"Suits me just fine." Mike winked. "It'll be a pleasure to have ya' move in. Much as I liked your old man, you're much prettier. I'll say this much, though, Jake Kincaid was one hell of an icon. When I first met him that day, toilin' in the vineyard...well, now, let's just say it was a day I'll remember."

"Yeah, for a while the vineyards kept him going, but not enough for a man used to basking in the limelight. You wouldn't believe all the hats, boots and other paraphernalia he got to keep from all those movies." Tess paused to look up toward her dad's wing. "It's gonna be real hard walking into his bedroom. I have to sort out his belongings, keep what I want and give the rest to charity. I have no idea how I'm going to do it, but I will. When I have this place restored, it'll be something the Kincaid name can be proud of."

Tess's view wandered across the courtyard again, sighing. "You should have seen him the day he bought this place. He was beside himself, his face all aglow, wanting a home to pass on to his grandchildren. He was like a little kid at Christmas. It was so gorgeous back then. It'll take a long time to rebuild, but I'd like to get started right away. Why don't you tell me about your friend's business?"

"You won't be sorry," Mike said, his boots crunching on the leaves and twigs surrounding the picnic area. "Red Spruce Landscaping, best on the island."

Tess found herself captivated by the twinkle in Mike's eyes, eyes with irises so bright that they shimmered in the sun like topaz jewels. Distracted by the unique shade, she was having trouble concentrating. They dazzled her. Realizing it had been a long time since she'd felt this way, something cold around her heart melted. It had been far too long since she'd allowed herself to feel anything. Ever since news of her father's death, she'd built a wall around herself.

Maybe it was time to let that wall down, and just maybe she was willing to give it a go with her ruggedly handsome neighbor. Thinking about that as they reached the picnic area, a smile curled her lips. "Here we are. Grab a seat; let's enjoy this gorgeous day, and while we're munching on these delicious muffins, you can tell me all about your friend's landscaping business. I'll just be a few minutes brewing that coffee."

Mike took off his hat and placed it on the table. "No coffee for me, thanks. I've been up since the crack of dawn so I've had my share of caffeine. Given a choice, I prefer the outdoors any day opposed to bein' all cooped up inside. Can't say I'm happy unless I'm out on the land or with my animals. I'm a morning person, up with the roosters, so I make a nice thermos full of steamin' coffee and head down to the barn. I like to spend my days off muckin' out the stalls and groomin' my horses. Nothin' like some fresh country air to energize the soul."

"I guess I've had enough caffeine," Tess said, brushing a blade of grass from her tank top. When she saw all the mud and grape stains soiling it, heat flushed her cheeks. As she tried to avoid looking directly at Mike, she focused on her new white sandals; they were ruined. Their color was now somewhere between a deep cherry red and mauve with thick globs of mud caked on the straps and heels. Here she was with this sexy hunk of a sheriff, looking like she'd just rolled in the mud.

Warmth crept up her neck and face, a slow but steady journey. She'd inherited her mother's Irish skin—fair complexion with freckles. She'd also been blessed with her mother's easy blush when embarrassed. Avoiding Mike's eyes, she did her best to make a graceful exit. "I'll go get us some bottled water, since I still have a few left. Later on this afternoon, I'll head down to the market and buy some supplies."

Her hand flew to her mouth. "Oops…I forgot I'm almost out of gas. Guess I won't be going anywhere."

"Well now, darlin', that's all taken care of." Mike bent down to pet Freddy. "You've got a full tank. While you were in the garden, I was up here fillin' your tank."

Mike was one of those neighbors who looked out for his friends. *I just might like having him around.* She smiled, a little more of that ice around her heart melting. "Thanks, Mike. No wonder Daddy thought the world of you."

"My pleasure, ma'am."

"So did your girlfriend forgive you for breaking the date last night?" The words tumbled out of Tess's mouth before she could stop them. What was it about Mike Andretti that made her drop her guard and just be herself? Then she felt a playful smile spreading across her face.

"No need to," Mike said, plopping down on the bench. "Seems she dumped me before I had a chance to dump her. Saw her this morning down at the bakery, sittin' outside on the patio with her new beau. They were sharin' a cappuccino, lookin' real cozy—like a match made in heaven."

"You got dumped by the woman you wanted to dump?" Tess tossed her head back and laughed. "How priceless."

"What can I say," Mike said, leaning down to scratch Freddy's ear. Then he looked directly into Tess's eyes. "Like I said, she wasn't my type."

Tess's breath caught when she saw her reflection in Mike's eyes. Her heart did a little pitter patter. Her words were thick, husky. "What exactly is your type, Sheriff?"

His smile was so easy it was impossible not to smile back. He brushed a twig from her hair, his face so close she could see the rings around his irises. She smelled the soap he'd used that morning, fresh, spicy and all male. His fingertip slid down her cheek, then he spoke, his voice low and husky. "Oh, ya' know, darlin'. Just your average girl-next-door type. The kind of woman a guy can be proud to take home and introduce to his mama."

Tess couldn't speak, but her heart was thumping loud enough to bring on the brass band. This man could get to her. She'd have to be careful and hang onto her heart, because as sure as the sun was going to set in the evening, this ruggedly handsome sheriff could crush it to a million pieces. The moment was broken when Freddy meowed loudly, demanding some attention.

"Hey there." Mike scooped him up. "Feelin' a little neglected?"

Freddy meowed and purred all the louder.

"You have a way with animals. I've never seen

my cat take to anyone the way he does you. Aside from me, he ignores everyone, snubs them. What's your secret?"

"Just love 'em. Got a few of these guys myself. Julio and Sir Walter. Then there's Hank, my big ol' Irish Setter. Thinks he's the cats' dad, kisses them good morning and good night. Had him since he was a pup. He follows me around when I'm out in the stable, tending to my horses and land."

"You sound like the Pied Piper," Tess said, enjoying the easy conversation. "I'm sure they all adore you."

"What can I say? I'm a sucker for strays. If a dog or cat comes to my door hurt or lost, I nurse 'em back to health and wind up givin' them a home. My land and the animals on it are the backbone of who I am, what I'm all about. I guess I'm a lot like you. Sparks fly in your eyes when ya' talk about the way these grounds once looked and will look again." He smiled, his dimple glinting. "Gotta love a woman after my own heart. Yes indeed, Tess Kincaid, I'm glad you'll be mistress of the manor."

Tess felt the heat rush to her cheeks again. Mistress of the manor indeed. She liked the sound of that, and she was pretty sure she'd like having Mike Andretti for a next door neighbor.

Picking a leaf from her hair, she flicked it to the ground, feeling as if the weight of the world had been lifted. She took in the scent of the ocean, the clover, the sweet wild flowers. She couldn't remember the last time she felt so relaxed, so at peace. "Well, I'll just be a few minutes. I'll run in, get that water and change my clothes before these stains are permanent. Be back in no time."

As Tess climbed through the thicket, she took in the splendor of the century old mansion; her heart swelled with pride. She'd make sure it would stay a Kincaid legacy for generations to come.

Chapter Six

His eyes narrowed, The Master crouched low in the deep underbrush of the forest, his camera focused on Contessa. Adjusting the lens, he zoomed in for a close up, the shutter snapping as he took the pictures.

He watched her and the White Knight walk across the vineyard, a jealous rage burning deep in his gut. He kicked the tip of his scuffed-up hunting boot into a tree branch that had fallen from a towering oak, his nostrils flaring.

A bushy-tailed squirrel scampered out from the clearing, chirring as it rustled through the foliage and up a maturing red spruce. The air was thick and dank with the smell of rot and wet earth. A falcon screeched as it swooped into the thicket, its carping cry foreboding.

Keeping vigil amidst a rich pallet of crimson, burnt orange and liquid amber, The Master's red hair and beard were the perfect camouflage. He scoffed to himself. Princess and White Knight were looking pretty cozy. Oops. Princess takes a skid in the wet leaves, White Knight to the rescue. Grabs her arm. Won't be long before White Knight makes a move. Princess notices tank top all covered in mud and turns beet red, oh so flustered. Capture the moment.

Snap snap. White Knight likes what he sees—pretty little princess down and dirty. Big smile. Princess in a centerfold.

The Master snapped photo after photo of

Contessa as she sauntered across the courtyard, her long hair rippling in the breeze. Nobody had hair like Contessa, the richest shade of mahogany, with highlights of burnished copper in the sun. The feel of it, as soft as spun silk. Closing his eyes, he could smell it, fresh and lovely, like wild flowers after a cleansing rain. The sway of her hips, as she undulated across the courtyard, was oh so inviting. His mouth watered, adrenaline and testosterone surging through his veins, arousing him. Then she disappeared into the mansion, the door slamming in her wake.

Oh how he had adored her, placed her high upon a pedestal. But she'd betrayed him, breaking promises with no regrets. He fingered the silver hoop earring in his left ear, the one she'd given as an emblem of undying love and fidelity. The bitch had done him wrong and would die in the final scene of his play. But not yet. He was having too much fun scaring her to death.

The Master chuckled at his own wit, thinking of the next scene. He couldn't wait.

The Master watched her enter the bedroom, a salacious rush surging through his blood. She stripped off her tank top, unveiling a pink and black lace push-up bra. Oh so sexy, full breasts spilling out. No silicone, Grade A large. Not a defect to be found. The Master drooled, licked his lips. Off go the shorts, sliding down long, shapely legs.

Snap snap. Barely there pink lace thong, triangle of hot pink covering the frontal view. Come on, baby, turn around and give us a thrill. She turns and opens her dresser drawer, displaying feminine wiles in satin and lace. She leans over, oh what a rush. Princess in a centerfold. Freeze frame.

****

Sitting in the picnic area, Tess and Mike enjoyed the muffins while soaking up the warm sunshine streaming over the harbor. A gentle sea breeze swooshed through the trees. A turtle meandered out of the pond to sun himself, and a dragonfly gracefully swooped down on the surface of the mirror-still water. Locusts buzzed with a chorus of crickets, performing a late summer symphony.

"It's still got that special something," Tess said, snapping a wild rose from its leafy green canopy. "It's always been magical here, like a sanctuary where birds harmonize with nature. Even though it needs a makeover, there's a quiet serenity that can't be broken or destroyed. I'm drawn to the peacefulness of the forest, the wildflowers framing the landscape, the hypnotic lull of the waves rolling into shore. The minute I pulled up the drive, I felt like I'd come home."

"Look over there." Mike pointed to a woodpecker drilling into the bark of a pine in a field of poppies. "Wish I had my camera. Check out that picture-perfect scene, all that satiny red carpeting the hillside. One of life's simple pleasures."

"I could sit here for hours," Tess said, rubbing some sunscreen on her arms and legs. "Thought I'd bring this down, along with some water. Even though my fair skin is sure to burn, this is a treat, sitting seaside soaking up the rays. Takes me back to when I was a little girl, trying to soak up the last rays of sunshine before my summer vacation with Daddy came to an end."

Mike dug into the goodies, fishing out a muffin bursting with blueberries. He wiggled the bag, a mischievous glint in his eye. "One more chocolate chip muffin in there with your name on it. If the Seaside Bakery doesn't convince ya' you've come home, nothin' will."

Tess snatched one, sank her teeth into it and closed her eyes in utter ecstasy. The chocolate chips melted in her mouth. "Mmmm. Ambrosia. When I moved to New York, I was so spoiled; I became a bakery snob. You know what they say—once you have the best, nothing else will do."

Mike winked. "Is that what they say?"

Tess felt her cheeks bloom a bright cherry red. Well she'd walked right into that one, hadn't she? She stammered. "Ah…I think I'll plead the Fifth on that one."

Mike finished his muffin, licking his fingers. "That was delicious. I could eat a dozen more." He patted his belly, his well-toned six pack Abs. "Good thing I work the horses with such vigor; otherwise, I might be getting that middle-aged spread."

"Hmm…" Tess studied him, conjuring up images of him taking off into the wild blue yonder on a bucking stallion, his bronze body gleaming in the sun, his streaked blond hair blowing in the breeze. Her gaze went to his bulging biceps, the tattooed horse sending a ripple of excitement through her. "Ah…I can't help but notice that rather interesting tattoo on your arm, the way it bucks when you flex your muscle. It's a real eye catcher. Is there a story behind it?"

"Well now, darlin', every picture tells a story, doesn't it? My buddy, Chip, the guy who owns the landscaping business, dared me to do it. We were out drinkin' one New Year's Eve and wound up at a tattoo parlor. Can't say I was thinking very clearly that night. How about it, Tess…got any secret tattoos?"“

Tess smiled, but she wasn't about to tell him she had a wild rose tattoo on her hip. She liked him. He was easy to talk to, easy to be with and she enjoyed his company. He was so refreshing after all the cool and aloof men she'd known in New York. Mike Andretti had a winning smile and a down-home country charm that made him one in a million. So far, this ruggedly handsome sheriff was doing a mighty fine job of winning her over. Her thoughts were broken by horses neighing in the distance. "So tell me how you came to live on the Wexler land. The way I remember, old lady Wexler was an eccentric woman and we were all afraid of her. She used to stand on her front porch, all stooped over her broom, sweeping leaves with a vengeance. Plus, she always had that creepy bird perched on her shoulder. They were quite a pair."

Mike guffawed, his laughter rolling across the acres. His golden brown eyes twinkled. "About that bird. Here's somethin' that'll tickle your fancy. Not only did I inherit the Wexler land, but I inherited the bird, Sir Galahad." He grinned, that slow, easy smile spreading across his face. "Sir Galahad must be several decades old by now but no one knows for sure. Talk about a character, that bird is one for the books."

"I hate birds." Tess shuddered. "Ever since that Alfred Hitchcock movie. After that, I developed a bird phobia, afraid they'd come get me."

"Ah...you'll just have to meet Sir Galahad. He'll change your mind. As far as how I inherited the estate...well now, that's real interesting. I was born and raised on Mount Desert Island, and as a teenager, I needed work. So I answered an ad for a laborer at the Wexler place. Right off the bat, I took a real shine to the horses and the land, and then once I got on the good side of Ms. Wexler, she gave me more hours. She taught me a lot about the horses. When she got all crippled up with arthritis, I made sure she got to her doctor appointments. Then, when she died, she left her entire estate to me—I was shocked."

Tess suddenly understood why her dad, a lonely old woman and strays took such a liking to the town sheriff. He was a simple man with a heart of gold, someone they could trust. Tess watched a butterfly flutter above a rosebush of Seven Sisters. Then she turned to Mike.

"When people and animals trust you, that says a lot about a person's character. It's easy to see you're a caring person, one who goes the extra mile to help a friend or neighbor. Daddy apparently thought the world of you which tells me you're someone I can trust, too. I'm glad you're my neighbor, Mike."

"Well now, darlin', that goes both ways."

Tess gestured toward the Wexler ranch. "Tell me about the horses. How do you fit it all in—the horses, the land, and the duties as the town sheriff?"

Mike smiled, displaying a set of straight, white teeth. "That's easy. First of all, as the sheriff, I work four days, so I've got a lot of extra time to take care of things. Secondly, I fit it all in...cause it's what I love doin'."

Just then, the hair on the back of Tess's neck prickled. She had the sudden feeling she was being watched, and following the feeling with her eyes, she looked up to the bell tower and gasped. A huge falcon was perched on the steeple, its piercing black eyes fixed on her. Shivers danced down her spine, her phobia of birds making her uneasy.

Noticing Mike's questioning gaze, she stammered. "Ah...sometimes I feel like someone is watching me. Maybe it comes from living in New York for so many years and developing eyes in back of my head. Like a sixth sense, I felt eyes burning a hole in my back, and just now, I spotted that creepy falcon on the steeple up there, see?"

Mike squinted into the brilliant sunshine, the corners of his eyes crinkling. "The woods and forests around these parts are full of peregrine falcons. It's their habit to perch high and survey their kingdom for prey. Nothin' to be scared of, darlin'. It's just a bird, a harmless bird keepin' vigil."

"Maybe. Truth is..." She hesitated and

shrugged. "Ah…maybe I shouldn't go into this, but the night before I came back here to the island, I got a rather disturbing fan letter. It was written in crimson red ink. Real creepy, like blood. It contained one sentence. *I'm your biggest fan.*"

"Did you call the police?"

Tess recalled how security had reacted, treating her as if dealing with a petulant child. Even though she knew her biggest fan had been in her condo, they didn't believe her. She was sorry she'd brought it up. But, after witnessing something similar last night in the ballroom, she decided not to hold anything back. "There's more to the story. You see, it was the night of the Romance Writers of America conference. The last night is the Awards Banquet for the RITA and Golden Heart, two of the most prestigious awards in the romance genre. I won the RITA. Then when I got home, there was a peculiar letter in my mailbox. It was addressed to Contessa. Other than my dad, no one knows me by that name. When I opened the door to my condo, someone had been in there. All the windows were open and it was pouring down rain. 'Moonlight Sonata' was playing on my CD player. I know I didn't leave the windows open nor did I leave the stereo on. The worst part, though, came when I ran for help. By the time security checked it out, there was no sign of disturbance. Even the letter, which I'd tossed on the floor, was gone without a trace. Security didn't believe me, Mike. But that night, I got a phone call from a man with a raspy voice." She stopped and caught her breath. "He…ah…said he'd been in my condo, going through my…panties. And…he said he was my biggest fan and was coming for me."

Chapter Seven

Mike studied her long and hard before speaking, his gaze searching. “I see a pattern here, Tess.” He shifted gears within a heartbeat. Warm golden brown eyes turned dark and broody. He measured her with an appraising stare. “So you’re tellin’ me with a few added theatrics, this has happened before?”

Tess shrugged, feeling foolish for bringing it up. “Look, Mike. I know how it sounds, really, but believe it or not, it’s true. This is the second time a bizarre event has happened to me. I’m well aware of how it sounds, and I have no explanation other than a hunch. Someone is trying to scare me. And guess what? It’s working. I haven’t been this on edge since the news of Daddy’s suicide. I have no one to turn to—no family, no siblings. Mama and Daddy both gone now. I’m all alone in this world. If someone is stalking me, following me from New York to New England, you bet I’m scared. That letter was real and so were the phone call and the music and the...” She stopped, tears pooling in her eyes.

“Tess...” Mike’s eyes softened, his hand resting on her shoulder. “Help me gather all the facts since this is the first I’m hearin’ about the fan letter. Let’s go back. I think we need to take a look at your life. I want a full list of your associates in New York, friend or foe, anyone you can think of, especially all nominees for the RITA. That’s a good place to start. We’ll go back to the night of the awards ceremony. Also, who knew you were comin’ back to Bar

Harbor?"

"No one…well, just my editor, and there's no way she's my stalker. The person who called me is definitely a man." Tess recalled the salacious things he'd whispered on the phone. She'd never forget the icy chill of those words. She looked into Mike's eyes and saw doubt. Her heart sank. "It's all true, Mike, really. His dark laughter haunts me. I'll never forget it, not for as long as I live. I have no clue who he is. I really never made any close friends in New York, and, outside of work-related events, I didn't have much of a social life. I spent most of my days and nights doing what writers do—write."

"You didn't date?"

Tess shook her head. "Not all that much, dinners and Broadway shows now and again. Nothing serious. You have to be a writer to understand, but it's a commitment, heart and soul. Between the research, the outline and synopsis, first draft through fruition, all the edits and galleys…well, there really isn't time for a busy social life. Then, as you become more popular, there are the promotional tours, interviews, and book signings. I'm telling you—it never ends. A writer is a recluse, a hermit. Computers are our best friends. So that's why moving here was so enticing. A change of scenery stirs the creative muse. I was so looking forward to coming home, but if my biggest fan has followed me here, threatening me in my childhood home, he's someone very clever—and very close."

"Tell me about the music, 'Moonlight Sonata'? You said it was playing in your New York condo, same as in the ballroom on the old Victrola? What's the link?"

"It's my favorite, has been since I was a little girl. Daddy always had it playing during masquerade parties, the haunting lyrics and chilling piano melody created the perfect ambiance. Even so, the melody is so beautiful I fell in love with the old classic. It keeps my childhood memories alive. Not only that, but it's so romantic. I even played it at my first piano recital when I was twelve-years-old."

Something flickered in Mike's eyes, just for a second. "You played it at a recital when you were twelve?"

"I sure did, brought the house down as I recall." Tess smiled, calling up the memory. "Got a standing ovation. Mama and Daddy were so proud, and to my delight and great pride, my piano teacher presented me with a dozen red roses, my very first bouquet."

"Okay," Mike said, his jaw clenched. "I'll want the name of that teacher, along with any guests you remember being at the recital. I'll also want the name of the studio where the recital took place. One more thing...give me the names of anyone who might know this is your favorite song. We'll get to the bottom of this, Tess, ya' got my word."

Tess nodded, the feeling she was being watched more intense than ever. She felt eyes on her, but couldn't tell exactly where they were. Despite the creepy eyes of the falcon, still peering at her from its perch on the steeple, she sensed evil from the deepest part of the thicket. Her insides turned to water. The falcon's beady eyes bore into hers, the black mustache on its white face daunting.

Just then, the powerful bird flapped its wings before taking flight into the thicket, its shrill screech chilling. Icy fingers of fear gripped Tess from the inside out.

Chapter Eight

Thinking about the falcon, the fan letter, the phone call, and all the bizarre happenings of the past week, Tess's sunny mood darkened. What had started as a bright new day had turned gloomy, despite the cloudless horizon. She stood up, brushing the crumbs from her denim shorts.

"Ah...look, Mike. I appreciate you being so neighborly, bringing these delicious baked goods and filling my tank with gas, but I need to buckle down and get to work. I spent time weeding out my garden, and now I should start on the inside. There must be a million things to do, and I know all twenty-four rooms need a good cleaning." She stared up at the window of her dad's room, feeling boneless. "I think I'll call a cleaning service. Got any to recommend?"

"Tess..." He brushed the tip of his finger along her forearm. "There's no rush to go in your dad's room."

"I know, but it isn't something I can avoid forever. Right now, it's too soon. The image I create in my mind of what he did in there is simply too intense..." She broke down, her voice cracking. She rubbed her temples, feeling lightheaded. "Who am I kidding? I can't go in there, see the bed, the place where he...I just can't."

"Believe me, I understand. There's no hurry, and just so ya' know, after the crime scene was investigated, it was all cleaned. I took care of it myself. Once everything was documented, the mattresses were removed. The frame is still there but with so much…" He stopped, his calloused hands rubbing Tess's chilled arms. "I'm sorry, darlin', but let's just say, they're gone. If ya' want, I'll help when ya' do decide to go in and clear out Jake's belongings. It's your call."

Tess shook her head, unable to speak as his words registered. She hadn't even given the bed a thought, hadn't even imagined the full extent of the scene. She felt nausea rise, turned and gagged, acid churning in the pit of her stomach. Coffee and blueberries mingled and rolled, producing a sour taste. She reached for the bottled water, but Mike beat her to it.

"Take a sip…real easy, now. What ya' need is some soda and crackers, good for what ails ya."

"That's what Daddy used to give me." Tess dabbed the beads of sweat from her forehead. She drank some water, feeling a little better. "We have a theater in the mansion, complete with a popcorn maker. I loved to have slumber parties where my friends and I used to sit, spellbound, as we watched a movie, gorging ourselves with soft drinks, candy and popcorn. It would never fail; in the middle of the night, I'd wake up crying with a stomachache, and Daddy would bring me soda and crackers."

"Never learned your lesson, huh?" Mike teased. "Stuff yourself silly, time after time. I can just see you as a little girl, all caught up in the movie, stuffin' your mouth full of junk food. Did it myself."

"It's one of those unwritten rules of childhood." Tess laughed, beginning to feel more like herself. "Gluttons for punishment. Now if I can just find my cat, I'll go back and get started, beginning with a tour of the entire mansion so I can figure out what to tackle first. Now, where is Freddy?" She scanned the hillside. "Freddy. Here, boy. Where is he?"

"There he is, baskin' in the sun in the middle of

all those tiger lilies down there. Watch this, I'll show ya' my animal magnetism. All my critters come runnin' when I call."

"Not Freddy," Tess said, somewhat amused as Mike put his thumb and forefinger between his lips, producing a shrill whistle.

The cat sprinted through the meadow like a streak of black lightning, straight for the sheriff. Mike looked at Tess, his golden brown eyes gleaming with satisfaction. "Told ya; animals adore me."

"You must be the Dr. Dolittle of Bar Harbor." Tess scooped Freddy up in her arms. "You'll have to teach me your techniques."

"Anytime."

They passed through a meadow where herbs grew wild and free, their blossoms sending a pleasant medley of thyme, basil, and sage through the air. Seagulls squawked in the distance, their sharp cries echoing across the water. Beneath sun-drenched skies, a deep sea fishing vessel set out for an excursion. As the tide rolled in, frothy waves crashed over the great rocks, producing a rhythmic lull.

Mike stared out to sea, shielding the sun from his eyes with his hand. "Just checkin' to see if my buddy's out there today. Chip has a sailboat. If he's not clearin' off someone's land, that's where he'll be. He enters the sailboat races every year."

In the back of the estate, high on the bluffs above the ocean, the bell tower loomed in eerie silence. An uneasiness crept through Tess, the feeling she was being watched more intense than ever. As they crossed the courtyard, she glanced up to the loft jutting out from the upper wing. Chills skated down her spine. She could have sworn she'd just seen someone wave at her from the dormer window. She sucked in her breath and mouthed the word. "Daddy?"

When the clock in the tower struck four, she nearly jumped out of her skin. She came to an abrupt halt, her mouth agape.

"Tess?" Mike watched her, his eyes narrowed. "You all right?"

Tess squeezed Freddy to her chest, her heart racing. She broke out in a cold sweat, blinked several times and looked at the loft window again. Nothing but sweeping pine branches, painting willowy shadows. Her skin felt drawn and tight. She felt as if she was being suffocated. She drew in a sharp breath.

"Tess, what is it?"

"I swore I saw someone up in the window, and it spooked me. Daddy always studied his script up there and when I came running home, he'd look down and wave at me. It freaked me out. I guess it was just a shadow from the pines, but the image was so striking for a second."

Mike dug into the pocket of his jeans. "Still got my key to your house. Jake gave it to me, just in case. Stay put and I'll go check it out."

Tess watched Mike barge through the door and into the house. She clung to Freddy, stroking his back. "It's all right, boy. You sensed it, too, didn't you? Someone was up there. I feel it in my bones." Tess felt eyes watching her, evil eyes from the deepest part of the thicket. Turning around, she peered up at the bell tower and the surrounding forests of Acadia National Park. The breeze swooshed through the leaves. Other than the warbling screech of a hoot owl, the woods were quiet. But Tess knew better. It was the calm before the storm. Someone was watching her.

"No one in there." Mike loped down the steps. "It's a century old manor, Tess, so there's bound to be dark shadows. With the recent death of your dad, it's no wonder you're easily spooked. Come on, I'll go in with ya' and make sure everything's cool."

"It's all right, really," Tess broke in. "I'm fine and would feel just awful if I took up any more of your time. First last night, and now your day off. Go on, really."

Mike was already marching up the stone steps to the veranda, holding the door open for her. "I'm the sheriff and I insist. Not only that, but we're neighbors and that makes ya' my responsibility, Ms. Kincaid. After you."

Tess entered the foyer, a smile teasing her lips. Mike Andretti's responsibility, was she? She put Freddy down, idly watching him scamper down the corridor. Then she turned to this man who was becoming very important to her—not just her next door neighbor, buddy of her dad's, or man of authority. Lord Almighty, he was handsome, in a rugged sort of way. Arms bristling with muscles, six pack abs, sun-bleached hair pulled back in a ponytail, that stallion tattoo—all wrapped up together, they gave him the look of a wild warrior. *Oh yeah.*

"So about my friend, the guy who has the landscaping business? Tess, did you hear a word I said?"

She hadn't. She'd been too busy admiring his mighty fine physique. She blinked several times, grasping enough of the conversation to come up with an answer. "Ah...sure. Whatever you think. If he's your friend and you trust him, then by all means, give him a call. The sooner the better."

"Great. Now let's take a little tour of the mansion, shall we?"

Chapter Nine

"This is like taking a trip through the Roman Forum," Tess said, her stomach tightening as they toured the garden ruins. "My mother took such pride in her roses when she lived here, not to mention her lady's slippers and orchids. The lavender was so sweet, you'd swear you were in one of those royal courtyards in England."

"Maybe Chip can spruce things up in here, too," Mike said.

As they approached her father's den, Mike stepped back to let her enter. Her gaze moved across a room fashioned with old-world influence; the den was large and spacious with Spanish decor. Rose-colored walls surrounded large windows with wrought iron fixtures. A Casablanca fan hung from the high, wooden-beamed ceiling and ebony tiles enclosed a stone fireplace. Featured above that fireplace was an imposing portrait of the great Jake Kincaid, rustling a bucking bronco. His unblinking stare beckoned, daring anyone to tame him.

Tess stood in front of that portrait now, awed by its jarring affect. His presence was so palpable the walls vibrated with his presence. It was impossible to imagine such a powerful man committing suicide. It didn't make sense, not for a man who'd been bigger than life.

Wiping the tears rolling down her cheeks, she gestured toward the portrait. "Daddy was so proud when he got the starring role in that old Western, *Vendetta of an Outlaw*. It was his biggest hit. Look at that ten-gallon Stetson. Once that thing was planted on Daddy's head, there was no getting him to take it off."

Mike brushed the tears from Tess's cheeks. "Those bewitching green eyes are much too pretty to be puffy. Come on now, darlin', just hang onto those good times. That's what I do. I like to think about the times we would share a laugh over a bottle of his vintage wine. We had some mighty fine times, me and Jake. There's no way I'm gonna let him rob me of those memories. So when I think of what he did, I just shove that to the back of my mind and focus on better times. That's what you ought to do, too; a good place to start might be that blue garden."

"You know about that?"

"You bet. Jake said he got the notion to plant a garden of forget-me-nots in your honor, just to show ya' you'd be on his mind until the next visit."

"Yeah," Tess said, looking into the eyes of the man in the portrait. "I liked the color blue so much. I said I wanted to plant all blue flowers, a place where happiness would always bloom."

"That's sweet." Mike stepped closer. "I saw ya' out there this morning', clippin' away. It was easy to see how much the garden meant to you, the sentimental value it holds. I know your dad was with ya' in spirit, Tess?"

Tess felt the heat radiating from Mike's body. An electrical current charged through the air, causing the tiny hairs on her arms to bristle. Her breathing grew shallow. "I adored that garden, especially the forget-me-nots. Daddy said he never heard of a blue garden before, but I proved him wrong. The lady at the greenhouse said there was nothing prettier than a blue border in a white stone arbor. So we planted flowers in all shades of blue. It looked so pretty. Daddy said it was fit for a queen."

"That's just what you are." Mike tucked a strand

of hair behind her ear. "Royalty."

Yep, Tess mused, *Sheriff Mike Andretti was gonna be the man who broke her heart.* Her mother used to tell her when the right man came along, there would be no mistake. Tess never knew what she meant by that statement, but she was beginning to understand.

"So which room will you attack first?" Mike asked, his eyes a shade darker.

Tess's heart skipped a beat. Then her gaze swept the spacious den. Cobwebs hung in every corner. Double hung windows were streaked with rain and grime, and the dark wooden panels that once gleamed were now dull and dusty. Worst of all, the closed-in den reeked of stale tobacco and the sweat of a man whose spirit had died long before his body.

Just as Tess turned to open a window, she heard footsteps on the staircase down the hall. Blocking all else out, she listened, her ear cocked toward the door. *Creak.* A sense of dread filled her as she remembered the hand she thought she saw in the loft. Then she heard it again. *Creak.*

"What is it, Tess?" Mike asked, a crease lining his forehead. "Haunted by old ghosts?"

Tess leaned toward him, whispering, "Did you hear that? A creak on the steps? Listen."

Mike held his forefinger to his lips, turned on his heels and crept to the doorway. Then he disappeared down the corridor. Tess followed slowly, her heart racing. Her pulse hammering. She peered down the hallway to the foot of the steps.

"Meow."

Mike stood there, holding Freddy. He winked. "Here's your cat burglar. Caught 'em red-handed."

Relief stormed through Tess. She knew she had to get over these phobias.

Returning to the den, she opened the double

hung window, bringing in the scent of the salty sea air. The curtains rustled, dust bunnies floated through the air in the sunlight. Tess's nose tickled. "Ah choo!"

"God bless ya, darlin'."

"I was just thinking about all the elbow grease it's gonna take to clean this den. As I'm sure you know, the den was Daddy's smoking room. See the cigar humidor over there on the wall? I bought that for him on his last birthday. There are even cigarette butts still in the ashtrays, some cigar stumps, too. When I was a little girl, Daddy used to smoke a corn pipe filled with cherry pipe tobacco. I can still smell the faintest hint of it. When I was younger, Mama kept after him to keep his den clean, even though it was his private domain. She took pride in making everything sparkle and shine, usually using bee's wax and lemon. If my mother could see the state of this mansion, she'd turn over in her grave."

"Funny thing," Mike said, scratching the stubble on his chin. "My dad smokes cherry pipe tobacco and my mom cleans with bee's wax. With that kinda connection, we've gotta be soulmates, destined to meet."

Tess smiled, his easy charm pulling at her heartstrings. He was getting to her. Another chunk of ice around her heart melted. "Do your parents live near here?"

"Right here on the island. Matter of fact, I go there for dinner every Sunday. After all of us kids left home, Mama and Dad rustled around that old house with no one to fuss over, so they turned the ol' homestead into a bed and breakfast. You'd like it, like them too. They're real friendly folks."

"They sound charming. You must be a chip off the old block, huh?"

Mike tipped his Stetson. "Apple never falls far from the tree. So when did your mother die, Tess?"

"Mama died five years ago of congestive heart failure. Truth be told, she died of a broken heart after the divorce. She stopped living, stopped caring about life. She just sat in her room, staring into space. She couldn't live with Daddy, but she sure couldn't live without him either."

"Damn shame when families bust up. Leaves emotional scars all around."

"Yeah." Tess lifted her eyes to the portrait of her dad once again. "How different life might have turned out if we had all stayed together as a family. But enough of the past. Let's talk about something else, okay?"

"You got it, darlin'. So where is Tess Kincaid gonna work, tap out the pages of her next best-selling thriller?"

Tess beamed. "The loft where Daddy used to study his lines. He always said it brought him good luck. It was his favorite room in the mansion, next to his den. Come on, let's check it out."

Taking the stairway to the landing, Tess turned right into a cozy loft. The sunny room offered a panoramic view of the rocky New England coastline. With autumn closing in over the harbor, the days were getting shorter. The last of the setting sun poured in through a skylight, bathing the room. A rare collection of butterfly face masks took up an entire wall. The bell tower loomed on the top of the hill across the courtyard, tall and mighty like a Gothic gargoyle.

"So what do you think?" Tess snatched a tissue to wipe the dust off the rosewood writing desk. "Some view, huh?"

"I'd say it's a writer's dream." Mike gazed as the sun disappeared behind the trees of Acadia National Park. "But I gotta be honest with ya. Lookin' at that gorgeous sunset, the way it's merging into coral, indigo and lavender blue, I'm thinkin' maybe it might stir your romantic muse, make ya' try your hand at a romance novel. Go on, take a look. That's what I call damn near perfect."

"It's truly beautiful," Tess agreed. "Watching the sky merge into all those hazy hues makes me wish I'd taken up art rather than writing. Pictures really do paint a thousand words."

She turned and brushed against Mike's arm, the bristly hairs tickling her skin. A surge of liquid heat soared through her, causing her blood to sizzle. The pulse in the hollow of her neck throbbed. His tall, muscular frame dominated the small loft. He was so close to her she felt his breath fan her face. He didn't say a word, but his body spoke a language all its own. His golden brown eyes burned with desire. Slightly breathless, she licked her lips. "Ah…you were saying?"

He moved toward her, closing the distance. He wrapped his arms around her waist, yanking her to his chest. His muscles bunched and quivered and his breath was ragged. He ran his fingers through her hair, fanning it out in wild disarray. His gaze held hers for a second before his lips swooped down on hers with a feverish rush, his tongue teasing and taunting. Every pulse in her body raced, every nerve ending twitched, every sensation intensified.

Just then, the bell in the tower rang out, its piercing gong echoing straight through her heart. The air hummed with silence. Tess's body trembled from the aftershock of the kiss.

Mike smiled, rubbing his calloused finger over Tess's cheek. "Ya' know what they say, darlin'. Timing is everything. But that was some kiss…been dyin' to do that since I first set eyes on ya."

His kiss left her completely spellbound. Her lips still throbbed and she could still taste him. Oh yeah. Mike Andretti would be starring in her dreams tonight.

Mike brushed her lips with a feathery kiss. “Can I tempt ya’ for dinner on the bluffs? It’s a beautiful evening and there’s nothin’ I’d like more than to spend it with a beautiful woman.”

Tess felt Cupid’s arrow pierce straight through her heart. “I’d love to.”

****

From the bell tower, The Master watched, nostrils flaring, breathing ragged. He yanked on his silver hoop earring and scoffed. So much for love and fidelity. He spit on the floor of the tower, unfocused eyes glinting with anger.

The slut. Pretty little princess falls from grace. White Knight didn’t wait long to put the moves on. Musta woke up with a boner the size of a baseball bat. The kiss had been x-rated.

They were no better than alley cats, going at it in the loft where he’d stood less than an hour ago. But all good things came to those who waited, and the best was yet to come. Pretty little princess down for the count. He was coming to get her. And when he did, he’d pounce on her like the big bad wolf.

Turning, The Master raced down the one hundred steps to crouch in the underbrush. No way was he about to get caught spying on Princess and White Knight. He was far too coy, far too clever. He was The Master.

Shrouded by blades of tall grass and shrubbery, The Master crouched down on a bed of fern and pine needles, spying. He watched them descend the stone steps from the mansion, his blood so hot it was about to quake. His eyes gleamed with jealous rage as he thrashed around in the tangled underbrush. Bristly pine branches slapped across his arms and shoulders; thorns scratched his bearded face. But he kept slashing, his muscular arms shredding through foliage. He fumed and struck out, spital drooling from the corner of his cracked lips.

His heart beat at a wild rhythm, adrenaline and testosterone pumping. Pretty little princess, oh how befitting, playing the role of damsel in distress. White Knight comes charging to the rescue in the pouring rain, Glock cocked and ready. Oh so gallant. A day later, Princess has him hooked. Comes a callin' with a bag of muffins. Oops. Could use a lesson in Romance 101. Shoulda brought forget-me-nots.

The Master watched Contessa and the White Knight cross the courtyard and descend the steep wooden steps to the beach, hand in hand. Anger rose within him. He fingered the earring and scoffed. The bitch, oh how she'd suffer for her betrayal. He watched her, looking oh so sweet and demure in her denim shorts and mint green T-shirt. Her thick mahogany hair was all wind-blown, giving her a sexy look that drove him crazy. How he remembered the way her hair felt, the way it tickled his skin, the way it smelled, so fresh and lovely like jasmine after a cleansing rain. The memories aroused him.

The Master kept vigil in the deep underbrush until Contessa and the White Knight faded from view. Furious, he stood up and stomped around. Crushing dry pinecones and acorns, The Master spotted the remains of a falcon in the underbrush, the acrid smell of decay pungent. Gagging, he kicked it with the tip of his hunting boot. Maggots fed on the rotted corpse. The eyes had been pecked out of the sockets, but its massive wings were still spread as if in flight.

The Master's thoughts spun round and round like a wheel in a hamster's cage. Then an explosion of neurons fired, giving birth to a brilliant idea.

Yes, yes, yes! His spirit renewed; he leapt high in the air.

The Master beamed. His dark laughter rolled through the forest. He rubbed his hands together, anticipating the look of fear on her face. A surge of adrenaline bolted through his system, giving him an all-time high.

Bravo! He was oh so brilliant, such a grand master. Tonight's performance would be oh so frightful. Pretty little princess scared speechless.

Chapter Ten

Magoo's was the perfect little seafood grotto with patio seating. It overlooked Frenchman Bay with its historic lighthouse on the rocky ledge at the entrance to the bay. Festive island music played as the sun disappeared.

"Good evening." The waiter appeared. "My name is Chuck and I'll be your server tonight. Can I get you started with something to drink?"

Tess looked up from her menu and smiled. "Can you recommend a good wine? Something not too dry, not too sweet, with a little kick."

"Our mead is very nice," Chuck said. "Wildflower honey, goldenrod and buttercup predominate the character, producing a lovely wine. The hint of clove gives it a little spicy kick."

"My goodness," Tess said, closing her menu. "After such a lovely, detailed description, how could I not try a glass. It sounds perfect."

"Excellent. And for you, sir?"

"I'll have a draft."

"I'll be right back with your drinks."

"I'm so glad to be home." Tess would never tire of watching the waves crash over the rocks. "Look at the seal out there."

"He's givin' ya' a Bar Harbor greeting." Mike gave her hand a playful squeeze, his golden brown eyes twinkling. "Gotta love it here on the harbor. Can't imagine livin' anywhere else in the entire world. Born and raised on Mount Desert Island, so I know these reefs and bluffs well. When I was a kid, my buddies and I spent hours huntin' down collapsed sea caves so we could skin dive and climb rock."

"Now there's something I haven't thought of in years," Tess said as the waiter presented their drinks. "My friends and I used to pretend we were pirates, hunting for sunken treasures in those caves. We'd spend all day searching for old coins, something to keep as a souvenir. All we'd ever find was seashells, but we'd let our imaginations run wild and pretend we'd found sunken treasure. Now there's a story dying to be written. See that, my creative muse is kicking in after just one day of sitting seaside."

"Are you folks ready to order?" The waiter appeared, pencil poised.

Tess sipped her wine and set it down. "I'm craving some Maine lobster with lots of butter and lemon."

"Very good, and you, sir?"

"Cheeseburger, medium rare, with an order of fries."

"I'll put those orders in."

Mike inhaled the brisk salty air. He pointed to a humpback whale about three hundred feet from the deck. "Seems all the sea creatures are rearing their heads to welcome ya' home."

"This feels wonderful." Tess leaned back in her seat, allowing the sea breeze to blow her hair all askew. In the distance, the fog horn blasted, producing a mewling echo so loud and unexpected Tess nearly jumped out of her skin. Clutching the edge of the table, she laughed out loud. "I'd forgotten all about that blasted thing."

Mike choked on his beer. Half sputtering, he let loose with a belly laugh that echoed across the dock. "The look on your face was priceless. Your eyes about popped out; man-oh-man, I sure wish I had my camera."

The waiter placed the food on the table. Tess eyed the lobster floating in a trough of butter and nearly swooned. She snatched one up. "I've been dreaming about these since I left the harbor."

"Nothing like good food, good company and good laughter."

Tess licked her lips. "These are absolutely delicious."

Mike reached across the table and dabbed at Tess's bottom lip. "Got a little butter, right there. By the way, did I mention I got a hold of my buddy earlier. He said his crew can start clearin' out your land anytime you like." He dug into his pocket. "Here is Chip's business card, Red Spruce Landscaping. I took the liberty of jottin' down my phone numbers on the back—home, work and cell. Why don't you give me your cell number? With all the power outages we have in these parts, we can't always count on land lines, so it's best to have a cell phone, too."

"I couldn't live without mine." Tess jotted her number on a napkin. "I rarely use a land line, but they're all over the mansion and I'm going to keep them. That was another thing Daddy collected, as you probably know, antique phones from classic thrillers. They're all over the mansion and some have very creepy rings. I'm telling ya, I could get a fortune if I sold them. However, they're all part of the good memories that haunt the house so I won't ever part with them, even if I don't hook them up."

"That's somethin' I find very curious. With your old man's passion for drama, I'm surprised he didn't star in films more befitting his personality."

Tess smiled. "There were so many times I thought that same thing while living in the mansion. I asked Daddy about it one day and he compared it to Halloween. He said if the spookiest holiday of the year occurred more than once every twelve months, the thrill would be gone. Daddy's passion for work and play were like night and day. His Westerns portrayed Jake Kincaid the man, his love of the great outdoors and adventure. Spooky collections and masquerades portrayed Jake Kincaid the boy, his love of thrill and excitement."

Mike pushed his empty plate aside. "Makes sense. Well, as relaxing as this is, it's time I tend to the animals. Plus, I'm on duty tomorrow, bright and early. I'll just get the check."

"That was delicious. Thank you very much for a relaxing evening; I really enjoyed it."

Mike took her hand as they walked through the rocky hillside. "I was thinkin' about how your dad explained keepin' his love of those two very different parts of his life separate. I guess that puts it all in perspective. Sounds like a good balance. Ya' know what they say, all work and no play makes Jake a dull boy."

The palm of Tess's hand tingled as they walked. Holding hands with Mike felt right, a perfect fit. She hadn't known him long, but she felt a strong connection brewing between them. She stared up at the stars twinkling in the blanket of blue velvet. The contentment she felt now almost overwhelmed her. She sighed, inhaling the fresh smell of sweet clover and wild roses from the bordering meadows. Her first evening out in Bar Harbor had been fun. She looked over and smiled. Mike Andretti was definitely getting to her.

Chapter Eleven

“Thanks for a wonderful day,” Tess said. “It did my heart good to have a relaxing evening on the reef. Good food, good wine and good company. This is just what I need to start my life anew.”

“Hey, do you remember the clambake down at the beach every Labor Day weekend?” Mike asked as they walked up the stone steps to the wrap-around veranda.

“Do I ever.” Tess’s mouth watered at the memory. “There’s nothing like the tantalizing aroma from that event. It was one of the high points of my visit each year. Clams never tasted so good, and it was a great way to end the summer.”

“It’s coming up next weekend. Wanna go? I’ll introduce you to a lot of local folks. Gotta warn ya, though. They might want your autograph. It’s not every day we get a best-selling author in our midst.”

“Sounds great. I didn’t realize how much I missed the island until I came back; folks in Bar Harbor just mosey along at their own pace in this private little enclave. It’s like stepping back in time to the days when fishing on the high seas was the only way to make a living.”

In the distance, several horses neighed, their whinnies carrying over the noise of the crashing waves rolling into shore.

“Well,” Mike said, looking toward his ranch. “Guess the natives are restless; time to feed ’em before turnin’ in for the night. Best be on my way. You gonna be all right, Tess?”

Tess already had her key in the lock. She turned to him and smiled. "I'll be fine, Mike. With all this fresh air and that delicious wine, I'll be sleeping well tonight."

"Good night, Tess." His lips touched hers with a feathery light kiss. "Sweet dreams."

Tess closed her door, bolting it. She tossed her purse on the floor beneath the tree stand. Out of habit, she kicked her shoes off and walked barefoot down the hall. She loved the feel of the cool marble tiles beneath her feet. After wearing a new pair of sandals all day, it felt like utter bliss.

Freddy rubbed against her leg, begging for food and attention. She scooped him up in her arms, comforted by his warm body and the low purr erupting from deep in his throat. Just then, there was a sharp tapping on the solid oak door. Carrying Freddy with her, Tess went to answer it.

Mike must have forgotten something. She unbolted the door and swung it open. "Mike?"

There was no one there. She stared through the blackness, but could see nothing. The crisp fall air blew in from the ocean, stirring the salty smell of the sea...and something else. She sniffed again, wrinkling her nose.

What in the world?

She looked around the well-lit courtyard and as far across her land as she could see. Nothing. The wind shifted just a bit, causing the stench hit her full in the face. She swallowed, trying to stop the gagging.

Confused, she stepped onto the porch and onto something soft and squishy. Her high-pitched screech rang through the courtyard. Freddy hissed and snarled, springing from her arms. She scrambled to shake off the cold mush oozing between her toes with her heart pounding. Still screaming, adrenaline pumping, she managed to give it a good swift kick with her foot, sending it into the light.

That's when she saw it clearly, the rotted corpse of a huge falcon, crawling with maggots. Sweat drenched her skin, the hair on the nape of her neck stood on edge. She swore she could feel the maggots sliding across her skin. Totally freaked, she hopped around like a jack rabbit, shaking her hands and feet, screeching like a wild bat.

Doing a sharp about face, she ran inside, Freddy hot on her heels. She bolted the door and backed up against it. She had to catch her breath. Her heart galloped, every nerve twitching.

A dead falcon on my porch?

A wave of nausea rose, making her so queasy she slumped to the floor, feeling boneless. She had to call Mike. How had it gotten there? Who had rapped at her door? Was her stalker out there in the woods? It had to be him.

Turmoil rolled in her gut.

****

From the bell tower, The Master basked in the rapture of another stellar performance. Power surged through his veins. Deep in the woods, the night predators thrashed through the thick underbrush, hunting for prey. His chest swelled as pride and excitement filled him. Oh what a thrill it had been to hide behind the willowy branches of the pines and watch the leading lady of his drama perform with such finesse. The look on her face had been priceless. Pretty little princess all bothered and bewildered.

She couldn't see a thing but she could smell the rotted corpse of the falcon. When she stepped outside in her bare feet, he'd nearly pissed his pants. The terror in her eyes, oh so delicious. Her kick had been outstanding. Score three points for Princess.

The best part of the show had been the dance, the grand finale to the evening. Bravo! The way she'd wiggled and squirmed, hell bent on shaking the maggots off her pretty little toes.

Her drama had earned the respect of the winged beasts in the forest. Bats and crows swooped into the deep underbrush, screeching as they flapped their wings. An owl hooted, its warbling echoing through the forest. The Master thrust his fist high in the air, his long red hair and beard billowing in the breeze. He whistled, the shrill sound silencing his onlookers. He took a sweeping bow.

Chapter Twelve

Hysterical, Tess fumbled in the pocket of her shorts for the business card with Mike's number. Grabbing her purse, she scooped out her cell phone, punching in the numbers with trembling fingers. The second he answered, she breathlessly begged, "Come quick. He was here, the stalker. He left his calling card, a falcon on my porch, a *dead* falcon."

Mike was there in a few minutes, checking every room, every dark corner. "Nobody's here, Tess."

"How do you explain the dead falcon? Surely you're not about to tell me that rotting bird was just my imagination, are you? Because just look at my feet. I need to take a shower and get this muck off me before I go stark raving mad!"

"Of course, I saw the bird. Who could miss the smell? But blamin' your so-called stalker for it is a stretch, Tess. With all the wild animals around these woods, it coulda been any one of a dozen creatures that deposited it on your porch."

"But it wasn't there when you dropped me off, and minutes later, I heard a tap at the door. I answered because I thought it was you; only there wasn't anyone there. When I caught a whiff of the disgusting thing, I went out to investigate and stepped on it."

"I dunno, Tess, but it's gone now, taken care of. Go on up and take a shower. I'll wait 'til you're done. Go on. You'll be safe, I promise."

Tess stood beneath the shower, allowing the piercing needles of hot water to drench her body. She pumped out a generous amount of rose-scented soap and worked up a hearty lather. Scrubbing her hair and skin with vigor, she soaped and rinsed three times, still feeling as if the maggots were crawling on her flesh. She paid special attention to her feet and toes, holding them under the water until they turned a flaming pink in protest. Only when the water turned cold did she stop scrubbing. Even after the hot shower, she was chilled to the bone and couldn't stop shaking. She towel dried and massaged scented lotion into her skin, her hands quivering. Her teeth chattered as she slipped into her plush green robe and fluffy slippers.

Unsure of her footing, Tess slowly made her way downstairs, her fingers tightly curled around the railing. Mike stood in the foyer, watching her closely.

"Feel better?" He perused her from head-to-toe. "Sure smell good. Is that roses?"

"It is and I do feel much better." She offered him a faint smile. Then because she couldn't help herself, she wrapped her arms around him and placed her head on his shoulder. She wanted him to envelop her in a strong embrace; she needed to feel life. She needed him. Heat soared from his entire body, warming her.

Her voice broke as she whispered, "Oh, Mike, I'm scared. I know you think it might have been an animal but I'm convinced he's out there. He's someone who knows me, knows my fear of the falcon. How did he get here only a few minutes after you left? Was he out there in the bushes, watching us?"

"It's all right, darlin'." He ran his hand up and down the small of her back. His voice was soft, gentle. "You're safe now. I'm sure it was a hell of a shock, steppin' on that dead bird, but I checked the entire mansion, all the grounds. No one's out there." He ran his lips along her cheek. "Go have a seat in the parlor and I'll get a snifter of brandy from the den. It'll help ya' get rid of the shakes. Join ya in a few minutes."

Tess did feel better after the drink. Warm heat filled her, but it was nothing like the heat radiating from Mike's body. He made her feel safe and secure. She could definitely get used to having him around.

Mike yawned, his broad shoulders drooping. "I'd best be on my way so I can get up at the crack of dawn to feed the horses before work. You gonna be all right, Tess?"

She stood on her tiptoes and kissed him. "I'll be fine, thanks to you. I really feel much better after my shower and the brandy." She offered a sheepish smile as they walked down the hall. "Bet you're real sorry I'm your next door neighbor, huh?"

He turned to leave, his boots clicking on the marble corridor. When he got to the door, he looked over his shoulder. "Not a chance, darlin'. Get some sleep, but remember, I'm just a phone call away."

Tess double bolted the door for the second time that night. The minute Mike left, fear of the unknown crept through her, burrowing deep within. Was she safe? Why did the hair on the back of her neck prickle?

She kept repeating to herself that she was just being ridiculous. "Maybe if I think it often enough, I'll start to believe it."

She decided to turn in. Mike had checked all twenty-four rooms, the showers, the closets and under the beds. No one was in the manor. Reaching the top of the steps, she made her way down the corridor to her bedroom. She flicked on the ceiling light, scanning the room. Freddy meowed, rubbing against her legs. She sat on the edge of her canopy bed, the mattress so comfortable she sank into it. A few moments later, the worries and fears of the day lost the battle. Not bothering to take off her robe, she kicked off her slippers and curled up, laying her head on the feather pillow. She'd just rest her eyes for a few minutes, then climb under the comforter.

****

Something jarred Tess from slumber. She bolted upright, her heart racing. The pulse in her throat jumped. Too much light. She blinked, allowed her pupils to adjust. Then she remembered leaving the ceiling light on…just in case.

Something was wrong. She heard noise from downstairs, something vaguely familiar. Curious, she stepped into her slippers and went to investigate. As she reached the last step, the hair on the back of her neck prickled. Goose bumps broke out on her flesh. The smell of hot buttered popcorn drifted to greet her, coming from the home theater in the west wing.

Just then an explosion of gunfire erupted, followed by the zing of bullets ricocheting off the cavernous walls. Tess's heart skipped a beat. Then it galloped at a wild rhythm, racing so fast she couldn't breathe. Every pulse in her body throbbed beneath her skin. Her hands were slick with sweat, her fingers slipping from the sleek mahogany railing.

She caught a glimpse of her reflection in the gilded mirror. Her green eyes were wide with shock and terror, her skin as white as snow. Then she heard it, her dad's deep belly laugh, rolling through the manor. Gasping, her hand flew to her mouth. "Daddy?"

Then another blast of gunfire, followed by the stampede of wild horses, their hooves pounding, their neighs frantic. More men whopping it up, bellowing over the thundering of horse hooves. "Yeeee haw!"

Like a magnet, Tess was drawn to the theater, the sound of her dad's robust laughter pulling her in like quicksand. Glimpses of her childhood flashed across her mind—sitting in the entertainment hall with her mom and dad, or with her friends, munching on hot buttered popcorn from the wall vendor, eyes glued to the screen. As she scurried down the hallway to the theater, excitement bolted through her. Her dad's booming voice and robust laughter were so real she wanted to run to him.

As she reached the arched doorway to the forum, her cat sat perched at the entrance, his stature stiff and rigid, his back arched. He stared straight ahead, his eyes focused.

Holding her breath, Tess turned into the huge auditorium and came to a dead halt, her heart hammering. Jake Kincaid took up the whole screen in living color, big as life on his bucking bronco, a ten-gallon hat on his head. He pointed his shotgun at an outlaw and said, "Come sunup, you'll be dead. Vultures are already circlin', ready to lick your carcass clean."

Just then, he turned full face, his penetrating brown eyes searing into Tess's. Emotions got the best of her and tears rolled down her cheeks. "Oh, Daddy."

His indomitable presence filled the entire theater. Badly shaken, Tess entered the theater and fell into one of the plush maroon recliners. She grabbed the armrests for support, her fingers tracing the built-in beverage holder. She sat, transfixed as her dad's image vanished from view like an apparition.

Her whole body trembled. Seeing her dad so vibrant and full of life had been surreal, a glimpse of the great Jake Kincaid in his glory days of Hollywood. Tess couldn't move, immobilized by the image of her dad. It had been years since she'd watched his first movie. Seeing him so happy and in his element made her weep. She was so caught up in the past she lost track of the present.

When all the house lights came on and the

velvet curtain closed, she snapped out of her revelry. Then she heard applause from the production room where the old projector ran; her heartbeat tripled. Thundering footsteps followed, tearing down the corridor. The front door slammed with a resounding bang.

Leaping to her feet, heart pumping, Tess fled down the corridor with the same speed as the enigma. She went to the bay window in the parlor, shoving the drapes apart to peer out. Her worst nightmare. She screamed, her shrieks reverberating through the mansion. A masked figure peered in, a face disguised in a dark ski mask pressed against the window. Beady eyes gleamed bright as fire.

Tess couldn't move, couldn't get her brain and reflexes to connect. Her heart jackhammered. Finally, she reacted, jerking the drapes closed with such force the wrought iron curtain rod came down, the whole ensemble shrouding her head and body in pleats of blue. Gasping and sputtering, choking from dust, she thrashed about, freeing herself. Her heart thumping, she jerked her head toward the window. The masked figure had vanished.

Tess cupped her hands over her mouth, racing for the powder room at the end of the hall. The meal she'd eaten churned, acid rolling, sour juices erupting. She barely made it.

She ran cold tap water and splashed it on her face, scrubbing her mouth out with toothpaste. Locking the door, she slid to the floor, her back to the entrance. Her entire body shook. She knew she had to call Mike, report this break-in to the sheriff. But she couldn't move, couldn't maneuver her legs. They felt like jelly. Her head was about to explode any second. She needed to just sit still for a minute, get control of this freight train racing through her head. She needed to catch her breath, get a hold of her emotions.

Who was stalking her, hunting her down? A slight tremor went through her, the image of that masked face pressed against the window, peering in at her. She couldn't see anything other than a dark ski mask, but there was no question it was a man.

It had to be the man who had followed her from New York City. Her instincts were on full alert, her sixth sense screaming to beware. The room began spinning, everything orbiting out of control. It was coming. It had been weeks since she'd had one, but she was having one now, a full-blown panic attack.

From deep within, a low keening started, rumbling through her like a volcano on the verge of eruption, crescendoing to a screeching roar. She folded her hands behind her neck like wings and shielded her head in her lap, wanting the world to stop revolving. She couldn't concentrate on anything other than the wild beat of her heart. The pulse in the hollow of her neck raced, her nerves twitched. She wanted to jump out of her skin.

All she could concentrate on was the blood thundering in her ears from the overload of adrenaline raging through her system.

She needed the anxiety pills in her purse. Using the edge of the sink for support, she hoisted herself up and stood on shaky legs. Her body was drenched with perspiration, her hands slick with sweat. She swiped both hands on her robe before opening the door.

Creeping down the hallway, searching dark corners, Tess was aware of every floorboard creaking, every clock ticking. Was he in one of the rooms, waiting to pounce? How had he gotten in? She knew she'd double bolted the door when Mike left. So how had the madman gotten in?

Her skin crawled, sweat beading from every pore. She'd been in bed, sleeping when he had been prowling through her home, making popcorn and setting up the old projector in the theater. *How*?

Her heart raced. She needed to call Mike, report the break-in. She had to get to a phone. She needed to get to her purse where both her cell phone and medication were. Her doctor had prescribed them to relax her during a panic attack. And if she ever needed an anxiety pill, it was now.

Finding the bag where she'd tossed it earlier, beneath the tree stand in the foyer, Tess rummaged through the contents, finding both pills and some bottled water. She downed a caplet, slugging back several gulps of lukewarm liquid. Her mouth felt as dry as sand. Putting the top back on the bottle, she fumbled through her purse, flipping back the Velcro tab to get her cell phone. The pouch was empty.

Feeling lightheaded, Tess sensed the walls starting to close in. She stumbled into the tree stand, grabbing onto one of the long looping hangers for support. The entire tree stand teetered, banging the wall. She took a deep breath to steady herself, wishing the pill would hurry and take effect. Where was her phone?

She found the business card with Mike's number. Crumpling it between her numb fingers, she headed to the nearest phone in the loft. Mike would know what to do. Her heartbeat slowed slightly as the medication took effect; Tess climbed the stairs to the loft. Closed off from the rest of the house, she'd always found comfort in the cozy enclave.

When she entered the loft filled with shadows, she gasped. Seeing her dad's vintage telephones in the light of day was one thing, but seeing them in muted darkness was rather jarring. The phone on the desk in the loft was a tombstone with the receiver being a glowing green skull, an eerie grin on its fleshless face.

As Tess picked up the receiver to dial the

number, she glanced out the window, startled to see the mountainside ablaze with flames, brilliant spears of orange and crimson spreading like wildfire. Panic hurled through her. How long before it reached the mansion? All those age-old birch and evergreens would go up like a house of cards.

Adrenaline pumping through her veins, making her fingers thick and clumsy. She punched in the numbers 9-1-1. She screamed into the phone the minute they answered. “Come quick. Fire at 1300 Mockingbird Lane. The Kincaid mansion is about to go up like a burning inferno. Hurry!”

Chapter Thirteen

In the distance, the sound of sirens squealed through the night as they made their way through the twisting hills overlooking Highway 3 and the ocean. Perched on the window, his owlish green eyes fixed on the bell tower, his back arched, Freddy hissed and snarled.

"Come on, Fred." Tess snatched him up in her arms, her hands shaking. She battled her decision to leave her laptop behind. *No time.* She grimaced, making a wild dash down the steps to the door just as the fire trucks came to a screeching halt in her driveway. She flung the door open.

"Where's the fire?" The fire chief stomped through the foyer in full uniform, his eyes searching. "Where is it?"

"How could you miss it?" Tess raced past him onto the veranda, confusion swirling through her head. She jabbed her forefinger toward the hillside where the flaming ball of fire had blazed only minutes ago. Other than the lighthouse in the harbor and the torch-lit lanterns in the courtyard, all was dark.

Flabbergasted, Tess's green eyes grew wide with shock and disbelief. "But I saw it from my window, it was coming straight for the house—honest." Her gaze darted wildly from the garden to the bell tower. She turned to the fireman, flustered. "I'm not kidding, really. I know what I saw...don't look at me that way. I'm not making this up or..."

Three other firefighters had gathered around,

anger glinting in their eyes.

The fire chief spoke into his mic. "Looks like a false alarm out here at 1300 Mockingbird." He ended the call, deep lines edging the corners of his mouth. "Look, miss, if this is your idea of a joke, you're in serious trouble. Seeing how fast the fire squad can make tracks when you call wolf can be very dangerous. When we're out here, chasin' our tails, someone out there just might burn to a crisp because we couldn't get to them in time. I could have you arrested for filing a false report."

"But…" Tess's cheeks burned with humiliation. "I'm not making it up…really. I saw a ball of fire from up in the loft; my cat saw it, too. His hair was on edge, his back was up, staring up at the hill leading to the bell tower—"

"Well that settles it." The fire chief signaled his team to leave. "As long as your cat saw the sorcerer's fire, that explains everything. We're outta here since we've wasted enough time. Get some help, lady. You need it."

"But—"

Just then, Mike Andretti pulled up in his sheriff's car, brakes squealing. He leapt from his vehicle, slamming the door. "Tess, are you all right? Heard it on my police radio. Is it out? Where was it? Where was the fire?"

"You know this woman?" The fire chief bellowed, climbing into his truck. "Get her some help. Either she needs glasses or she's crazy as a loon. Either way, Mike, she's unstable."

Tess and Mike wordlessly watched the fire trucks peel out of the driveway, an uncomfortable silence hovering between them. The wind swooshed through the towering evergreens, causing an eerie whistle.

"Let's go inside." Mike's shaggy blonde hair rippled in the breeze and he raised an eyebrow. "We need to talk. Better put on a pot of some mighty strong coffee."

****

The coffee maker spewed, permeating the air with the rich smell of hazelnut. Getting two mugs from the cupboard, Tess filled them with the gourmet blend, her mind on what she'd seen. She turned to where Mike sat watching her from the breakfast nook, his golden-brown eyes broody.

She cleared her throat. "Ah...I never did get to the market, so I hope you like your coffee black."

"That's fine."

Tess set the coffee mugs down, the steaming liquid sloshing onto the pinewood table. Scuffing along the black and white diamond-tiled floor in her slippers, she pulled a bag of sugar cookies from the walk-in pantry. Opening it, she bit into one, her teeth chomping into the buttery treat. "I have to eat something before I pass out."

He gave her a sidelong glance. "After all that lobster? What happened, Tess?"

She chewed her cookie, chased it down with a sip of coffee. "I don't know where to start. From the minute you left, there has been a chain of bizarre happenings. He was in here, while I slept. I don't know how he got in because I know for a fact I bolted the door when you left. Exhausted, I went to bed. Something woke me, something hauntingly familiar from my past."

She shivered just a bit and pulled her arms in closer. "I went to investigate, and when I came down the steps, the smell of popcorn was coming from the home theater down in the west wing. Daddy's movie was blasting on the screen, his first Western. I heard clapping from the projector room just before someone tore down the corridor. I chased him down the hall but couldn't make myself go outside after him. When I looked out the window, I saw him...peering in. It startled me so much I yanked the curtains shut and they toppled down on my head."

She absent-mindedly rubbed her head where she had a bit of a bump from the rod hitting her. "Then I had a panic attack. I managed to get to my purse so I could take an anxiety pill to settle my nerves. I was just about to call you when I saw the fire on the hill, just below the bell tower. It was spreading…coming straight for the mansion."

Mike sipped his coffee, watching Tess over the rim of his cup. He reached across the table for her trembling hand. "Tess. Get hold of yourself…take a deep breath. You're ramblin' ninety miles a minute and I'm havin' trouble keepin' up here. You're tellin' me all these things went down in the course of what?" He checked his watch. "Less than two hours? That's a stretch and it's gotta end. There is no fire on the mountainside, no burning bush or ball of flame. I don't believe someone was in here popping popcorn and playin' games with the projector in the theater. I'm sorry, Tess, but I think it's time to take action. As the sheriff, I gotta recommend a trip to the emergency room for an evaluation. This has gone on long enough. Go on, get your purse and toss a few things in an overnight bag. You're dealin' with an awful lot here and the mind can play tricks when under stress."

"I'm not crazy." Tess snatched her hand away. "Of course, I'm under stress, but I'm not one to see optical illusions or go crying wolf. I saw fire rolling down the hill from the bell tower, and so did Freddy. His back arched the way it gets when he spies someone he doesn't like. You said it yourself. Animals sense things, like they have a sixth sense or something. I know what I saw, inside and out, and I'd swear to it on a stack of Bibles. Don't you dare tell me he wasn't peering in my window at me because I damn well know what I saw."

"Easy, Tess." Mike stood up. "Please, just get your stuff."

Tess's mouth dropped open. The words caught in her throat. "No, Mike, please don't make me go. I'm not crazy, really."

Mike's eyes softened a bit. "It's all right, Tess. The best place you can be right now is the hospital. They'll give you somethin' to calm your nerves. Callin' the fire department for a false alarm is serious, a criminal offense. Let's go."

Tears spilled down Tess's face. "Please, Mike. I don't know how to explain all these weird happenings, but I'm not crazy. Please don't make me go to the hospital."

"I'm not sure what to make of you, Tess. Gimme a break, huh? Ever since you rolled into town, you've been seeing things, smelling things, hearing things. I know you have a lot to deal with since your dad's suicide, but I'd say it's about time for you to get some help, some serious therapy. Now come on, let's hit the road."

Chapter Fourteen

From the deep woods, The Master slinked, yanking off his ski mask. His long red hair and beard stuck out in wild disarray, full of static electricity. Unable to suppress his laughter a second longer, he leapt high in the air and let the laughter roll. *Ha, ha, ha*! His hat was off to Contessa on this grandest of nights. Bravo! His princess had outdone herself with another stellar performance.

Yes, yes, yes!

Tossing his head back, he howled at the full moon glinting in the starless sky. Reliving the events of the evening, The Master beamed. Contessa had mesmerized her audience with her expressive green eyes, oh so bewitching. The perfect goddess. Creeping into the mansion to set the stage had been so theatrical. *Lights, camera, action.*

The best part had been playing with dear old Daddy's projector, and oh what a thrill to pop corn in the old fashioned wall vendor. *Snap, crackle, pop.*

Scaring Princess to death was the name of the game. And oh how she screamed. The look of sheer terror in her eyes when he'd pressed his mug up to the window. What a rush. Brought the house down. Pretty little princess tangled up in blue.

The most memorable part though was when she wasn't aware of his presence. She was so arousing as she slept, the sweet smell of roses surrounding her. The desire to crawl in bed with her and shimmy her out of her green robe had been oh so tempting. But good things come to those who wait, and he could wait. The best was yet to come. The things he would do to Princess were oh so naughty. It would be show-stopping when he finally revealed all to her. *Yes, yes, yes.*

Birds of prey thrashed about, cries of the wild erupting from the lowest thrush of the thicket. A falcon screeched as it swooped down from its perch. Undulating pine branches painted willowy shadows on the floor of the forest, bristly needles swooshing in the wind. The air carried the dank smell of rot and decay. Maturing red oaks reached upward, gnarled branches groping in the dark.

Totally in his element, The Master nibbled on a handful of buttered popcorn. He dug into the pocket of his hooded jacket. Tilting back his head, he cupped his hand to his mouth, dumping in the buttery treat. Chewing the freshly popped corn, he spit out the kernels. Brushing his hands on his jacket, he picked up the nighttime binoculars and spied into the mansion.

Princess and White Knight were having a lovers' spat. White Knight doesn't believe her. Poor little princess. Oh what a tangled web we weave. Oops. If looks could kill, White Knight would be down for the count.

Come on, Princess, hit 'em with your best shot.

****

Tess staggered, the room spinning. Her eyes felt funny, unfocused. Her temples throbbed from the stress. Too much pressure, too much in one night. She turned on her heel and twisted her ankle.

"Tess." Mike was by her side in a heartbeat, guiding her back into the booth. "Easy now, there ya' go. What just happened?"

Pulsating pain spiked in her left eye, so severe it felt as if her eyeball were being nailed to her brain. She bit her lip to keep from crying out. The light was too bright, too intense. She cupped her hands over her face, blocking it. She sucked in her breath. “My head…ankle…”

“I’ll get an ice pack.” Mike ran off to the freezer, returning with a bag of frozen peas. “Prop your leg up across the booth and I’ll wrap these peas around the swelling. Come on, the sooner you get it iced, the better.”

Sharp needles of pain radiated down the left side of her face. The tendons in her ankle screamed in outrage. She watched Mike lay the peas across her lower leg, his fingers probing. The bright lights scorched her eyes. She wanted to die. She put her head down, tears streaming. “Turn off the lights…please.” The walls narrowed, enveloping her. Her stomach rolled. The coffee and cookies turned to acid, threatening to come back up. She needed her medicine. She tried to get comfortable but couldn’t. Nothing would help but the prescription pills in her purse. She had to get to them, even if she had to crawl.

“Tess…” Mike rubbed her back, massaging little circles with his thumbs. His fingers kneaded pressure points, easing some of her pain. But not enough.

“I’m takin’ you to the hospital; it’s time a doctor checks you out.”

Tess couldn’t move, too much pain. She wanted it to stop. Nausea threatened again, stronger. The room kept spinning, the walls caving in. The floor rushed toward her, the black and white tiles making her so dizzy she saw stars. She looked at Mike, his frame a fuzzy blur. “Please get my purse in the hallway…under the tree stand. I need my migraine medication…zipper compartment. The lights, please…please turn them off.”

“Hang on, darlin’.” His hand hit the switch as he rounded the bend. “I’ll be back in a flash.”

Tess slid into a fetal position, kicking off the bag

of peas. They hit the tile floor with a subtle thud. She cradled her arms around her head for a pillow. Her left eye hurt like the dickens, piercing bullets of pain that squeezed tears. She felt sick, disoriented. What was taking Mike so long? Then she heard him, thundering down the corridor, his heavy footsteps making her head pound. Feeling his presence loom above her, she opened one eye and peeked up at him. "Did you find them? In my bag? Please I need one along with a glass of water. Hurry, Mike."

"There's no migraine medication in your purse. Just a sample package of these."

"What?"

He flung them in her face. "Anti-psychotic pills."

Tess felt as if she was trapped in a nightmare. How could all these bizarre things be happening. She pulled herself upright, using the table for support. Her eyes unfocused, she blinked back the tears.

Even though the kitchen was dark, the lanterns in the courtyard pierced her eyes like hot laser beams. Squeezing them tight, she buried her head in her arms and slid to the table. Her voice sounded muffled, distant. "This is no time to be pulling a prank. I need my migraine medication before my head explodes."

He muttered something under his breath. Then he turned on his heels and stomped across the floor to the light. He snapped on the switch. Fluorescent light flooded the room. In long strides, he stalked to the table, booted heels clicking. He thrust the package on the table, the rustling making Tess's nerve endings tweak. Red hot fury blazed in his eyes. He huffed out a breath. "This medication is used to treat mental disorders—patients who see and hear things that simply don't exist. In other words, for those who hallucinate."

"Mike, why are you doing this to me?" Tess

looked up, shielding out the bright light with her hand. She squinted through unfocused eyes. "I need my pills! Please, I'm begging you."

"I'm taking you to the emergency room." Mike scooped her up in his arms. "You need a complete mental evaluation. Jake would want me to take care of his daughter, and, as the county sheriff, it's my duty and obligation. Let's go."

Overwhelmed with pain and unable to speak, Tess gave up the fight. The hospital would give her something to stop the raging pain.

The draft in the corridor rippled through Tess's robe, sending goose bumps skating up her spine. She buried her head in Mike's neck to block out even the slightest light. The muskiness of his skin nauseated her. The minute they were outside, the brisk air hit her face. She sucked in greedy gulps of air, cringing when Mike fled down the steps, the thumping making the pain unbearable. She grimaced, curling tighter into Mike's arms, their hearts beating in unison. Finally, he set her in the passenger's side of the sheriff's car, secured the seat belt around her, jumped in the driver's side to start the car and then tore down the road, tires peeling.

****

Silhouetted in the shadows of the mighty pines, The Master watched the White Knight deposit Contessa into his vehicle and peel out, burning rubber down the driveway, pinecones and broken twigs snapping beneath his tires. As the sheriff's car rattled down the twisted road that cut through the sloping hills of Mount Desert Island, his brakes squealed in protest. Reaching the bottom of the rocky terrain, he turned left and headed toward town, the engine growling as it picked up speed. The faster he drove, the louder the rumble.

A minute later, the first streak of light peeked through a canopy of sugar maples, the dawning of a new day. A woodpecker drilled into the bark of a scrub pine. And just beyond, the low branches of a birch tree flitted as a black-capped chickadee peeked out. From the treetops, the blue jays bickered.

The Master stood tall and mighty, his red hair and beard blowing in the breeze. He dug into his pocket, pulling out a hot pink cell phone. He turned to his audience of winged beasts and grinned at them.

Chapter Fifteen

"Hello, Ms. Kincaid." The doctor entered the room, flipping through the admission papers. "I'm Dr. Wilson. How long have you suffered from migraines?"

"They started several months ago, when my dad died. I need something for the pain," Tess said, her eyes pleading. "Please, this has to be the worst one yet and I misplaced my medication. I twisted my ankle when I slipped earlier. I can't put any pressure on it. I think I sprained it."

"A nurse will be in after I examine you." The doctor felt the bones in Tess's foot, her fingers probing. "She'll give you a shot to tackle your migraine. I'll order an X-ray for your ankle, although I don't think anything's broken. Let me take a listen to your heart and lungs."

The doctor pressed the stethoscope on Tess's chest, the cold metal icy against her bare skin. The medicinal scent of alcohol and disinfectant filled her senses, the sterile smell making her queasy.

"How long have you been taking the anti-psychotic pills?"

"I've never taken them," Tess insisted, rubbing her throbbing left temple. "I have no idea how those sample pills got into my purse, but someone broke into my home tonight, the man who's stalking me. He must have planted them in my purse when he stole my migraine pills and my cell phone. Please…please, can I have something for the pain?"

The doctor scribbled in the chart, then looked at

Tess. "Just so I understand. Are you saying you feel someone is stalking you, broke into your home, switched your medication and stole your cell phone? Is that what I'm hearing, Ms. Kincaid?"

"That's right." Tess sighed as she resigned herself to telling the story one more time. She knew her words were coming out but with equal certainty, knew they weren't being heard. While she was in too much pain to open her eyes, she knew the look of disbelief that would be on the doctor's face. "He had to have planted the anti-psychotic pills in my purse to make me look like I'm crazy. Now can I please have something for this freaking migraine?"

"How long has it been since you've taken your anti-psychotic medication, Ms. Kincaid?"

Tess buried her face in her hands, tears rolling down her cheek. "I know how it sounds, but please listen to me. It all started in New York." She forced herself to share more of the story, although everything inside her told her it was a waste of time. "Okay, you've heard it all; now would you please give me something for this freakin' pain!"

"Who is he? Who is stalking you?"

"I don't know. Please, believe me."

"All right, Ms. Kincaid. I'm going to send the nurse in with a sedative, something to make you more comfortable. A lab technician will be in to draw some blood. Once you're feeling a bit better, I'm going to recommend a psychological evaluation from one of our social workers. Since you're not harming yourself, or anyone else, I can't force you, but I strongly advise it. Not only that, but the sheriff feels it's necessary. We're trying to help you get to the bottom of your symptoms, Ms. Kincaid. Is that all right with you?"

Tess raked her hands through her hair. "Whatever…yes. As long as you give me something for this pain. *Please!*"

The doctor peered at Tess. “All right, Ms. Kincaid. That’s all for now. I’ll send the nurse right in with something. I’m going to consult with your doctor in New York, the physician who prescribed the pills for your anxiety. Get some rest and I’ll see you in the morning.”

Just when Tess didn’t think she could take the pain a second longer, the nurse came in with a shot, jabbing it into her backside. Within a few minutes, the drug had taken affect, putting her out of pain and into a deep and well-needed rest.

****

The following morning, Tess toyed with a breakfast made up of bland scrambled eggs, dry toast and a cup of decaffeinated coffee. Feeling tired and groggy from the after-effects of the medication, she craved a cup of premium blend beans. But, she mused, shoving her eggs from one side of her plate to the other, at least her migraine was gone. It left her feeling jumpy, on edge.

A cacophony of noise—nurses chattering, wheels squeaking, dishes clinking—unraveled Tess’s nerves. She pushed her tray out of the way and cranked her bed back a notch, trying to get comfortable. Hearing soft footsteps padding down the corridor, she looked up. Her doctor stood in the doorway, piercing blue eyes studying her through wire-rimmed glasses.

“How do you feel this morning, Ms. Kincaid?” She entered the room, her loafers scuffing on the floor. She flipped through the pages of Tess’s chart.

“I feel much better since my migraine’s gone.”

“Good. Your blood pressure’s a little high today. Let’s take it again.”

Tess held out her arm while the doctor wrapped the cuff securely. She squeezed the pump a few times. Then air hissed. “Much better. I got in touch with your doctor. He tells me you’ve been suffering from anxiety attacks since your father’s suicide. He also confirmed he never prescribed or suggested any anti-psychotic pills for you."

Tess looked directly into the doctor's eyes. "So now do you believe someone broke into my home last night and switched the medication?"

The doctor studied her, sharp eyes searching. "I can't say, Ms. Kincaid. I'm a physician, not a police officer or therapist. I only know what I witnessed last night. Your behavior warrants an evaluation by one of our social workers. You seem to be seeing, hearing and smelling things that simply don't exist. If I were to state my professional opinion, I'd say these delusions are the aftermath of your father's suicide. The results from your blood work show no trace of the medication, but there are levels indicating you've been taking your anxiety pills. Now let's talk about side-effects."

The doctor finished putting away the blood pressure cuff and turned back to Tess. "Everyone has a different tolerance to drugs. Sometimes it takes changing the medication a few times to obtain the required result. Also all pills have side-effects. The one you're taking for anxiety has quite a few so I'd like to change your medication to something milder, less invasive. Try the new pills and see if your symptoms lessen. In order to reach the desired effect, you have to stay on the medication which can take several weeks."

The doctor handed Tess a prescription. "Have this filled and see if you don't feel better. In the meantime, discontinue your present medication." The doctor lifted the lid of the tray, peering at the uneaten food. "You didn't eat very much. No appetite this morning?"

Tess eyed her breakfast. Her stomach rolled. Actually, she was very hungry and would love nothing better than a muffin from the Seaside Bakery. She shrugged. "I guess it's the medication."

"You should try to eat something, even the toast. The social worker will be in shortly. Buzz if you need anything."

Tess stared at the walls, zapped of all energy and life. They didn't believe her; no one believed her. They all thought she was traumatized.

Mike, the doctors, the nurses. What's the use?

She felt as if she was just babbling on. The more she babbled about being stalked, the more they'd medicate her. She stared at the new prescription the doctor had written. New pills to replace old pills. The vicious circle went around and around. Where would it end? She thought of the psychology classes she'd taken in college. The mind was a tricky foe. It could bend. It could snap. It could break. How long would it be before her mind snapped?

She heard more footsteps coming down the corridor. A woman walked through the door, dressed in a pair of navy dress slacks and a crisp white polo shirt. Her auburn hair was pulled on top of her head in a ponytail, accentuating her huge gray eyes.

"Good morning, Ms. Kincaid. I'm Melissa Young, the social worker assigned to give you a psychological evaluation. How are you feeling today?"

"Frustrated," Tess said, fumbling for the right words. "I'm not crazy, honest. My stalker is real, not some enigma, some figment of my imagination. I feel as if I'm losing my mind, but know in my heart, I'm sane. Please believe me."

"Let's start with your migraines. Do you get them often? And if so, is there any pattern?"

"They started six months ago when I received word my dad committed suicide. He shot himself in the home where I lived as a child, the home I've inherited."

"Dr. Wilson reports you feel someone is stalking you, watching you from the woods surrounding your house. She has also documented you heard voices and footsteps in your home, saw a man peeping in your window, and believe he planted anti-psychotic pills in your purse. The sheriff reported you called the fire department because you saw fire on the mountainside. Tell me about these things, Tess."

"I know how it sounds, but they're all true. I recently moved into my father's estate, the home I lived in as a child. There's a bell tower on the bluff behind the manor. Last night, I was up in the loft at midnight, looked out and saw fire on the mountainside, a burning bush rolling toward the house. I called the fire department, but when they got there, the fire was gone. I don't know how to explain it, but I know what I saw."

The social worker made notes in her chart. "Let me get this straight. You looked out on the hill and saw a burning bush. Yet when the fire department got there, it was gone."

"Yes."

"Maybe it was a reflection of some sort. Or maybe you were tired and your eyes were playing tricks on you. Do you wear glasses?"

"No." Tess huffed out a breath. "What's the use of all this repetition if no one believes a word I say?"

"Tell me about your stalker."

"He's trying to make me think I'm delusional, but he's real. He's told me he's my biggest fan and sent me a letter, written in a child's squiggly handwriting—big, bold and in bright red, like blood. He's also called and told me he's enjoyed running his fingers through my panties. The thought of his creepy voice makes me shudder. He has to be stopped."

"Tell me a little about your childhood home, Ms. Kincaid. Why would you move back to a home that's haunted with such mortality?"

"I loved living there when I was a little girl,

thought of it as my sand castle on the sea. Daddy knew that and left it to me for that very reason. It broke my heart when my parents divorced and Mama and I moved to New York. I lived for the summers when I'd return to spend three glorious months in my sand castle. Daddy used to be a Hollywood actor, but when he was no longer in the limelight, depression set in and he began drinking. I had no idea, no clue he was so despondent, thinking of taking his own life."

"All right, Tess. I'm getting a pretty good picture of your mental health and I'm seeing a definite pattern. You've been dealing with a horrendous amount of stress in the past several months which has been compounded by migraines. Additional complications have occurred because of the anxiety pills you've been taking. All medications have side-effects, especially when combined. Even though the percentage is low, there have been cases where migraine medication can cause mild hallucinations."

The social worker looked up from her notes. "Have you considered alternative treatments for your migraines? Maybe a chiropractor? This could help your migraines and do wonders for your anxiety level. Without the medication and their side-effects, I think these optical and auditory illusions will dissipate. The mind is fragile, Tess, but I see no reason to label you as mentally unstable—or to request further evaluation. However, I do *strongly* advise you try alternative treatments such as massage therapy and chiropractic joint manipulation to deal with your migraines." She leaned forward in her chair, her voice softening. "You're dealing with guilt and grief, and the added stress from moving into the home where your father shot himself. I'll leave the number for our grief counselors and support groups. Sometimes, talking out your fears and guilt with others is the best remedy. Try and relax. If there are too many disturbing memories in your home, consider selling."

Tess interrupted, her eyes full of questions. "Let's say everything you've just said is true. How do you explain the sample package of anti-psychotics in my purse and my migraine pills vanishing into thin air?"

"I can't." The social worker stacked her papers neatly and placed them in a briefcase. "It's possible you stopped in a clinic and talked to a professional about your father's suicide. Sometimes we simply don't remember things when our minds are plagued with shock, especially something as brutal as suicide. The doctor might have suggested you try some of the anti-psychotic pills to help your hallucinations. Since they are free samples, there is no doctor's name on the pills and no way of confirming a diagnosis. You might have simply slipped them into your purse without remembering. As far as the missing pills, that's no big deal. You made a major move and could have easily left them behind. I'll give you my card with contact information if you need to talk or discuss this any further. Take care, and don't hesitate to call if you have any questions."

Tess watched the social worker leave the room, wondering if it had been the side-effects of the pills that had caused her to see, hear and smell things. She had to admit she never even glanced at the pamphlets that came with the medication. She'd pitched them in the nearest trash can. But still, something just didn't sit right with her.

Especially the anti-psychotic pills. She'd never been to a clinic. Surely, she wasn't so far gone that she'd waltz into a clinic to tell a stranger she was hallucinating. Would she? No, she was certain someone had been in her New York condo that night, same as the mansion. Sure, she'd taken a migraine pill and fallen into a deep sleep the first night he'd called her in New York, but she hadn't taken any pills when she came home earlier. Nor had she taken any pills the night she returned to the bizarre scene in the ballroom here.

Confusion and anger bubbled from deep within. Frustrated and needing to release some of the pent-up emotions she was feeling, she hurled her balled-up fist into her pillow. Feeling a bit better, she took a deep breath and composed herself.

No one believes me. Fine. Once bitten, twice shy. If nobody was willing to help her hunt down her stalker, she'd just do it herself. After all, she knew a thing or two about psychopaths. She wrote about them and had researched them thoroughly, so she'd just think like the detectives she wrote about. She'd trap whoever was creating chaos in her life.

Tess took a shower, her mind spinning. She'd play along; she'd even try the massage and chiropractor because she could use some help relaxing. Tess knew her stalker was real, not just a figment of her imagination. He was out there, watching and waiting for just the right opportunity to pounce on her, catch her off guard.

She wasn't about to let her guard down for a second. Living in New York City had taught her a thing or two about self preservation. Honed from years of experience, she had eyes in back of her head. Tess knew she was being watched from deep in the woods, from up in the bell tower. She could feel his creepy eyes on her, following her every move.

Tess sat in bed, waiting for Mike to come and pick her up. She was still dressed in her green robe, the one she'd had on the night before. She tapped her fingers on the bedstand, fidgety and nervous. She hated hospitals, and if she didn't go while the going was good, they might change their minds and keep her. The phone rang, the loud jingle slicing through the deafening silence. She rolled her eyes. If that was Mike, saying he'd be late, she really would go nuts. She picked up the receiver. "Hello."

Nothing.

Just as she was about to hang up, she heard it. Manic laughter sounding as if it was coming from the final circle of hell. Chills skittered up and down her spine. She dropped the phone, but the psychotic laughter echoed all the louder.

****

Mike heard her screams clear down the corridor. He tore down the hallway, heavy footsteps thundering, doctors and nurses hot on his heels. Tess's screams escalated to piercing shrieks. Heart pounding, Mike flew across the threshold and came to a dead halt.

Tess sat crouched in the corner of her bed, knees up to her chin, green eyes wild with fear, mouth wide open, wretched screams spewing. Her arms were winged like a bat in flight, her fingers tangled in huge wads of hair. The phone's receiver dangled from a cord on the floor.

"Sedate her," the doctor ordered. "Before she does any more damage to herself or someone else. She needs to be sedated and restrained. Hurry."

Tess just pointed to the phone, her eyes pleading with Mike's.

He picked up the receiver and slapped it to his ear. His mouth dropped open, his eyes huge with disbelief as he listened to the insane laughter.

Chapter Sixteen

The Master stood in the grand ballroom of the mansion, cackling. Unable to stifle himself, the manic laughter bubbling from deep within grew louder, more insane. He placed the phone back on the cradle. Visualizing Contessa's face, gales of hysteria spewed from his gaping mouth. He thrust his head back as he imagined her horrified expression, her bewitching green eyes full of fright. Oh what a thrill. Racing in circles, his chilling laughter echoed off the walls. Totally spent, The Master heaved a heavy sigh, beads of sweat drenching his nude body. He clapped with delight.

Bravo! Hat's off to another stellar performance. What a wall banger. Indeed yes. Calling her from the grand ballroom had added the perfect suspense to his thriller.

Yes, yes, yes.

What a clever Master he'd been the night before. Calling the hospital on a hunch had paid off in spades, pretending to be none other than the sheriff himself. Oh how theatrical. The nurse had been very willing to sing like a canary. Pretty little princess, bouncing off the walls, tucked in for the night all sedated. Welcome to the funny farm.

While the cat's away…the mouse will play.

Oh how he had played. The things he'd done were oh so naughty. He'd loved going through her panties, the feel of the silk thong in his hands, oh so slinky. The touch of it, the ecstasy of running his fingers through the black lace crouch, oh so arousing. The fantasies he'd conjured up.

While playing with her naughty nighties, he'd come across the perfect little number for closing night. Oh what a thrill. He imagined how she'd look in the black lace teddy, her voluptuous body all wrapped up in black silk and lace. He'd enjoyed rubbing the pretty pink rosebuds between his fingers, the ones embroidered in just the right places. The ultimate had been sleeping in her pink canopy bed, his naked body snugly cocooned between her satin sheets, her black lace panties clutched in his hand.

The dawning of a new day found him bright-eyed and bushy-tailed. After perking a pot of gourmet coffee, dear old Daddy's superior blend, he'd been wired tight as a bongo drum.

Yes, yes, yes. Good to the last drop.

Now he'd opened up the stage to far more drama, letting White Knight in on the action. It wouldn't be long before the grounds were crawling with cops. The time had come to raise the stakes, add a bit more adventure to the greatest show on earth.

Racing to the window, blocking out the creaks in the old manor, he pressed his ear to the curtain and listened. A beat, then he heard it, barely discernible over the wild thump of his heart, but there was no mistake. They were coming, the rumble of engines growing louder. Then he spied them, three unmarked patrol cars. And a few minutes later, Bar Harbor's finest were out and about, scanning the woods for the big bad wolf.

The Master turned around, his heart pumping. Oh what a rush. Adrenaline surged through his blood, thundered in his ears. He rubbed his hands together, hissed in a breath, air whistling in the hollow cavern of his missing tooth. Surged with a bolt of adrenaline, he broke out in laughter, leaping high in the air and cackling like a wild hyena.

Catching a glimpse of his reflection in the mirror behind the bar, he grinned and saluted himself.

He took a little peek through the curtains, every nerve in his wiry body twitching. He scoffed to himself. They were on the wrong track. They could scan every inch of the deep dark woods, search every corner of the bell tower. While they scratched their heads, retracing their footsteps again and again, he'd be behind the curtains, getting the stage ready for the next scene.

He turned to his audience of wax gargoyles and took a sweeping bow. His gaze scanned the massive hall. He splayed his arms out and grinned at them.

Surged with adrenaline, The Master got busy. He had work to do, but first things first. It was time to hose down in Princess's pretty little shower, lather himself silly in her scented creams and lotions. He couldn't wait.

Shrouded in a mist of steam, The Master stood in the shower, needles of hot spray saturating his body. The water hammered against the sliding glass doors like hail stones. He inhaled, allowing the scent of roses and jasmine to fill his senses. He pumped out soap and shampoo, lathering his rock hard body to a fevered frenzy. He felt wonderful, so wonderful. Oh what a rush to stand in Princess's shower, losing himself in her sweet essence.

Closing his eyes, he imagined her in the shower with him. Oh what a thrill.

Yes…yes…yes.

****

Mike watched Tess sleep, so quiet and subdued. It had taken two interns to hold her down while a nurse sedated her. Even after a shot of what he assumed to be some pretty powerful stuff, she still thrashed about in the sheets, kicking and screaming, eyes wild with fear. He couldn't blame her. For the rest of his life, the image of her yanking her hair would be burned in his brain.

Was it any wonder she'd gone bonkers? No one believed her. Then getting the chilling phone call had been the straw that broke the camel's back. Who was this demented psychopath? Who was stalking Tess? How did he know so many personal details about her?

Whoever it was knew of her father's passion for theatrics, her intense fear of falcons, and that her favorite song was "Moonlight Sonata." Whoever he was, he was one step ahead of them, probably laughing his ass off every time he pulled one over on Mike. But no more. The search was on.

Frustrated, he pinched the bridge of his nose, never taking his eyes off Tess. If he hadn't heard that psychotic laughter with his own ears, he would have gone on thinking she was nuts. He could only imagine the nightmare she had been living, but that was about to end. He'd find her stalker if he had to search every corner of the woods.

Her stalker wasn't some figment of her imagination, some enigma. He was real, which called for a full-blown investigation. When she woke up and felt up to it, he'd give this matter the attention it deserved, something he should have done the minute she reported the first break-in.

Tess stirred, a slight whimper escaping her lips. She rolled her head from side-to-side on her pillow, her thick mahogany hair fanning around her face. She said something low and muffled, indiscernible.

She was a flawless beauty, perfect in every way. Her heart-shaped face was so lovely. He traced his fingertip along her cheek, awed by its incredible smoothness. It felt soft, like the petals of a rose after a spring rain. Fresh and lovely, a peaches-and-cream complexion. Her eyes fluttered, her long eyelashes curling over her cheekbone. Her lips moved, as if she was trying to speak. Then they stilled.

He touched them, running his finger along her pretty bow-shaped lips. She moaned softly. He felt something for this woman. Yet he hardly knew her. Why did his stomach go into spasms every time he looked at her? *Primal male reaction*, but he knew better. Deep in his gut, he knew it was a lot more than testosterone raging through his veins, a whole lot more.

Leaning over, he brushed her lips with a feathery light kiss. "Shh…it's all right now, darlin'. You're safe and sound. I'm right here by your side. No one's gonna hurt you."

She was so pretty lying there with all that mahogany hair tumbling around her shoulders. He ran his fingers through it, smoothing out the tangles. It felt like spun silk. The sun picked up the highlights, shimmers of burnished copper. Drawn to it, he got closer, wanting to inhale its scent. He had the sudden urge to bury his face in it, lose himself in all those silky tresses. Closing his eyes, he indulged himself, just for a second. It smelled clean, like a garden of wild flowers.

As much as he wanted her to go on sleeping, getting some well-deserved rest, he wished she'd wake up so he could question her. Guilt gnawed deep in the pit of his stomach. He berated himself for not believing her. What kind of a sheriff was he if he couldn't even rely on his basic instincts? Rather than take the time to investigate, he'd written her off as a nutcase, a deeply disturbed woman unable to cope with her father's suicide. The things she'd reported had been downright bizarre. No one believed her stories—everyone was willing to write her off as a paranoid schizophrenic. He'd been the worst culprit, the county sheriff, the man who insisted she be evaluated. How could he live with that?

Just then, the sheets rustled. Tess stirred, blinked a few times and opened her eyes. Even jaded by the sedative, they were a startling shade of beguiling green. Stormy as the sea and twice as bewitching.

"Mike?" She fluttered her eyelashes, trying to focus. "Is that you?"

He leaned closer. "It's me, Tess. I'm right here. Take it easy, darlin', real slow. Can you sit up?"

"I'm thirsty; my mouth is so dry."

"Best let me pour, darlin'. Your hands are too shaky." Water sloshed into the Styrofoam cup. He held it to her lips. "Try a little sip."

****

She gulped the cold fluid, the muscles in her throat pumping. Her gaze swept the room, as if trying to reacquaint herself with her surroundings. When her eyes settled on the phone, her pupils grew large with fear. Catching her breath, she recoiled, licking her parched lips.

"He called before...my stalker. I know you think I'm nuts, but I'm not. He cackled like some demented fool over and over again, insane laughter you'd have to hear to believe. It was bone chilling, psychotic. I don't know who he is or why he's doing it, but he is trying to drive me berserk. Believe it or not, he called and—"

"I know."

"What?"

Mike sat down on her bed, the mattress sinking from his weight. He took her hand in his, giving it a little squeeze.

"I know, Tess. I can't tell you how sorry I am for thinkin' you'd gone off the deep end, but when I came in here before, you were pullin' at your own hair and screamin' like a wild woman. I saw the phone danglin' by the cord and picked it up. I heard it, Tess, and I'm so damn sorry. I swear, with God as my witness, we'll catch this lunatic and put him behind bars. You've got my word on it—guaranteed."

Tess's eyes grew misty. She swiped at tears rolling down her cheek as she let out a long, pent-up breath. Her voice cracked, "Thank God."

He reached for the bouquet of wild flowers on the stand. The cellophane wrap rustled when he handed them to her. "For you, darlin'. Your favorite flower, just a little token to cheer ya."

Tess brought them to her nose, a smile teasing her lips. Her bewitching green eyes glistened with tears, making them sparkle like emeralds. She toyed with one of the petals, tracing the outline with her fingernail. Her voice was thick with emotion as she ran her hand along Mike's cheek and moved a little closer. "You remembered my favorite flower, forget-me-nots. They're beautiful. Thank you, Mike…for the flowers but more importantly, for finally believing me. I can't tell you how good that makes me feel, sharing this heavy burden."

She reached for his hand, intertwining her fingers with his. "With your help, I'll simply refuse to be his puppet. For so long now, he's been calling all the shots, making all the moves. If he said jump, I'd jump. If he said run, I'd run. If he said scream, I'd scream. Well…no more. The first step to combating fear is conquering it, head on. Instead of sticking my head in the sand, being afraid of my own shadow, it's time to do everything in my power to learn his identity."

She took another sip of the water she held as she thought back over the previous discussion. "Like you said, with all he knows about me, he has to be someone from my childhood. Let's go back to the mansion and start searching. The clue to this puzzle has to be in the mansion. Think about it. He has to be someone from my past. If I go through some old photo albums, maybe something will jog my memory. It's time to deal with this stalker. So how about it, Sheriff—do we have a deal?"

Mike pulled her into a tight embrace. "You betcha, darlin'."

Tess pressed her lips to his and whispered the words. "Sealed with a kiss."

****

Rolling along Highway 3 and the ocean, the sweet smell of clover and the sea breeze blew in the open windows of Mike's cherry-red pickup. Tess closed her eyes, loving the way the warm sunshine felt on her face and arm. She had so much to do, but no idea where to begin. She remembered stacks of photo albums—pictures of beach parties, slumber parties, birthday parties—all tucked away in her bedroom closet. She'd dig them out and scan them, hopefully shed some light on the mystery.

Mike tweaked her knee. "Tell me about the hysterical laughter on the phone. Have you ever heard it before?"

"No." She stopped, a distant memory skittering across her brain. She turned to Mike. "Wait, it was so long ago I'd forgotten all about it, but there was a party where Daddy dressed in a straightjacket. When the guests arrived, his body quaked with manic laughter, much like what I heard on the phone."

Mike made the turn at the fork in the road, stopping to let a white tail deer and her fawn cross into the blue shadows of the woods. "So we're ninety-nine percent certain we're dealin' with someone who knew you when you lived here all those years ago." He arched an eyebrow. "Ever get around to makin' that list, the one with the names of guests at your piano recital? We need a place to start, Tess. Once I have some names, I can run them through our database. If any of them have a record, it'll show up."

Tess thought of her childhood friends, the kids who she'd hung out with on the harbor. She ran her hand through her hair, trying to conjure up something, someone who might have held a grudge. She looked at Mike. "I'll make that list and go through some old albums I have stashed in my closet. If that doesn't pan out, there's gotta be some in the attic."

Mike drove through the wrought iron gate. Draping vines of bougainvillea grew wild, thickly intertwined in the rusty black sconces. Sleek ebony panthers graced either side of the entrance, their marble bodies arched in attack mode. The engine grumbled as it took the grade, gears shifting.

The crisp autumn breeze stirred the delicate fragrance of the wildflowers Tess held. She sniffed, glanced over at Mike, and gave him a smile. Then she noticed all the cars in the drive and the men scouting the grounds and woods. "Who are they?"

"Once I heard that laughter blastin' on the phone at the hospital, I called the police to come out and search the grounds, see if there was anything to find. Looks like they're still out there."

As they neared the estate, several policemen came into view, searching the grounds and courtyard. Craning her neck, Tess spied them far back in the thicket, probing the underbrush with broken tree branches. A policeman crouched in front of the parlor window on a kneeling pad, a large kit at his side.

"What's he doing?" Tess asked.

"Dustin' for prints, 2-D footwear impression. They're usually taken on the inside, startin' at the entryway. They'll be back tomorrow to search the inside for prints, both latent and physical."

"Latent?"

"Prints not obvious to the human eye. They can be lifted, using tools in the fingerprint kit."

Just then, a falcon soared across the courtyard to the steeple on the bell tower where it perched.

"I thought I'd seen the last of that bird last night. Don't tell me he resurrected. Didn't you say you got rid of him?"

"Relax, darlin'." Mike pulled in the drive, brakes squealing. He gestured toward the woods. "Gotta be a whole cult in these parts. They love to perch high, so your steeple is the perfect nesting ground. Best bone up, darlin', 'cuz they're here to stay."

Seagulls swooped, their squawking echoing in the bluffs. The buoy bell clanked, its gong reverberating through the island. Peering as far as the eye could see, Tess wondered how she could have ever fancied this overgrown dell as her sand castle on the sea. What once stood tall and mighty over acres of well-manicured vineyards now resembled a haunted house shrouded in thick rot and decaying birch trees. Then there were the woods, crawling with cops and peregrine falcons.

Mike got out of the truck to talk to a few of the officers, his cowboy boots crushing through dry branches and foliage. One of the officers pointed, his arm spanning the width of the woods and thicket. Tess could tell by his expression they'd found nothing.

Deciding to get out and see what was going on, she grabbed the door handle. Just as she was about to hop out, she caught herself. She was in her robe and slippers, same as the night before. She stared at her reflection in the rearview mirror, shocked by her appearance. Dark circles shrouded her eyes, her complexion looked chalky, and her hair was a tangled mess. She looked a fright.

The police seemed to be wrapping things up. Robust voices carried through the air for a minute before car doors opened and shut, tires spinning as they drove down the driveway.

Tess leaped out. "What did they say? Did they find anything?"

Mike shook his head, his golden brown eyes scanning the woods. "Nope. Looks like he's long gone. Chances are...he won't be back. This place'll be crawlin' with cops every day. They're gonna do a search, keep an eye out. But, I don't like the idea of you stayin' out here all alone after all that's gone down. So ya' got two choices. Either move in with me, or I'll be campin' here. What's it gonna be?"

Tess thought about that. She didn't like the idea of being scared out of her home, but she really wasn't looking forward to spending the night all alone in the mansion after *he* got in. She met his gaze. "I'd love for you to stay, Mike. I'd feel a lot safer with you around."

Wordlessly, Mike went to his truck and opened the glove compartment. When he came back, he had his Glock, his gaze searching the courtyard. "Let's go."

The minute Tess walked into the foyer, her skin prickled, every hair on edge. Water gushed from the lion's head mounted on the brick wall, pulsating jets surging from its gaping mouth. When she'd left, the fountain had been unplugged. She stopped dead in her tracks, her sixth sense warning her to beware.

"He's been here," she whispered.

Mike's fingers tightened on his gun, his eyes hard as stone. He released the safety, doing a semi-circle around the entryway, his eyes searching.

Tess's heart raced, her pulse hammered. "He's in the ballroom. Can you smell something burning? Hear the music?"

Chapter Seventeen

"Shh," Mike pressed his forefinger to his lips. He leaned over and whispered in her ear. The bristles on his chin scratched her cheek. "Stay put while I go check it out."

"Not on your life," she whispered. "There's no way I'm staying here all alone."

Creeping down the barrel-shaped corridor, her heart in her throat, she scuffed along, her back to the wall. Muted sunlight filtered through stained glass windows, painting willowy shadows on the walls. Just as Tess passed a portrait of her father, the picture fell, tumbling to the floor with a crashing bang. The sound of shattering glass splintered the air. Tess's heart skipped a beat.

"Daddy?" she whispered, her eyes searching, feeling as if he were warning her from the grave to beware.

"It's all right, Tess," Mike whispered in her ear. He touched her face, his calloused hand gentle. "Keep close."

She bit the inside of her lip. An eerie whistle hissed through the corridor like the haunting echo. Despite the cool draft, sweat trickled down her neck and chest. With her back to the wall, she scaled it, elbow-to-elbow with Mike, very aware of the close proximity.

When his arm draped in front of her, easing her closer to the wall, she felt his muscles bunch when he brushed against her breast. A little thrill shot through her.

Blending into the dark paneling, camouflaged in shadows, Tess shimmied along, adrenaline pumping. Between copper lanterns, portraits of her dad loomed in eerie silence, his penetrating gaze so palpable it made her shudder. His piercing brown eyes seemed to watch and follow, his unblinking stare unnerving.

The back of her head brushed spider webs loose, veiling her face in a silken mesh. Shuddering, she flung them off. The thought of a hairy legged spider crawling in her hair made her quiver. Dust bunnies filtered through the air in the muted light. Her eyes began to water. She fought the urge to sneeze. A dampness seeped into the mansion through cracks and crevasses, the air cloistering...like a mausoleum. Tess sucked in her breath. A cold hollow wedged its way deep inside her chest.

Then the air changed. Every hair on her body bristled, every muscle flexed.

Cool air drifted out of the ballroom, carrying the scent of burning candles and cigarettes. Music floated through the corridor, the seductive undertone hauntingly familiar. The music was hypnotic, mesmerizing. Tess could barely think over the loud beat of her heart.

Every sense screamed to beware. She was about to come face-to-face with her stalker, her biggest fan. But over the hammering of her heart and accelerated senses, her will to put an end to this deadly game prevailed. She had to face him, find out who was behind this bizarre masquerade. Anticipation mounting, she made the turn at the end of the corridor and came to a riveting halt.

A female wax gargoyle stood in the doorway, long blonde hair billowing in the breeze. Her glass eyes shimmered with madness, an eerie smile on her face. In one hand, she held a mission bell, the other reaching out for a candle.

Music played from the old phonograph, the plucking of guitar strings laced with seduction. A breeze blew in through open terrace doors, stirring the sweet scent of jasmine from the candelabras.

Two wax nymphs stood at the bar, glass eyes shining bright in the candlelight, pliable fingers wrapped around flutes of pink champagne. Lit cigarettes burned in ashtrays. From behind the bar, a winged monster served drinks.

In the center of the ballroom, two gargoyles held a pose as if they were dancing, their waxy bodies closely pressed together, their reflections glowing in the mirrored ceiling. From the old phonograph in the corner, the hypnotic music played.

Tess gasped, her hand clasping her mouth. "Oh my God!"

Mike raised his gun, circled the room. "Come out with your hands up. Hancock County Sheriff. Put your hands where I can see them."

After checking the terrace and every corner of the ballroom, Mike put in a call to his sergeant. He turned to Tess, his eyes blazing. "Don't touch anything. The team'll wanna dust for prints."

Tess stood frozen in place, still unable to believe her eyes. "You're telling me when the police were out there combing the grounds, not one of them spotted these open terrace doors and someone moving around in here? Not one of them detected the smell of burning tobacco and candles? How the hell did he slip past all of them?"

Mike gestured to the bar, then to the candles and terrace doors. Then he ran his fingers through his shaggy blonde hair. "Take a look around, Tess. The candles have barely begun to burn and the ice is still fresh. It takes approximately ten minutes for a cigarette to burn down. So what's that tell ya? We're dealin' with one clever son of a bitch. He knew the cops were out there and he waited until the coast was clear before adding the theatrics. We both know the curtains were drawn before we left, the doors locked. So he must've moved the gargoyles around while the cops searched the grounds. Then, the second the coast was clear, he got busy, lighting candles and cigarettes, playin' bartender. Then he opened the curtains and doors. Don't ya' get it? He's been in here the whole time."

"But..." Tess stammered, her eyes searching. "How? How did he get in when everything was locked, double bolted even." A slight tremor shot through her. Between the gargoyles and the staged performance, she was about to unravel. The seductive plucking of guitar strings crawled inside her skin. Tess looked at the pink champagne on ice, the mirrored ceiling, the surreal setting.

"What's that?" Mike pointed to the part of the ceiling uncovered by mirror. Hunks of sodden plaster hung in huge strips. Water dripped, making a plopping sound on the cherry wood floors. A second later, the entire section of ceiling caved in, water gushing out in torrents.

"That's coming from my bathroom!" Tess cried out. She looked at Mike, her eyes huge with fright.

Like a bolt of lightning, Mike dashed through the hall and down the corridor, cowboy boots clicking in his wake. The air crackled with electricity. Hot on his heels, Tess caught up, scuffing along as fast as she could on her still throbbing ankle.

As she reached the foot of the staircase, she looked up, her heart dancing a wild rhythm. Tess stood frozen, rigid as stone, unable to move. Her right foot was on the first step, her left hand clutching the railing so tight her fingers went numb. She couldn't move, just couldn't get her mind and body to connect. The force of water crashing on her shower door was deafening, like hail stones. Shower water never sounded like that. It was all wrong. Icy fingers of fear clutched around her heart. Her inner voice warned her to run for her life. Heart hammering, the flight-or-fright syndrome kicked in, forcing her to make a snap decision. She had to find out. She tore up the steps, two at a time, the pain in her ankle forgotten.

Mike's silhouette disappeared around the corner of the upper landing. A floorboard creaked beneath his weight. Heart galloping, Tess raced to catch up.

She reached the first landing. Sunlight glinted through the skylight in the loft, painting long shadows on the wall. Like groping arms, they reached out, causing Tess's heart to catch in her throat. Every sensation hummed with adrenaline. She reached the top of the second landing, just in time to see Mike's left hand turn the brass doorknob of the bathroom, his right hand gripped tight around his gun.

The door wouldn't open, wouldn't budge. Steam had sealed it shut. Then a loud boom, a swift kick with his cowhide boot. The door flew open, steam billowing out, the scent of roses and jasmine potent. She sucked in her breath and gasped.

"Mike, watch out!"

Pellets of water beat against the glass door, louder and louder. But louder still was the thumping on the glass paneled door. The ceiling fan rotated in an eerie rhythm, stirring the heavy scent of roses through the mist. Tess caught a glimpse of a silhouette behind the shower door.

Mike stepped back, fingers squeezed around his pistol, ready to fire. With his other hand, he thrust the shower door open, sending it skidding down the tract. Just as it hit the wall with a jarring bang, a huge brown bat flew out, eeking, flapping its wings as it soared off, leaving a puddle of water in its wake.

Tess screeched, crossing her arms over her head

and shielding her face, ducking to avoid the bat. Just then, heavy footsteps pounded up the staircase, picking up speed through the corridor, louder and louder, coming to a riveting halt at the doorway.

"Police. Freeze."

Chapter Eighteen

"What the hell's going on here?" the chief demanded, his hard-boiled gaze fixed on Mike. "Did ya' call us all the way out here to catch a bat?"

"No." Mike's golden brown eyes blazed, teeth clenched. "What we're dealin' with here is a stalker, a very clever psychopath. After what I've witnessed in the past hour, I'm convinced he's been in here the whole time, settin' the stage while your men searched the woods. It's like he's some theater freak with some sick fetish for the dramatic. Gotta see the ballroom to believe it."

The chief barked orders to the crime scene officer. "Shut the water off, dust for prints." Then his cold eyes met Mike's. "You're tellin' me he was in this shower, left the water on, closed the door, set the scene to make it look like he was in there?"

"Yeah," Mike said, scanning the shower floor. The cap was off the shampoo, liquid soap knocked sideways, pump off, thick globs of rose-scented gel caked on the lip of the tub. "That's exactly what I'm tellin' you. Whether the bat got in through some crack in the wall or was left by the nut to add theatrics is anyone's guess. I—"

His words were cut off by Tess's screams, coming from her bedroom.

Like a wild stampede, they fled to her, Mike at the head, the chief and officer in the rear by a hair. Tess stood in the entrance of her bedroom, white-knuckled hands grasping the wooden framed archway.

Open balcony doors banged in the wind, lace sheers swooshing. The salty sea breeze blew in, stirring the scent of roses through the room.

The satin sheets and pink duvet lay in a crumpled heap at the foot of the brass canopy bed. Dresser drawers were wide open, black silk stockings hanging out. Panties lay askew on the floor, along with sheer peek-a-boos and lacey lingerie.

The chief let out a low whistle. "Bag all this, get those sheets and pillow cases, the panties, too. We're gonna wanna check for DNA. Make sure ya—"

Tess broke in, her green eyes glassy with shock. "I can't believe he's been in here, in my bed. He…he…" She pointed to the crumpled sheets, to her panties. "The pervert…went through my…"

"Come on, Tess." Mike took her in his arms. "Let's go down in the kitchen and let these men do their work."

"Where's the bat?" Her eyes searched the dark hallway. "Is that winged beast still in here?"

One of the crime scene investigators looked up. "No, ma'am. We opened the door and he flew right out."

****

Sitting in the breakfast nook, Tess's entire body shook with shock. She could feel nerve endings snapping beneath her skin. She was on the verge of a major conniption, a complete meltdown. One more shock and she'd pop. When the coffee maker spewed and hissed, she nearly jumped out of her skin.

Taking a deep breath, she allowed the rich aroma of hazelnut to sooth her frayed nerves. Closing her eyes, she blocked out the past hour and drew comfort from the aromatic scent of the gourmet beans, until the clattering of cups broke into her meditation. Mike pulled two ceramic mugs from the cupboard. He poured the coffee, sloshing a generous snifter of brandy into one. She looked out the window, the golden rays of the sun casting an amber glow on the courtyard.

"Here ya' go, Tess." Mike placed a steaming mug of coffee on the counter. Then he sat in the booth across from her, his brown eyes broody. He brought the cup to his lips, never taking his eyes off her. But even so, Tess got the feeling his mind was a million miles away, reliving every second of the unfolding drama. She could see his wheels turning.

"How did he get in, Mike? It's like he has an inside connection, a way of slipping through the cracks. This is totally bizarre. I've even gone so far as to dissociate myself, pretend it's a story I'm writing instead of my real life drama. I'm stumped. As many thrillers as I've written, all the research about getting into the mind of a psychopath, I keep hitting brick walls. I have no idea how he's getting in and setting the stage without ever being seen or heard. How he keeps one step ahead of all of us, including a team of investigators, is a mystery to me."

"What do you do when you hit a brick wall in a plot and you're on a deadline?" Mike asked. "Come on, Tess. Think. Use reverse psychology. Pretend this is a fiction opposed to real life. How would ya' solve this mystery?"

Just as Tess was about to speak, thinking of her stalker as a character in her latest suspense thriller, the chief of police and the crime scene officer came lumbering down the corridor, footsteps thundering.

"Got what we need." The chief took a seat on the bench, the vinyl cushion crunching beneath his weight. "Dusted for prints, both latent and visible. Man, that's some freakish scene in the ballroom, a real theater production. We're dealing with a very clever psychopath, someone who enjoys the hunt every bit as much as the drama. He's always a step ahead of us. Since he comes and goes whenever he pleases, he's someone who knows the layout of this manor like the back of his hands. Any idea who that might be, Ms. Kincaid? Know of someone holding a grudge, a score to settle?"

"Call me Tess." She smiled faintly. "I've been sitting here driving myself crazy, trying to figure out who he is. I'm sorry, but nobody comes to mind. All I know is this stalker, whoever he is, knows things about me, personal details of my life, things that were never reported in newspapers or magazines. I'm talking about things that go back some twenty years, when I lived here with my parents. It's downright creepy. The fact he gets in here when I know for certain all the doors and windows are bolted is driving me nuts."

Tess took a sip of her brandy-laced coffee, then another. Too jittery to hold the cup, she plunked it down on the wooden counter. She sighed. "It all started back in New York. Then he followed me here and has been stalking me ever since. He's coy and very cunning. The way he sets up the ballroom with such theatrics is reminiscent of my father's masquerades; it's downright chilling."

Tess took a deep breath, looking at Mike. "He has to be someone who knew Daddy very well, someone who was a guest at these parties. But how he made fire appear on the mountain is another mystery. As far as I know, it has no connecting link to the masquerades. As many props as Daddy used in the ballroom, none of them was ever remotely connected to fire. This doesn't make sense. Who is he and how is he getting into my house?"

The chief reached into his pocket for a fresh pack of Marlboros. Turning them upside down, he tapped them on the table. He worked the string, unwrapped the cellophane, scrunched it in his hand. Fishing out a cigarette, he struck a match to it.

Smoke filtered through the room. A sheepish expression flashed in his eyes. He looked at Tess. “Ah…sorry. Bad habit. Mind if I smoke?”

Tess waved her hand and stood. She walked to the counter, returning with an ashtray. “I don’t mind. Daddy always smoked in here. The smell of cigarettes in the kitchen is natural. Can I get you a cup of coffee, Chief?”

“Thanks, a black cup would sure hit the spot.”

Tess poured the coffee, grateful to have something to do with her hands. She placed it in front of him and took a seat. “So the million dollar question is how is this stalker getting into my house when everything is locked up?”

The chief flicked his ash into the copper ashtray. “Let’s start with suspects. So there aren’t any enemies jumping to your mind. Any fans you met along the way to fame who send out a red flag?”

“Not that I’m aware of.” Tess pressed her forefinger to her lips. “I’ve gotten lots of fan letters over the years, but not one of them was ever the least bit threatening. Not until the one in the mailbox right before I left New York, claiming to be my biggest fan.”

The chief scribbled notes. “Anything else?”

“I feel his eyes on me, from the woods behind the bell tower. Whether or not this has any bearing on the case, my friends and I used to play up there when we were kids, pretending it was a medieval castle.”

Something flashed in the cop’s eyes. “You and your friends?”

“That’s right,” Tess said. “My parents divorced when I was very young, but every summer, I returned here to stay with my dad. I played with the kids who lived around here, or came in for the summer to stay at the beach.”

“Do you remember their names?” The chief

asked, his pen poised. “Could be an angle to explore.”

“Ah…” Tess pondered, gazing up toward the bell tower. “Let me think. I knew most of them only by first names. Jimmy, Marcy, Danny…and let me think…there was a Bobby, yeah Bobby.”

“Have you heard from any of these kids since?” The chief jotted down more notes. “Maybe when you became a best-selling author?”

“No.” Tess finished the last of her coffee. She walked to the sink and rinsed out her mug. She gazed out the window, her eyes fixed on the huge peregrine falcon on the steeple of the tower. “He’s watching me. I can feel his eyes from deep in the woods.”

The chief exchanged a look with Mike, then he cleared his throat. “Ah…Ms. Kincaid. Are there any trap doors in this mansion you’re aware of? Some hidden wall? This old manor’s gotta be what…close to a century old?” He glanced around, his gaze sweeping the room. “It’s been my experience that most old houses have hidden walls, hiding places, sometimes vaults within the panels.”

Tess’s heart skipped a beat. A hidden passageway? That had never occurred to her, but it made sense…a lot of sense. Yet she knew of none, nothing had ever been mentioned. Could it be? She walked back to the table, a bit shaken. Totally shocked, she stammered. “Not that I know of, and with Daddy’s love of the thrill, surely he would have mentioned it or used the hidden doors somehow to his advantage, even if it was to scare Mama and me. Like I said, Daddy was the king of the practical jokes.”

“All right then.” The chief stood to leave. “That’s it for now. If you think of anything, anything at all, don’t hesitate to call. Just as a precaution, Ms Kincaid, you shouldn’t stay here all alone. We can’t provide round-the-clock security for you…sorry to say, it just isn't in the budget."

Mike broke in. "I'll be staying here with Tess until this stalker's behind bars."

"Good," the chief said as he left. "I'll see myself out. I'll be in touch."

After the front door closed and locked into place, Mike looked at Tess. "Do you own a gun?"

"What?"

"I wanna teach you how to defend yourself...and the sooner the better."

Chapter Nineteen

"You want me to do what?"

"That's right, darlin'." Mike's gaze met hers. "Like it or not, it's high time ya' learn how to use a controlled weapon. As county sheriff, it's one of my duties to determine whether or not a person should obtain a license to operate. Granted, the shoe's generally on the other foot. Folks come to my office and apply for the license. After runnin' the proper checks, makin' sure there's no criminal record or mental instability, a license is granted. I can't make ya' learn how to shoot a gun, but I also can't think of a woman who needs to learn how to protect herself more than you. I can teach ya, down at the shooting range or the local college."

Tess went to speak, but no words came out. She blinked several times, trying to comprehend one more shock. She licked her parched lips. "I…can't, Mike. I could never shoot a gun…not after what Daddy did. Please try and understand what you're asking." Tears spilled down her cheeks. She swiped them with the back of her hand. "I just can't. My answer's no."

Mike was at her side, wrapping her in his muscular arms. "Shh. Hush now, darlin'. It's all right. Course I understand, more than ya' know. Don't you think I see your dad's body every time I look at a gun? But someone's out to get ya, and this is no time to be weak. I can't be with you every second and neither can the police. If push comes to shove, wouldn't ya' feel better knowin' how to protect yourself?"

"I don't wanna think about that right now." Tess swiped at a tear rolling down her cheek. "No more today. I just can't take another moment of this unending drama."

"All right, we'll put the discussion on hold…for now. What you need is some food. I know ya' haven't eaten all day; in fact, I could use a bite myself."

"The cupboards are empty," Tess said, her gaze sweeping the kitchen. "I never did make it to the market. There's nothing in here except coffee, tea and cookies, the ones Daddy left in the pantry."

"Need more than that." Mike picked up the phone. "I'll order a pizza. What do you want on it?"

Tess shrugged, rolled her shoulders. She wasn't hungry but knew she had to eat. She heaved a sigh. "Surprise me."

****

After the delivery of pizza and cokes, Tess and Mike munched in silence, each deep in thought. In spite of her lack of appetite, the minute the loaded pie arrived, the tantalizing aroma of spicy tomato sauce and grilled pepperoni teased her taste buds.

Digging into a slice, then another, Tess washed down the comfort food with a hearty gulp of coke, feeling considerably better. She licked the juice from her finger, savoring the taste. She watched Mike take a bite of his pizza, hot juice squirting out of the corner of his mouth. The tip of his tongue darted out, catching the sauce before it dribbled down his chin. A surge of hormones bolted through Tess, turning her blood to liquid heat. A warm sensation rushed to her cheeks. When he caught her watching him, he leaned over the table, taking her mouth in a hungry kiss.

"Been dyin' to do that all day, darlin'."

"Ah…I think we should discuss our sleeping arrangements. I can't even go in my bedroom after that pervert slept in my bed and I certainly don't wanna be alone in this house if there's even the slightest chance he's in here, hiding in some hidden panel. Why don't we build a fire in the parlor and camp out in front of it. I'll go up and get those photo albums so we can go through them. Come to think of it, I might still have my old diary up there. Yes, I'm sure of it."

Tess started to walk toward the door but hesitated before turning around, reaching out her hand to Mike. "Come with me, please…I really don't wanna go in my bedroom alone after he's been in there. Plus we have to get some blankets and pillows from the upstairs linen closet. And I want to grab a sweat suit, get out of this robe."

"You're right, Tess. Finding your diary could give us some key insight, maybe trigger some memories you have filed away. Good thinking. Just let me make a call to a buddy of mine, see if he can drop by my ranch to feed the animals."

Mike slapped himself. "Damn. Almost forgot with all the excitement. My buddy Chip and his landscaping crew are comin' out here first thing tomorrow, bright and early."

Tess raised an eyebrow. "How early?"

"Seven, could be even a little earlier."

Tess tossed the empty pizza box into the trash. "Well, it'll be good to get the land cleared out, some of those dead trees and unruly foliage. At least it's something I have control over around this place." She looked at Mike. "Ready? If memory serves, the photo albums are on the shelf in the back of my closet. I used to have to get a chair to get them down. But with your height, you can probably reach them." She smiled up at him. "I knew you'd come in handy."

"Lead the way, darlin'."

****

Mike knelt on the stone hearth before the fireplace, whistling a tune. He pitched in a birch log from the brass basket and struck a match to it. Dry wood snapped and popped, the fire's amber glow spreading upward as bright as a sorcerer's flame.

Tess sat on an old patchwork quilt in front of the fireplace, going through the albums. Every time she turned a page, another memory unfolded. She stopped when she got to her twelfth birthday party. A warm, fuzzy feeling nestled deep in the pit of her stomach. A smile formed on her lips as the memory of that special day exploded in living color. The party was in the grand ballroom. Helium balloons floated about and the wax gargoyles were adorned in party hats. A huge castle cake was on a table in the center of the hall.

Mike brushed his hands on his jeans and joined Tess on the quilt. "Looks like some birthday bash. Cute kid, even if ya' were a tad on the chubby side."

Tess nudged her elbow into his ribs. "I was pleasantly plump, that's all. I loved to eat, especially sweets. That cake was delicious, pure chocolate fudge, baked fresh at the Seaside Bakery."

"Who are those kids?"

"My friends from the beach, the ones I told you about. The girl with the pink, beaded tank is Danny, short for Danielle. The boy with the red hair and freckles is Bobby. Then there's Marcy, the girl on my right in the white sundress, and there's Jimmy in the Star Wars T-shirt. Oh...look at Mama and Daddy, all smiles for the camera. This was the year before Mama and I moved to New York."

"So are any of these pictures triggerin' any memories? Any reason one of the kids might hold a grudge?"

"The only thing these pictures are doing is bringing back nice memories, especially since my twelfth birthday party was the last thing we ever did as a family."

"When is your birthday?"

"July 4th."

"A real firecracker, are ya' darlin'?" He kissed her cheek.

"And you? When's your birthday, Sheriff?"

"Christmas Day."

"Oh, poor baby." Tess patted his chin. "I betcha feel cheated, huh?"

"No way. I get twice as many presents as my brother and sisters. So, did ya' go through your diary yet?"

"I will as soon as I'm through with this album. Look…this next picture has Daddy posing with one of the wax gargoyles, the winged beast, and one of the kids is with him. I don't know who it is with that face mask on, but it's Daddy's Venetian, black velvet devil mask. I don't remember this picture being taken. I wonder who it is. Hmm. Maybe it'll come. Let me read my diary, see if there are any clues."

"I'll just go through this album over here." Mike got up and stoked the fire with the brass poker. Flames shot up, hissing and snapping, stirring the rustic scent of birch as he returned to sit beside her.

A few minutes later, Tess looked up. "Here's something interesting. I wrote that I gave Bobby a silver earring, a buried treasure I found when we were out snorkeling. Funny thing, I don't remember that at all. But it's no wonder. Like I said, we played sunken treasure and were always trading trinkets we found." Tess yawned, closing her diary. "I think that's enough for tonight. I'm really beat and you did say your friend's coming over at the crack of dawn. Besides, I don't think I'm gonna find anything in either this diary or the pictures. It's just kid stuff."

"Sure wish I could help, darlin'. Guess old memories keep the good times from fading out." Mike uncurled his long legs, stood up and stoked the last of the burning embers with the poker. He pitched another log in the grate, stepping back when it snapped and crackled. Bright orange flames shot upward. He brushed his hands on his Wranglers. "Isn't this nice, sittin' in front of the roarin' fire with me instead of being all alone in this big old house?"

"It sure is." Tess watched Mike fiddle with the log, feeling a fire in her belly as hot as the raging inferno he'd created in the hearth.

He sat next to her on the old patchwork quilt, his eyes growing dark as he gazed into hers. He moved closer, running his long fingers through her sleek mahogany tresses. "I love your hair; it's so pretty. The way the light from the fire flickers against it, making it look like burnished copper, all those colors." He nuzzled closer. "And it smells so wonderful..." He moved a little closer, gazing into her eyes.

His words were like a soft breeze. She had to strain to hear them but her heart seemed to know, as its beat raced and all traces of tiredness were gone.

"There's something between us, darlin', can't you feel it? You're always on my mind. I think I fell for you the moment your dad showed me all your pictures and told me stories about you growing up. I felt like I knew ya when I saw you in the flesh for the first time, out there in the raging storm, looking so hauntingly beautiful. Darlin', I nearly came apart at the seams. I wanted to take you in my arms, but I couldn't. You were scared to death, desperate for someone to believe you were being stalked. I'm real sorry about all this, Tess. I promise, with God as my witness, I'll find this maniac and nail him, put him behind bars where he can never scare you again."

Tess's eyes filled with tears. She touched his face, running her fingertips along the contours of his cheekbone. "The first time I saw you out there in the pouring rain…Sheriff Andretti, you stole my breath. I couldn't speak, all I could do was watch you. For a moment, just seeing you, made everything else going on fade away. You looked so dangerous, so determined, and so very masculine. Your eyes were dark and brooding…you have the most amazing eyes, totally mesmerizing, all those different colors. Right now, in the glow of the firelight, they look like liquid gold with sparks of emeralds. You steal my breath, Mike Andretti."

His voice grew husky, his eyes dark with desire. He kissed her, pulling her into his arms, his words coming out as a groan. "You drive me crazy. Tell me you want me, darlin'."

Tess melted into his kiss. His mouth was warm and wet, tasting of pepperoni and hot Italian spices. The stubble of hair on his chin tickled her and butterflies fluttered in her belly.

"You are so beautiful," he said, his teeth grazing the tender flesh at the hollow of her throat. "Your skin smells so good, tastes so sweet. Is that…roses?"

"Sachet of roses," she purred, arching her neck back. "I'm glad you like it."

"I think it's a love potion," he whispered in her ear, his voice low and husky. He pulled back slightly to look at her, desire burning in his eyes. "I gotta tell ya, darlin'; it's workin'. I'm tumblin' head over heels."

"Me, too."

Mike's mouth swooped down on hers, devouring it with savage hunger. "Tess, I need you."

His tongue separated her lips, teasing, taunting, delving deeper and deeper. His hands slid her sweatshirt up, his lips kissing a seductive path up her torso.

Tess ran her hands through his hair, undoing the band securing his ponytail. Thick locks tumbled down to his shoulders, giving him the look of a handsome Greek god. Her hands made their way up his chest, burying her fingers in a silky bed of pleasure.

"I want you," she whispered.

As the roaring fire shrouded them in a cozy ambiance, Mike gently pushed her down on the patchwork quilt, kissing away the last of her fears.

Chapter Twenty

She had to be dreaming. No sooner had Tess fallen asleep in Mike's arms when a roar blasted from outdoors, followed by the thundering boom which shook the room. Alarm bells shrieked in her head. The stalker? Her temples throbbed as she bolted upright. Her pulse raced. Realizing Mike was gone, her heart skipped a beat. Where was he? She was all alone and her biggest fan was trying to bulldoze his way into the manor.

Then it hit her. The landscaping crew. She glanced up at the clock on the mantel. True to Mike's word, the crew had arrived before seven. The comforter rustled as she untangled herself. Freddy meowed, simultaneously purring and rubbing her.

Tess craned her head toward the window where the buzz cut through her last nerve. Streaming sunshine poured through a crack in the pleated drapes, the glare blinding. "Freddy, I guess the landscapers have arrived."

Wrapping herself in the quilt, she padded across the icy hardwood floor in her bare feet, rolling her head from shoulder to shoulder to work out the kinks. She parted the curtains and peered out

Several bulldozers and caterpillar cranes crawled along the sloping hillsides of the estate, hoisting rocks and heavy debris from the unruly landscape. Gnarled branches timbered from the trunks of towering red oaks. Stumps were extricated, split and sliced before being put into grinding machines. Other trees were trimmed and reshaped, giving them a fresh makeover. Wood splinters and soil hurled in all directions, creating a thick cloud of dust and freshly dug earth. In the center of all the chaos, Mike towered, perched on a bulldozer, removing the topsoil layer, pushing it into an out-of-the-way stockpile. As if sensing her presence, he looked over and met her gaze. Casting a wicked wink, his arm shot upward as he mouthed the words, "Mornin', darlin'."

Shaking her head, unable to wipe the grin off her face, Tess backed up, the heavy curtain panels folding together with a gentle swoosh. Memories of the night before surged through her like a bolt of electricity. Seeing her man sitting atop a bulldozer, looking hot and sexy in the early morning sun made her want him all over again. Damn the man. Where did he get his energy? After a night of passionate lovemaking, there he was, all bright-eyed and bushy-tailed, lending a hand to his buddy.

Freddy meowed, a frantic cry for breakfast. He wanted to be fed and there would be no peace until His Royal Highness was taken care of. "Come on, Fred. Let's go see about breakfast and some strong coffee."

Slipping into her sweatsuit, she scooped up the whining feline and headed to the kitchen, depositing him at his dish. He weaved in and out of her legs, meowing. Sighing, she jiggled some cat chow into his dish and put on the coffee. A few minutes later, the heavenly aroma of hazelnut wafted through the kitchen. Tess opened the windows facing the front yard, allowing the crisp morning air to filter in, bringing in the smell of freshly mown grass.

The side door opened and the air was suddenly charged with electricity. Mike had his arms around her in one fluid move, sweeping her up in his arms and twirling her around. "Mornin', darlin'."

"Morning." She caught her breath as she slid

down the length of his body, her arms locked around his neck. When her feet touched the ground, their lips fused together in an erotic kiss that left her wanting more. She caught her breath, staring into his golden brown eyes. “You could spoil me with a greeting like that.”

“That’s what I wanna do,” he whispered in her ear. “Spoil ya’ rotten. Is that coffee I smell?”

Tess smiled up at him. “Your timing is perfect. Wanna cup?”

“You bet.” He nibbled on her ear, kissing the side of her neck. His voice was husky when he whispered the words, “Last night was perfect, darlin’, and so are you.” He deepened the kiss. “And I do like that wild rose tattoo…right here. Very sexy.” His fingers trailed down to her upper thigh, leaving shivers in their wake. “How about a shower?”

****

Dressed in a peach T-shirt with glittering seashells and a pair of cotton shorts, Tess sat on a lounge chair with her photo albums, diary and notepad, drinking coffee while searching her brain for clues. Her hair was still damp, fragrant with the scent of jasmine shampoo. She’d have to change brands, knowing the pervert had been in her shower, using her toiletries. Sensing Mike’s presence, she looked up. Her heart did a little dance. Dressed in uniform, he stole her breath.

“I’m on duty this morning.” He leaned down to kiss her. “You’ll be perfectly safe with Chip and the gang working outside. I’ll stop back for lunch, but if you need me, I’m just a call away.”

Tess beamed up at him. She traced his badge with the tip of her finger, her voice a soft purr. “I just love a man in uniform. You look so dangerous, so sexy.” She stood and stretched on tiptoe to kiss him. The moment their lips met, an electrical current flowed through her and it quickly advanced to movement that left them both breathless.

"Be good, now; don't start something we can't finish." Mike smiled and lightly brushed her lips with his. "But definitely keep the thought for later. For now, try and think of more names of the kids around here who you used to play with. I'll see you in a few hours."

****

The sound of car tires coming up the driveway broke into Tess's thoughts. She squinted, shielding her eyes from the relentless rays of the early morning sun. A woman hopped out of a red sports car, carrying a huge bag from the Seaside Bakery. Tess's stomach growled and her mouth watered, which reminded her she still needed to get to the grocery store.

There was no doubt who the woman had her sights set on. With a big smile on her face, she sauntered across the lawn to Chip. When she stood on her tiptoes to plant a big kiss on his lips, his face bloomed a bright cherry red all the way up to his gleaming bald head. Hoots and whistles erupted from the crew. The woman waved at them, her golden blonde curls tumbling down her back. "You boys ready for a donut break? Got y'all a treat from the bakery, glazed donuts and muffins."

There was something familiar about the woman. The more Tess stared, the stronger the feeling. She knew her from somewhere. It was her curls, all those big bouncing curls and the way she used them to flaunt herself. And that slight Southern twang. A second later, the woman was running toward Tess at full speed, a huge grin on her face.

"Well…as I live and breathe! Tess Kincaid, is that really you?"

A huge smile spread across Tess's face as she jumped out of her chaise lounge, racing to her childhood friend. They collided in a huge embrace.

"Mandy? Oh my gosh, I kept thinking I knew you from somewhere. It was your hair—and the way you tossed it back—that finally helped me figure it out. You look great, haven't changed a bit! How do you stay so young-looking?"

"Oh, honey," Mandy purred. "It's that big burly guy over there. Now if I could just get him to share my enthusiasm, we'd be all set, but I have to admit chasing him is half the fun. You remember how I always loved the chase, even as kids. Hey, do ya' ever hear from any of the old gang? Danny, Bobby, Jimmy?"

"Grab a seat," Tess said. "As a matter of fact, I was just going through some old albums. Come on, I'll get you a cup of coffee. You couldn't by any chance spare a muffin from what you brought, could you?"

"I brought plenty so I'll go steal a couple from the bag. The guys will never miss them." Mandy continued talking as she started to back away. "This is so great. I read all your books and have always wanted to get in touch with you. This must be fate, running into you like this. Can you believe I never left the harbor? I've set up my own business down on the dock, my hair salon. You'll have to come on down and I'll give ya' the works."

A few hours later, Tess and Mandy had caught up on things. Tess filled her friend in on the bizarre happenings of late.

"So that's why you're not in the pictures." Tess brushed her hands after devouring a muffin. "It's all coming back to me now. You had food poisoning and had to miss the party."

"But I sent you a gift though, one of those mystery books you loved so much. You always did say you'd be an author some day and look at you now."

Tess's smile faded, a feeling of dread dampening her light-hearted mood. "But seriously, Mandy, is there any reason you can think of that one of these kids might hold a grudge?"

"Not that I know of." Mandy blew a kiss to Chip. "We were just kids, playing kids' games. Those were the days, huh? Hey, ya' know, I do kinda remember Bobby having a crush on you. Wonder what happened to him? He was always talking about the movies, said he wanted to be a director or something when he grew up. Listen, honey, I gotta run. I have a girl coming into the shop in about twenty minutes. Let's get together, okay? Are you gonna be at the Labor Day beach party?"

"I wouldn't miss it. The sheriff asked me to go with him."

"Are you two an item?"

Tess smiled. "You might say that."

No sooner had Mandy left when Mike pulled up in his sheriff's car, a bottle of water in his hand. He slugged some back and kissed her, his lips wet.

"So did ya' come up with anything while I was gone?"

"I spent time looking…but, hey, you'll never guess what happened? Chip's girlfriend stopped by with some baked goods for his crew. I kept thinking I knew her and finally figured out it was Mandy, one of those friends we've been talking about. It was great to catch up. If not for Chip, our paths might not have crossed, at least for a while."

"Chip's been datin' her off and on. Was Mandy able to shed any light on the mystery?"

"Not really, but she did mention Bobby had a crush on me. She also remembers him wanting to be a director when he grew up."

Mike's eyes took on an icy glaze. "Did she remember his last name? This could be a lead, Tess."

"No, she doesn't have any idea what happened

to any of the kids. I don't think Bobby's childhood crush has anything to do with the stalker. What would be the point, after all these years?"

****

The Master whistled as he strutted through the tunnel, feeling oh so clever. A mouse skittered by, twittering as he disappeared into a hole in the wall. The Master swiped spider webs as he walked, heading for the secret panel in the wall. He stopped when he reached the wine cellar. He yanked the rope light, showcasing Daddy's finest in soft light. Choosing a bottle of nicely aged red, he checked the label. 1969. He uncorked it, humming a tune.

The Master guffawed, dark laughter echoing through the tunnel. He slugged some back and smacked his lips, oh so delicious. Hat's off to Daddy. Filled with adrenaline as he prepared to stage the next scene, he trudged onward, stopping when he reached the other end of the tunnel. Punching in a secret code, the doors to the freight elevator parted and The Master stepped aboard.

Envisioning the coming attractions, a sense of power surged through him. He smiled to himself. Such a clever master, slinking through the tunnel like a thief in the night. And Princess Contessa, mistress of the manor, oh so baffled and bewildered. His flesh tingled with excitement. Charged with energy, he thrust his fist high in the air. Hail to *the king of drama.*

But the best part of the show was watching the pretty little princess twitter under his thumb. The fear blazing in her bewitching green eyes was so satisfying. Knowing his theatrics had spooked her senseless made his blood tingle with dark rapture. He licked his lips in eager anticipation. The fantasies he'd conjured up were X-rated and oh so naughty, like a missile shooting off into space…blast off.

Yes, yes, yes!

The ancient freight elevator creaked as the doors parted. Stepping out, adrenaline pumping, he raced up the stone steps. Spying the brass plaque on the wall, his pulse twitched a wild rhythm. He walked into a spider web, thrashing about, spitting and sputtering. A dank draft hissed through the tunnel, producing an eerie whistle. Like a lynching post, a sinewy rope ladder swayed from the rafters.

The Master charged toward the brass panel, his fingers tingling. Reaching it, he stroked it, his heart thumping like a bongo drum. Quivering with an overload of adrenaline, he punched in the password to grant access to the kitchen pantry.

Contessa.

The Master preened. Oh how befitting. Daddy's little princess. With a hitch, the floor of the pantry parted and The Master reigned.

Climbing up the rope ladder with the agile moves of a monkey, he stepped into the kitchen pantry. He reached into his pocket and pulled out a mask. Shrouding his face in it, he grinned to himself. And from behind the mask, he cackled like a wild hyena.

****

Tess sat on the chaise lounge, pulling her knees up to her chin as she watched Mike. He put his thumb and forefinger between his lips and whistled, then shouted across the land to one of the guys. A burning heat nestled deep in her belly, singeing her cheeks with a healthy glow. The things he could do with those lips. Yes indeed, Mike would definitely be the focus for her next novel. The perfect male personified.

Noticing how much land had been cleared since dawn, Tess was impressed. The crew had some diligent workers, literally moving mountains with all their muscle power. A group of stagnant grandfather maples had been cleared, giving way to a handsome canopy of thriving, healthy trees. The grounds were beginning to take shape.

Her gaze went back to Mike. He leaned over the water pump to refill his bottle, giving her a rather attractive view of his well-toned backside. His sandy blond hair was tied back in a ponytail, accentuating his high cheekbones and sparkling eyes. Her gaze traveled down his rock hard body, one that she itched to touch again.

Breaking the direction her thoughts were headed, Tess decided she was hungry. She'd worked up quite an appetite the night before. Some cookies would really hit the spot, along with another cup of coffee for some caffeine. Losing some sleep was catching up with her and she really wanted to tackle the rest of the diary and jot some names down from her piano recital. Yawning, she settled in to soak up just a bit more sun before going into the house to gather her snack.

A gentle breeze swooshed through the pines, stirring the sweet scent of wildflowers and roses. The last roses of summer mingled with the dank smell of fall. Somewhere out there, amidst the rustling of autumn leaves, her stalker lurked. Where would it end?

From the harbor, the seagulls scavenged on the sand for food, squawking and squabbling. The sea called to Tess, timeless and romantic. Shaking her head to clear her thoughts, Tess knew if she didn't get up now, she would probably still be sitting in the lounge come evening.

As she entered the house, ideas began to bloom in her head about a romantic hero on the high seas. Her hero would definitely have shaggy blonde hair, a rock hard body and warm golden brown eyes with sparks of liquid jade.

Just as Tess turned the brass knob on the

pantry door, the bell in the tower gonged, startling her. She wondered if she'd ever get used to those piercing chimes. Probably not, she decided, opening the pantry door. Just as she went to grab the cookies from the shelf, a gloved hand snatched the box from the other side. A face, obviously masked, popped up, grinning at her.

Chapter Twenty-One

Screaming like the hounds of hell were hot on her heels, Tess turned and bolted for the door, pulse hammering, heart in her throat. A high-pitched keen erupted from her, louder and louder, rising to a screeching howl. She stole a glance over her shoulder, expecting the creep to snake his arms around her. Running, tripping, she skidded on the kitchen tiles, slipping and sliding, adrenaline pumping.

Charging through a side door leading to the courtyard, she wrenched the screen back with such force it banged against the house before slamming into her shoulder. She kept running, crying hysterically. “Help!”

The crew had stopped for lunch and was gathered around the picnic table. The air hummed with testosterone, male voices and laughter. Fast food bags lined the table, the smell of onions and fries wafting through the air. The raspy vocals of Rod Steward warbled across the courtyard. All laughter came to an abrupt halt when Tess snaked around the table, hair flying in the breeze, arms floundering, eyes wide with shock as she slammed into Mike’s cast-iron chest.

“Tess?” His muscular arms draped around her waist, catching her before she slumped to the ground. “Easy, darlin’. What is it?”

“He…he…” She pointed to the kitchen window, gasping for breath. “Pantry…on the other side of the shelf.”

Mike's warm hazel eyes grew dark and broody. His muscles flexed as he reached for the gun strapped to his waist. He broke loose from Tess, racing for the door, boots clomping. He craned his neck over his shoulder. "Stay put. I'll go check it out."

****

Entering the mansion, Mike flung the screen door open. He released the safety on his gun. The loud click shattered the silence. His heartbeat tripled, adrenaline pumping through his veins.

Crossing the threshold to the kitchen in one fluid move, he blocked out the voices drifting in, the clanking of the harbor bell, the squabbling of seagulls. Every sense was tuned for the intruder. His instincts hummed with adrenaline, his heart racing. The pantry door was wide open, fully ajar, giving way to a walk-in butler's pantry as big as a room.

The shelves were barren, raspberry tea and chocolate syrup the only staples. Stepping inside, he looked around, spotting a rope light hanging from the ceiling. He searched for a hidden button, some type of latch that would lead him to the other side. Nothing.

Disgusted, he blew out a breath, air hissing between clenched teeth. Reaching into the back pocket of his jeans, he pulled out his cell phone and called downtown.

"Yeah, looks like the stalker strikes again. Send the crime team out for prints. This entire mansion needs to be swept for a hidden passageway. Gotta be a tunnel leadin' straight to the kitchen pantry."

****

Mike strutted through the side door to the courtyard, screen slamming behind him. The crew had finished their lunch break and had resumed clearing the land, saws hissing, bulldozers grinding.

Tess sat on the picnic table, sipping a coke, talking to Chip.

"Thanks for keepin' an eye on Tess." Mike slapped his buddy on the back. His gaze locked with Tess's before he took a seat on the picnic bench, wooden legs scraping cement. "No sign of him, darlin'. But no doubt, there's gotta be some secret tunnel, some hidden passageway to the pantry. That's how he's been gettin' in and out."

Tess traced a drop of water rolling down the side of the can. "Well, with Daddy's love of the thrill and his passion for scaring people to death, there's no way he knew about some secret tunnel."

"Damn." Mike replaced the Glock in the holster and stared up at the woods. He ran his hand through his hair. Perspiration stained the underarms of his shirt. "He's always one step ahead of us. Whoever he is, he's one clever son of a bitch." His eyes seared into Tess's. "Can ya' describe him?"

"Ah, look…" Chip popped the last fry into his mouth and gathered his trash from the table. He winked at Tess before taking off. "Lunch break's over, best be getting back to work. A pleasure to meet ya, Tess, even under these circumstances. Hope you'll be at the beach party this weekend."

"That's what I came back for." Tess managed a faint smile. "We'll talk more at the party, when things settle down a bit. At least I hope so."

Chip put his hard hat on and strutted across the courtyard, his work boots scuffing on the rough cement.

Mike massaged Tess's neck and shoulders, kneading out the tension. Leaning close, he whispered in her ear. "I'm so sorry, darlin'. We gotta catch this dude; is there anything at all you can tell me about him?"

Tess sipped her coke, then turned to Mike, meeting his gaze. "He scared the livin' daylights out of me. When I opened the pantry door, the last thing I expected to see was a hand snake out and snatch the cookies…just when I did." She shuddered. "To think I nearly touched the pervert's hand, the same filthy fingers that probed through my panties." She combed her fingers through her hair. "Ah…let me think. He had on a latex face mask, distorting his features. So I can't describe him. Plus, I only got a glimpse of him when he popped his head up like a weasel. But wait…there was something. Let me think."

Tess struggled to remember, tapping her memory and forcing herself to slow down and think details. "I've got it; his front tooth's missing."

"Good." Mike got close, brushing his lips to hers. "That's a start and…"

The low rumble of a van climbing the driveway interrupted, tires plowing over limbs and tree branches.

Mike lifted his hand in greeting and turned to Tess. "I called my sergeant and asked him to send the crime scene to investigate, scan for a hidden passageway. I'll just show them the pantry and be right back." He leaned over and kissed her. "You're safe out here; Chip and the crew are right out there and I'll be back in a flash."

Mike strutted to the team of investigators, his gait brisk, confident. Several men leapt from the van, doors slamming. A spark of energy ignited between them as an agenda was discussed. Grabbing a few kits from the van, the team loped up the stone steps to the manor, Mike in the lead. Despite the danger, or maybe because of it, a surge of heat hurled through Tess, coiling deep in her belly. Memories of the night before rushed into her brain and every pulse quickened. She remembered his touch, the scent of his skin, the bristle of his hair on her bare flesh. She licked her lips, sucked in her breath. Reaching for the coke can, she tilted it to take a drink, considerably cooling the temperature in her mouth, but her very core still raged like a burning inferno.

Then she thought of the man in her pantry, the stalker.

Her biggest fan?

Tess's flesh turned cold. A slight shiver prickled her skin. For all she knew, he'd been in her house for a long time, prowling around the rooms. What kind of a sick pervert was he? Who was he? Someone from her childhood, one of the…

"Howdy, ma'am." A lumberjack of a man appeared in front of her, his blue eyes gleaming with an unnatural brightness. He tipped his bright yellow hard hat to her. Getting very close, almost in her face, he placed his hands on either side of her on the picnic table. He chomped on a wad of gum and blew a bubble, popping it in her face. "Didn't mean to scare ya. Boss said we need to keep an eye out for ya'."

"Ah…yeah." Tess tried to back away from him, feeling trapped, pinned in by his massive form. His breath reeked of apple gum, the smell so sweet she wanted to gag. He was way too close and way too creepy. Something about him struck her as familiar, his bright blue eyes maybe. When the seagulls squawked overhead in the harbor, something skittered across her mind, but only for a moment. In that fleeting second, she smelled apples, felt the sun on her back, heard gales of laughter drifting across the courtyard. Then it was gone. She blinked several times. "I'm sorry. Do I know you? Have we met somewhere?"

"No, ma'am." He backed off when he saw Mike coming. "Can't say as we have."

"You're on the clock, Will," Mike said, slapping him on the back. "Chip ain't payin' ya' to flirt. Get back to work."

"Sure thing, Sheriff." Will shuffled across the courtyard, his heavy work boots dragging on the cement. Turning on the power mower, he heaved it across the land with the strength of a bull, shredded green grass spewing in the air, shaving the countryside into a velvety carpet of fragrant green clover.

Tess stared, mesmerized, trying to place him. Something gnawed at her. She'd met him somewhere before, but where? She turned to Mike. "Who is that guy?"

"Will?" Mike cast a sidelong glance. "Did he offend you in some way?"

"No, but there's something about him...his eyes, I think. I swear I've met him before. I can't explain it, but it's the closest thing I've ever experienced to déjà vu. For a fleeting second, I was a child again, playing in the courtyard, laughing, light at heart. And it all came about when I saw that creepy guy's eyes, smelled his sickening sweet apple gum."

"His name's Will Gentry," Mike said, tracing his fingertip along Tess's jawline as if to reassure her. "Been with the crew for years. Might be a tad slow-witted, but he's a dedicated worker, never missed a day's work in five years. Lives down on the harbor with his uncle. Chip gave him a job, lets him mow grass, not on the hill, just on the flat land. He's a loner, never socializes with the others, even during lunch breaks. Likes to garden, gotta real passion for cuttin' grass. Will's harmless, really. Doesn't drink or smoke. Bout all he's guilty of doin' is chewing gum all day."

Just as Tess was about to say something, the side door opened, screen door banging, hinges squeaking. One of the investigators yelled across the courtyard. "Got something in here, Sheriff. Best come take a look."

Chapter Twenty-Two

A feeling of apprehension washed over Tess as she crept down the barrel-shaped corridor, hand-in-hand with Mike. His grip tightened around her hand as they neared the den. An eerie whistle hissed through the hallway. Pictures of Jake Kincaid loomed between the copper lanterns, his unblinking stare unsettling. As they neared the den, the sultry vocals of Patsy Cline drifted out, the bittersweet lyrics laced with heart-wrenching pain. Fingers of dread tingled down Tess's spine. She bit her lip, knowing she was about to witness something other-worldly yet again.

When she stood at the threshold to the den, she gasped, squeezing Mike's hand so hard she felt her nails dig into his flesh. Behind the scarred up mahogany bar, a wax gargoyle towered, all gussied up in a white Oxford shirt, shoestring tie and horse-head belt buckle. Perched on its head sat her dad's ten-gallon hat. An open bottle of whiskey sat on the bar, the gargoyle's waxy fingers gripping the neck of the jug. A cigarette burned in the ashtray, thick smoke curling up, filtering through the air. The wax figure's glass eyes gleamed with brightness, a ghostly smile on its bloodless lips. The chilling image was reflected in the smoky mirror behind the bar.

With a jarring hiss, static crackled across the den, and from hidden wall speakers, Jake Kincaid's robust belly laugh shook the walls. A second later, his low, husky voice came through loud and clear. "Ya' ol' coot, how's 'bout doin' a few shots with me?

Come on, pardner, rustle up a chair."

Tess slid into Mike's arms, gasping. "Daddy!"

Mike's muscular arms held her, snaked around her waist, nestling the top of her head beneath his chin. "Hush now, darlin'. It's all right. It's another staged performance, a real mean prank."

Tess's strangled words caught in her throat. "He...he's dressed like Daddy, and..." She gestured with her hand. "That's another one of Daddy's old Westerns, one of his favorites, Shotgun at Dawn. It's...so surreal, hearing his voice quake with such vitality."

"Got it." One of the team scuffed across the cherry wood floors. "The movie's playing in the home theater down at the end of the corridor. No sign of the perpetrator." He turned to Tess. "Ya' know how the hidden wall speakers work, Ms. Kincaid?"

Tess nodded, still awe-struck by the chilling image of her dad behind the bar. "Yeah, there are controls in all twenty-four rooms. It's a high-tech panel Daddy had installed years ago because of the size of this mansion." She caught a glimpse of her reflection in the bar mirror. Her tangled hair lacked its usual sheen. Sweat beaded her upper lip, and deep purple shadows haunted her eyes. Instinctively, she ran her fingers through her hair. Then she forced herself to look away and focus on the investigating officer. "Come on, I'll show you."

"Put these on first." He handed her a pair of latex gloves. "Don't wanna smudge any prints the perpetrator might've left."

Tess's sandals scuffed along the wooden floors. She walked to the edge of the bar where the Victrola continued to crank out Patsy Cline's "Sweet Dreams." She pressed her forefinger into a slight depression. With a gentle squeak, a hinged panel unfolded from the wall, revealing a set of buttons with a variety of numbers. She pointed to the seventh button. “That’s for the theater.”

“Much obliged, ma’am. We’ll wanna dust for prints.”

Tess backed off. Mike guided her to one of the Naugahyde highback chairs at the bar. The smoke gagged her. She coughed, her eyes smarting from both tears and smoke. Dust coated the ash burns on the surface of the wood. She gazed at the old phonograph in the corner, the sultry vocals getting to her. When things were good between her parents, they used to dance to country love songs and “Sweet Dreams” was one of their favorites.

Staring across the room at her father’s picture, she met the gaze of the man in the portrait. Fresh tears pooled in her eyes. “Oh Daddy.”

Tears streamed down her cheeks. Filled with nostalgic memories, she looked at the wax figure behind the bar. Her heart skipped a beat as she visualized her dad fishing out one of his cigarettes. Spotting his gold engraved lighter on the bar, she swore she heard the flick of fire, tobacco catching as the tip went up in flame. The way those waxy fingers gripped the neck of the whiskey bottle was something she’d seen her dad do so many times. The entire setting was creepy, surreal.

Mike joined her, his calloused hand touching her cheek. “Need anything, darlin’?”

“Just to catch this nut. Any sign of him?”

“Sorry to say, he’s slipped through our fingers yet again.” He scrubbed his chin with his hand. “I sat here in the den with your old man now and again, samplin’ some vintage wine, smokin’ a cigar while shootin’ the breeze. I’ve seen the wax gargoyle, keepin’ vigil at the arched entry. So the perpetrator moved it behind the bar and dressed it up to look like your dad.” His golden eyes met her gaze, held it for a second. “We never left the parlor last night, so apparently, he’s been in here the whole time. And then again today just in time to light that cigarette."

Tess's hands trembled, her lips quivered. "Do you think he saw us? When we were..."

"Shh..." He caressed her neck, his fingers massaging tiny circles. "We won't even go there."

The crime scene investigator broke in. "Look here, Sheriff, we've stumbled upon something interesting."

The team gathered around a painting just to the left of the entryway, a chocolate brown Thoroughbred with a white stripe down its nose. A gilded frame ensconced it. One of the investigators pointed a gloved finger to the frame. "There's a microscopic chip beneath it." He depressed it with his finger, and with a gentle hiss, a hidden panel opened, revealing a walk-in steel vault full of guns.

"Holy shit." Mike whistled, walking in. "Look at this."

Double barrel shotguns were neatly stacked in a glass case on the adjacent wall. In cubbyhole compartments, a variety of Western guns gleamed in the muted light.

"I recognize a good many of these." Mike scanned every weapon. He hoisted his fingers through his belt loops and gestured with his chin. "There's a Colt 1878 Lightning, a 75 Remington and a Real McCoy—to name a few."

"Those are the guns Daddy used in his movies." Tess stared in awe. "I never knew about this vault, but I do remember Daddy didn't want guns around me and Mama when we lived here. And with all my friends in and out..." Her voice faded off. "Is it any wonder?"

"So we've discovered one hidden passageway in this old manor," Mike volunteered, his gaze searching. "But this doesn't lead to the pantry. There's gotta be another passageway, a trap door somewhere."

Feeling a bit nauseated, Tess fled to the bathroom at the other end of the den. Dizzy, her eyes unfocused, she didn't see her cat lying on the floor until it was too late. She tripped over him, stumbling, her heart pounding. He hissed and snarled and ran for his life. "Sorry, Freddy. Didn't see ya."

Hurrying, her feet slid out of her sandals, slapping on the cold hardwood floor. Barely making it, she barged through the door, slamming it behind her. The room was dark, no windows. She flicked on the light switch, illuminating the room in brilliant white light. Gagging, she knelt before the toilet and choked, a bad case of the dry heaves, her eyes bulging, the veins popping in her neck. Resting for a few seconds, she pulled herself up and went to the sink to splash cold water on her face. Bleary eyed, dead tired, and completely unnerved, she blinked a few times, squinting to read the writing on the mirror. Then she gasped. The letters glaring at her were written in what looked like blood.

I'm coming to get you, Contessa.

Tess screamed at the top of her lungs before slumping to the floor in a massive heap. A split second before her world went dark, she heard laughter from deep within the walls.

Chapter Twenty-Three

Hearing Tess's screams, Mike tore across the den, the heels of his boots clicking on the scuffed-up floors. Reaching the bathroom door, he charged through, his pistol raised, both hands tightly gripped around the steely metal. He saw the writing on the mirror and then looked down to see her sprawled out on the floor; his heart leapt to his throat.

"Tess!" He knelt down by her, relief storming through him when he felt a thready pulse. He brought her wrist to his lips and kissed it. "It's all right, darlin'." He craned his neck over his shoulder, toward the door where the team had gathered. "Someone call an ambulance."

An hour later, after the paramedics had declared Tess to be in good health, all things considered, she sat in the kitchen with Mike, playing with the fast food he'd ordered.

She bit into the turkey sub, chewed slowly and chased it down with a gulp of coke. Never taking his eyes off her, Mike dipped his hand into the bag and pulled out a sandwich. The paper rustled as he unwrapped it; the aroma of smoked turkey and onions filled the air. Biting into it with gusto, he watched Tess play with her food. His heart hurt for her. He looked into her misty green eyes, cloudy with tears.

"Come on now, darlin'. Part of the reason ya' passed out is due to lack of food. When you mix that with shock…well, go figure. Now eat. And drink that coke. It's good for what ails ya'."

"I know," Tess said, her gaze searching the room. "He's gotta be in here, hiding, waiting to pounce. You saw what he wrote on the mirror—he's coming to get me. I'm scared, Mike." Tears spilled down her cheeks, mascara streaked on her face.

Mike reached over, took her quivering hand in his, giving it a comforting squeeze. "I know, darlin'. Soon as you can pack a bag, I'm takin' you to my place. We just can't take any more chances."

Tess shook her head, tightening her grip on Mike's hand. "I can't think of anything I'd rather do, but Freddy has to come with me. Is that okay? I mean you already have so many animals."

"He's a part of you, Tess. Of course, you can bring your cat. He'll fit right in at my house, you'll see."

"That's what I'm afraid of." Tess smiled. "Freddy isn't exactly what you'd call a social butterfly. He prefers solitude and his own space."

"We'll work it out. So let's go pack a few of your things and then we're outta here."

"Well before I pack, I really must use the powder room," Tess said, heading toward the door at the end of the kitchen. "I'll just be a minute."

"Wait," Mike fled past her, air swooshing. "After what happened before, let me check it out first."

Feeling confident no stalker lurked in the powder room, Mike stood guard at the door, waiting for Tess. While she was out of earshot, he pulled out his cell phone and made a call downtown.

"Yeah, listen. After what's been goin' on over here at 1300 Mockingbird Lane, my radar's on full alert. The death of Jake Kincaid was ruled a suicide, even though an autopsy was performed. Might not be a bad idea to take another look. If my suspicions are right, someone missed something on the investigation."

"Hey, Mike," one of the investigators lumbered

into the kitchen. "Got all we need for now. We've searched this whole manor and can't find any other hidden passageways. How he's coming and going is beyond me."

When Tess came out of the powder room, her jawline was set, her full lips puckered into a pout. "Listen, Mike. I've been thinking. You couldn't find any sign of a hidden panel in the pantry and neither could the crime techs. I've agreed to move in with you until this stalker is caught, but dammit, this is my home. I can't help but feel I'm missing something. I've been wracking my brain for something Daddy or one of the hired help might have said about a secret panel, but nothing comes to mind. Before we leave, let me have a crack at it. If I go in the pantry and drift back in time to when I was a little girl, maybe something will jog my memory."

Mike huffed out a breath. He stood there studying her, thumbs hoisted through the loops of his pants. Then he nodded curtly. "All right, Tess. Let's go in and have another look. Can't hurt. Knowledge of a trap door or hidden panel might be tucked away in the back of your mind. Been my experience that returnin' to the scene often triggers a clue to solve the case. Come on."

****

Tess stood in the center of the pantry, childhood memories flashing through her brain. The walk-in pantry was bigger than the entire kitchen in her New York condo. Spying all the spider webs draping from the corners, she cringed, knowing how meticulous her mother had been about cleanliness. She'd once fired a cook for not dusting the pantry shelves each morning. Tess turned, doing a semi-circle, searching every corner, every crevice.

She envisioned Maddie, the cook who ran the kitchen like a drill sergeant, giving her a good tongue lashing for sneaking into the pantry and hiding beneath the bottom ledge. One time when Maddie came in to pluck a bag of granulated sugar from the top shelf, Tess leapt out and screamed "Boo!" Maddie screeched to the high heavens, the sugar slipping from her grasp, the bag splitting wide open as it hit the floor. Hand on her ample hip, Maddie made her get a broom and dust pan to clean up the mess.

Tess pressed her forefinger to her lip. What had possessed her to hide beneath the bottom ledge and frighten poor Maddie to death? Could she have known of a button unlocking a trap door?

Getting on her hands and knees, she crawled under the ledge, sneezing when a cloud of dust shrouded her face. Tess looked up and felt around for a depression that would cause the pantry to swivel to the other side.

Isn't that what those old mystery books always portrayed? Biting her lip, squeezing her eyes to keep the dust out, she felt every inch of the ledge. All she got was a splinter, causing the tip of her forefinger to twitch with pain. Unfolding, she stood up in the massive pantry, feeling the four walls, her fingers itching to find the key to the other side.

Nothing. Frustrated, her heart thudding against the wall of her chest, she skimmed every shelf with her finger, surface and beneath.

Nothing. Where is it?

How was the stalker getting into the mansion from the pantry? How did he know something she didn't when she had lived here and had explored every inch of the mansion in her youth? Her father had been the king of practical jokes.

Well, the last laugh was certainly on her, wasn't it? Balling up her fist, she punched the wall once, then twice. Her knuckles ached. Then her voice broke. "Where is it? Dammit, where in the hell is the freakin' trap door to the other side?"

Mike stepped in and enveloped her in his muscular arms. “Shhh. It’s all right. Let’s go.”

****

After the crime scene and landscaping crews packed up and left, Tess and Mike descended the steps and wandered to his vehicle. Heading to the old Wexler estate, cool country air blew in through open windows, renewing Tess’s spirit. Her fears seemed to literally vanish into thin air. Mike lived in a rural setting where the air was fresher, scented with the sweet smell of hay. The sounds of nature exploded all around her. Blue and white herons chirped from age-old birch trees. Tess looked up just in time to see a magnificent golden eagle soar gracefully over a neighboring hayfield.

The truck’s engine grumbled as it took the grade, heavy tires crunching leaves and fallen tree limbs. The sun peeked through the fall foliage, a brilliant ball of fire blazing through the amber leaves of autumn.

The minute Tess got out of the truck, she was greeted with the neighing of horses. Just then, one of the ranch hands dashed out of the barn, heading for Mike.

“Jezebel’s in labor, boss, Best come quick.”

Mike grabbed Tess’s hand, dragging her across fallen limbs, twigs and pines toward the barn. Rushing through the Dutch doors, cool air enveloped her. Horses stomped from inside their stalls, their hooves clomping, their cries restless. The smell of horse manure and hay filled her senses. She spotted the laboring mare at once. The horse stomped, chomped her jaws and turned her head down to stare at her belly during a contraction. Her neck and shoulders were soaked in perspiration.

Mike eased the mare through the worst of the pain, meeting her gaze, singing words of encouragement. When the contraction passed, the mare looked adoringly at Mike, her big brown eyes filled with love and devotion. Tess teared up, struck by this act of bonding between man and horse.

When Mike picked up his flamenco guitar from the corner and sat crossed legged in front of the mare, Tess's heart melted. The gentle strumming floated through the barn, the lilt of the Latin music sweetly sensual. Drawn to the hypnotic lull, Tess stared in awe.

Her body felt boneless, awed by the sight that met her eyes. Her man truly was a horse whisperer…and so much more. She felt untethered, her heart soaring as the heavy anchor that had weighed her down freed. The outside world and all its turmoil simply stopped revolving. At this moment in time, nothing was more important than the miracle of birth. And she was a part of it.

Mike could not be a more doting birth partner than if he truly were the father. She bit her lips, shedding unabashed tears. She sighed, grateful to witness this miracle. A warm feeling eased through her, pulling at her heartstrings.

As if reading her mind, Mike looked up and smiled. His golden brown eyes were bloodshot, tiny lines pinching the edges. His face was drawn, his jawline firm and rigid. "Tess, I'm glad you're here to see this. Come sit with us. It won't be long now."

"I see that," Tess said, joining Mike on the barn floor. She spoke softly, overwhelmed with a maternal instinct she had no idea she possessed. "Hello there, Jezebel. So you're about to have a baby, are you? Aren't you pretty, all that sleek chestnut hair and white stripe down your nose. Your foal will be a beauty, just like its mama."

"You're good with horses," Mike said, gently holding the small guitar made of Spanish cypress, plucking the strings with outward flicks of his fingers, producing a rhythmic roll reminiscent of the clicking of castanets.

Completely mesmerized, Tess watched Mike caress the instrument with loving strokes. Her heart melted, seeing this vulnerable side of him, so loving and devoted to a mare foaling. It touched her in a way nothing ever had. She watched Mike, the muted sun shrouding him in partial light. His eyes never once left the mare's, the non-verbal communication painting a picture words could never express.

Tess bit her lip, convinced beyond a shadow of a doubt that Mike Andretti truly was too good to be real. Her heart did a little pitter patter in her chest, emotions tugging at her insides, squeezing her like a tight embrace. The horses in the surrounding stalls softly whinnied, harmonizing with the gentle plucking of guitar strings.

Just then, Jezebel had a major contraction, so hard she laid down in a bed of soft hay, her neck and shoulders drenched with sweat. She snorted and whinnied, rustling around for comfort.

"Won't be long now," Mike whispered, quietly plucking the strings, the sweet lilt relaxing the mare.

Tess gasped, unable to stop herself as Jezebel rolled to her side and began pushing, the contractions in full swing. Then a little chill went through Tess as the two feet of the foal popped out, followed by the nose, greedily sucking in air.

"You're almost there, Jez," Mike said, maintaining his eye contact with the mare, whispering to her in between plucking on the strings of the guitar. "There's my girl; you're doing real good. It's just about over. Come on, baby, you can do it. Just a little more pushin'."

"This is amazing." Tess whispered as she stared in awe.

"The foal can breathe on its own, now that the nose is out. Here it comes, look."

The foal dropped out, its long legs slipping to the ground. It was a girl. She tried to get up but fell over, scuffling to her feet to try again. Jezebel watched, staring at her foal, finally breaking eye contact with Mike.

"That was so beautiful." Tess reached out and touched Mike's face. "You stole my breath." *And my heart.*

Mike kissed her, his lips so feathery soft she shuddered. Standing up, he stretched, his warm eyes glassy with unshed tears as he watched the foal bond with her dam. He turned to Tess, his golden brown eyes glistening like drops of morning dew. "Nothin' is more precious than the gift of life."

Tess nodded, unable to speak. Emotions tore down the last of the brick wall she'd built around her heart. Sighing, she whispered, her voice breaking. "It brings everything full circle, doesn't it?"

"It sure does."

Tess stared at the mare and her newborn, mesmerized by the miracle of birth. "Witnessing such an awesome experience was just the medicine the doctor ordered. Made me forget my woes. So where did you learn to play with such finesse? You're a very fine musician."

Just as Mike was about to say something, an officer strutted through the door. He took in the scene at a glance, his hard brown eyes softening for a second when the foal stood up and suckled her dam. Then he cleared his throat. "Ms. Kincaid, I'm Detective Jones. We met at your father's funeral. I'm glad you're here. This involves both of you; actually, I'm here on official police business."

"This is about the prints, the DNA you found, isn't it?" Tess asked, toying with a lock of her hair. "They found something, didn't they?"

"Yeah," the detective said, coming a bit closer, his boots scuffing on the stable floor. "There were fibers of red hair on the pillow case and sheets, along with DNA and sperm. We also got some very clear prints, but…there's something else. We need to talk, Ms. Kincaid. There's news regarding your father."

Tess's heart picked up a beat. "What about Daddy?"

From behind the stall gates, the horses shuffled and kicked, threw back their heads and whinnied a split second before the day turned as black as night. A minute later, a crashing bolt of lightning splintered the sky, followed by a clap of thunder that shook the walls. The horses chortled, heads peering over stall gates. Buckets of rain beat on the barn roof. With a sudden gust of wind, the door slammed shut with a bang.

Mike placed his hand on Tess's shoulder. "Darlin', let's step out of the stall and let my ranch hand finish up with Jezebel."

Without even fully realizing it, Tess was drawn into the walkway, closer to information she instinctively knew she didn't want to know. She felt Mike's arm come around her shoulder, thankful for the strength and warmth it provided.

"What's this all about, Detective?" Tess knew she couldn't put this off. "Why are the police involved?"

"I wish there was an easy way to tell you this." The detective touched Tess's arm, then his brown eyes seared into hers like lasers. "There were a few inconsistencies with your dad's death and we've been checking into it."

"Inconsistencies?" Tess's gaze darted nervously from the detective to Mike. "Like what?"

"We did an autopsy on your dad due to somewhat suspicious circumstances surrounding his death. There were a few discrepancies, such as the location of the bullet hole, the fact that no gunpowder residue was on his hands and he had bruising on his wrists."

"This is all news to me," Tess said, her eyes searching. "As far as I knew, it was a suicide. Why is this the first I'm hearing about these suspicious circumstances?"

"We always do an autopsy if there is a question of whether a person's death is a homicide or a suicide. Your father's autopsy came back pending, and unfortunately, the results were misfiled in our database."

Tess closed her eyes as she waited for the answer. "What are you telling me, Detective?"

"I'm sorry, Ms. Kincaid. Your father did not commit suicide. Jake Kincaid was murdered."

Chapter Twenty-Four

"Oh my God!" Tess cried out, collapsing in Mike's arms. "No! Who killed Daddy? Who?"

"We don't know for certain, Ms. Kincaid. Homicide is investigating, but we know the name of your stalker from the fingerprints and DNA. His prints are in our database because he has a record; in fact, he was released from the Broward County jail six months ago after serving a murder sentence. His name is Roberto Smith. Do you know this man?"

"Ah..." Tess stammered, raking her fingers through her hair, her mind spinning. "I really can't say. It doesn't ring any bells, but it's a rather common name. I keep thinking he has to be someone from my childhood, someone who knew me well and was familiar with the layout of the mansion. There was a Bobby, I recall, but I never even knew his last name. He had red hair and freckles. He showed up one summer and that was it. None of us ever saw or heard from him again. What possible reason would he have to come back here to stalk me...or to kill Daddy? If only I'd been at the estate that night...maybe Daddy would still be alive."

"Come on now, darlin'." Mike ran his hand down her arm. "There's no use in playin' the what-if game."

"How about you, Mike?" the detective asked. "You and Jake Kincaid were neighbors, friends even. Did he ever confide in you about any gambling debts, any seedy characters he was worried about? A woman or a jealous lover?"

"Never," Mike said. "All Jake ever talked about was how much he missed the old days when he starred in all those westerns, partied with some of the bigwigs of Hollywood, and how damn proud he was of his daughter."

"Now that I think about it," Tess said, emotion wedged in her throat. "It all makes perfect sense. Whoever killed Daddy is my stalker. You all thought I was nuts at first, reporting things no one else saw or heard. From the first night I entered the estate, I felt eyes watching me from the woods. He's out there, and he has access to the manor through some secret passageway no one can find. He's out to get me, kill me."

"We'll find him," Mike said, scanning the horses. Spooked by the thunder and lightning, they stomped and kicked stall doors, snorting loudly. Pouring rain hammered on the barn roof. The foal suckled all the louder, greedily taking milk from her dam.

"We'll catch him," the detective said. "We all know how coy and cunning he is. Let's try to keep rational and stay cool. Now that we have a name, something to go on, we're one step closer to catching Roberto Smith. Oh, there's one more thing that links Roberto Smith and your stalker. Not only did Smith's parole officer inform me Smith has never shown up for his parole meetings, but she said he does indeed have a missing front tooth."

"What was this Roberto Smith in jail for?" Tess asked. "Did you say murder?"

"Yeah, ten year sentence. Smith walked into a Florida convenience store one night and killed the clerk, all for twenty bucks. The kid he murdered was a nineteen-year-old college student, trying to make his tuition fee."

"So Roberto Smith has killed twice…that we know of," Tess said. "Which means he won't have any qualms about killing me."

The detective turned to leave. "I'll put out an all points bulletin to keep an eye out for Roberto Smith. He's armed and dangerous. Since he has access to your estate, no doubt he's helped himself to a gun. We already know he used your dad's pistol to kill him, and then, to stage the suicide, he left it at the scene. Do you know how many guns your dad owned, Ms. Kincaid? Can you take inventory?"

Tess's skin grew even more chalky, drained of all blood. She shook her head and heaved a sigh. "No, I'm sorry, Detective. I really have no idea how many guns Daddy owned. Until I got news of his death and then saw his vault, I never even knew he owned a gun."

"How about you, Mike?" The detective's penetrating gaze was sharp and demanding. "You knew Jake Kincaid fairly well. Y'all ever discuss guns? He ever show ya' his stash?"

"No. Like I said when the crime scene techs stumbled on the steel vault, I was in the den shootin' the breeze with Jake many times and the subject of guns never came up in conversation."

"All right." The detective turned, stopping in front of Tess. "Watch your step, Ms. Kincaid. Roberto Smith is close and just waiting for the right opportunity to pounce. Don't give him any reason to catch you off guard. My advice is not to return to the Kincaid estate, least 'til he's caught."

"Believe me, I'm not going to do anything foolish," Tess said. "How did the autopsy prove Daddy was murdered?"

"First of all, there were two gunshots to the head—one to the temple which we thought was the only site. However, upon looking further, there was another one just behind the ear and his hair was initially covering it," the homicide cop said. "A person who commits suicide generally puts the gun in the mouth or the temple, single shot and the first one we saw. However, even if one shot doesn't result in death, the person will more than likely pass out and be incapable of pulling the trigger again. In addition, your dad had no gunpowder residue on his hand, something he would have had *if* he had pulled the trigger. There was also bruising on both of his wrists, which indicates your dad put up a fight. It's even possible he knew his attacker. Watch your back, Tess."

The rain slowed as the homicide detective got into his unmarked vehicle. He was stuck in the mud, his tires spinning circles, mirky water splashing in all directions. After a few tries, the wheels caught and he headed down the driveway. Tess fell into Mike's arms, her chest heaving, wretched sobs pouring from her very soul.

"Why would Roberto Smith want to kill Daddy? How could this man come into his room, shoot him in the head and stage it as a suicide? What was the motive? And why come after me now?"

"I don't know, darlin'." Mike brushed her hair with his hand, threading his fingers through her long mahogany tresses. "But we're gonna get to the bottom of it, I promise, and homicide won't give up until they have Roberto Smith behind bars. In the meantime, though, it's you I'm worried about. I don't want you going anywhere alone. I want ya' here with me, where I can keep an eye on you."

"But you're not here all the time. You're the county sheriff and have a million responsibilities to deal with. How can you—"

"Hush now, darlin'. Put your worries on my shoulders. When I'm not here, I'll have a guard on ya', that's all. We're not takin' any chances."

"I'm scared, Mike. Truly scared. The last time I felt this vulnerable was when my parents divorced and I was forced to leave my dad and my home. I still remember how alone I felt, so lonely I thought

I'd die."

"It's all right. You've got me and I'm not goin' anywhere. Let's head on up to the house and get you and Freddy all settled in."

"Yeah, poor thing's probably getting restless in his cat caddy in your truck. I could use some strong coffee to jog my memory. I'm apparently blocking something from my childhood. If only I knew Bobby's last name. He did have red hair, but why would he want to kill Daddy and why me? We were never anything but good to him. It wasn't as if I invited everyone to my party except Bobby. He has no reason to hold a grudge, or in this case, a vendetta. I can't imagine it's him."

"Could the masked guest at your birthday party have been Bobby?" Mike asked, scratching his chin. "Think about the link. The unidentified kid in the picture had an apparent attraction to the wax gargoyles in the ballroom, proven by the photo, and had on the same mask you said the gargoyle was wearing in the ballroom the first night you came back here, the night you called me. Makes sense. I'll bet the Bobby from your childhood and this Roberto Smith are one and the same—your stalker and your dad's killer."

Connecting the dots, the hair on the nape of Tess's neck prickled. She stared at Mike, her eyes haunted. "I remember now. Bobby did have a real love of the gargoyles, the face masks...and something else."

"What is it, darlin'?"

"Bobby loved the theater. He asked me far more than the other kids if he could come over and watch the movies in our home theater, check out the production room. One night, Daddy even took him back and showed him how the projector worked. Oh my God. It must be him."

"Good." Mike took her in his arms. "That makes

us one step closer to catching him."

Tess drew from his strength and his warmth. "Oh no, Mike, I left my laptop back at the house. Can we go back and get it? I sure don't want him getting into my files and documents, all those personal addresses and phone numbers."

"You betcha, darlin'. Let's head out between raindrops."

****

Mike pulled into Tess's driveway. "Looks like the storm knocked out some tree limbs. The crew'll be back tomorrow, first thing, so they'll clear all that debris away. Stay put; I'll run in and grab your computer. Be back before ya' miss me."

Tess watched Mike dodge mud puddles, doing his best to stay dry. Raindrops splattered on the windshield from the leaves of red oaks and maples. The sun peeked out from behind murky clouds. Just as Mike raced up the stone steps, his foot landed in a puddle, splashing his leg with water. He shook his foot, obviously trying to get the water out of his boot.

Tess suppressed a giggle that turned into a muffled gasp as her gaze caught a field of blue, dozens of freshly planted forget-me-nots in her white stone arbor. Roberto Smith had invaded her sanctuary. The hair on the nape of her neck stood straight up, every nerve twitching. Her sixth sense screamed to beware. Her pulse hammered. The entire blue garden had been weeded and planted with her favorite wild flower.

Angry and frustrated, throwing all caution to the wind, Tess stomped out of Mike's pickup, avoiding mud puddles. When Freddy cried, she went back and released her cat from his cage so he could relieve himself before he had an accident. Slipping in the wet grass, sandals squishing, she skidded to a halt in front of her blue garden, awe-struck. Where was he? She turned and peered into the woods, her eyes searching the thicket.

From deep in the woods, a falcon cried, its shrill cry chilling. Even before Tess looked, she felt beady eyes watching her from the bell tower. A niggle of fear skittered down her back, chilling her to the bone. She spotted the falcon keeping vigil on the steeple of the tower. His piercing eyes bore into hers, his penetrating stare so intense she felt it clear down to her toes.

Freddy tore off to the edge of the land, snarling and hissing, his back arched.

"What is it, boy?" Tess silhouetted herself against the trunk of a towering pine. A breeze rustled through the rain-sodden branches, showering Tess in a bucket of raindrops. Shivering, her nipples puckered beneath her soaked T-shirt. Her teeth rattled from the chill. The woods were quiet, dark and dense. She couldn't see anything, but she sensed evil from deep in the thicket.

"Come on, Freddy." She fled across the lawn to snatch him. Just as she reached him, the ankle she still favored gave out, sending her sailing over a slick patch of leaves. With a thud, she hit the ground, dazed and helpless, the damp dank earth filling her senses.

Wincing, she propped herself up on her elbows, pain zinging through every bone and muscle. She smelled apples, then she heard his voice, low and muffled.

"Hurt yourself, miss?"

Tess craned her neck, popped her head up. Will Gentry stared down at her, his bright blue eyes gleaming. Then in one clumsy move, he snaked his fingers around her wrist and yanked her up, his hand as big as a ham hock.

Chomping on his gum, he sputtered, "You ain't safe out here all alone."

"What do you want?" Tess snatched her arm

from him, backing up. Adrenaline gushed through her. Her heart pumped fast and furious, so hard it thundered in her ears. “Why are you watching me, following me? Leave me alone, hear? The sheriff's just inside. He'll be out in two seconds flat to kick you off my land.”

“It ain't me ya' gotta fear, ma'am.” His jaw worked hard, the sweet apple scent nauseating. “It's the man in the woods.”

“Who?” Tess's gaze darted from Will Gentry to the bell tower. What should she do? Should she scream for Mike? Where the hell was he? What was keeping him so long? And why wasn't her cat clawing this Will Gentry to death? She wished she had a dog; a mean pit bull would rip his lungs out.

“Gotta go home.” Will shuffled from foot to foot, his unblinking stare disarming. Then he stabbed his forefinger in his chest, his motions jerky. “Cross my heart and hope to die…stick a needle in my eye. The man in the watch tower is gonna get ya'.”

Tess's heart jackhammered, blood pumping hard. Will Gentry slowly shuffled away, his stocky frame painting shadows on the grass. He made his way into a patch of trees, disappearing into the woods like an apparition. Tess huffed out the breath she'd been holding, her heart slowly tapering down to a normal rhythm. Freddy rubbed her leg, meowing loudly.

“Yeah.” Tess scooped him up in her arms, snuggling him close to her shivering body. “So where were you a few minutes ago? Not exactly my knight in shining armor, are you?”

“Tess,” Mike grabbed her, his eyes narrowed, lips stretched into a thin line. “What the hell's wrong with ya', woman? Didn't I tell ya' to stay put? Don't you know the danger you're in out here? An armed and dangerous criminal's on the loose, heart set on huntin' you down and killin' you. So ya' wanna tell me why you're out here in the open like some sittin' duck?"

"He...he..." Tears poured from Tess's eyes. "He planted forget-me-nots in my blue garden. He knows, Mike. Don't you see? Roberto Smith knows my favorite flower and planted them in my blue garden while we were gone. Unless it was that creepy Will Gentry. You just missed him; he's probably still scuffing through the thicket. He told me to watch my step. Said the man in the watch tower's gonna get me."

Mike sighed and took Tess in his arms. Sandwiched between them, Freddy snarled and hissed. Mike took her hand. "Come on, darlin'. You are soaked; let's get you home and warmed up."

****

Walking up the crushed oyster-shell walkway to Mike's home, Tess took in her surroundings. Scarlet, salmon and creamy white roses bloomed in the wooden arbor spanning the length of the parapet, their sweet essence filling the air. Chickadees softly tweeted from sugar maples. Glistening drops of rain fell from lemon and orange trees, plopping into puddles on the ground.

A dog yipped and whined the minute he heard Mike's footsteps. When the door opened, a large Irish Setter leaped on him, showering his face with doggy kisses. "Easy, Hank, there's a good boy. Say hello to Tess. There ya' go, be nice."

An excitable setter jumped on Tess, yipping, slobbering. Two cats circled in and out of her legs, purring, motors rumbling. They sniffed Freddy through his cat caddy. From the other side of the parlor, the parrot squawked.

"Bad boy, Mike. Wipe your feet."

"Did he just say what I think he said?" Tess asked, looking toward the cage. Her rigid shoulders eased, the knots in her neck loosening. "How did he know to say that?"

"Years of practice." Mike set Tess's suitcase and laptop at the foot of the stairs. "Like I said, Sir Galahad was old lady Wexler's parrot. I used to work as her stable boy, and when I'd come in after a rain, she'd tell me to wipe my feet. If I didn't, I got a tongue lashin' for tracking up her rug."

The bird flapped his feathered wings.

"So that's the infamous Galahad."

Mike grinned. "It's just a regular pet farm around here."

"Dare I let Freddy out of his cage?" Tess asked, noticing how unusually quiet he was.

"Let's go for it," Mike said, unlocking the caddy. Freddy refused to budge, still as a stone statue, claws fully extended. Walter and Julio sniffed him, greeting him with robust meows.

Freddy came out hissing, making a beeline for one of the rooms, Walter chasing him.

"Looks like we're gonna have some adjusting to do." Mike winked. "Now that we're all acquainted, let's go get settled. I'll rustle up somethin' to munch on. Go on, take a look around and make yourself at home. Wanna beer?"

"Ah..." Tess stared at her sopping wet sandals, making puddles on the floor, and her muddy clothes. Wiping her feet on the weather-beaten entry rug, she grabbed her bag. "Before I get a tongue lashing, I'd better go change. A beer sounds great."

"Straight up the steps, any room you like." Mike stole a kiss as she brushed past him. "Clean towels are in the bathroom pantry, first shelf."

Chapter Twenty-Five

"This is gorgeous," Tess said, doing a semi-circle around the Mediterranean parlor. "All these arched motifs add such character. I love all the blue undertones, combined with the different shades of turquoise and green."

She walked across the plush gold carpeting, her bare feet sinking into folds of butter-soft thickness. Hand-hammered lamps with Scavo glass cast a warm amber glow on the room, adding a cozy ambiance. She sunk into an emerald green sofa accented by a tumbling array of fringed pillows in burgundy and gold. A wrought iron fireplace was enhanced by filigree fixtures.

"All these colors bring the place to life. I just love it."

Mike smiled, handing her an ice cold bottle of beer. He set a basket of warm tortilla chips and some salsa on the coffee table, before taking a seat next to her. Walter immediately plopped on his lap. "Glad ya' like it. It's Moroccan design, a rich blend of Berber, Arab, Spanish and French."

"It adds energy to the room," Tess said, noticing how all the animals had gathered. Julio jumped on her lap and Hank lay at her feet, panting for attention. Freddy eyed them from behind a Moucharabieh screen.

Mike scratched Walter's ear, his eyes on Tess. "I can't take much credit for the designing. Ms. Wexler did it all and loved every minute of it, the more exotic, the better. She was an eccentric old woman with a whole slew of superstitions."

Tess's lighthearted mood lessened a tad. She felt a chill, but the heat radiating from Mike's body soon warmed her. She took a chip, dipped it into the salsa and ate it, chasing it down with a hearty gulp of beer. She gestured to the opposite wall. "I love that fireplace. Do you use it a lot?"

"Have been lately," Mike said, massaging her shoulder, his calloused fingertips sliding under the neckline of her shirt. "Fall nights on the New England countryside get pretty chilly. How about I build one now?"

Tess took another sip of beer, feeling more at home than she did in the house next door. She smiled up at him. "I'd love it."

The springs in the sofa squeaked as Mike got up. Tess watched him walk across the room to the fireplace, his well worn jeans softly scuffing, denim brushing denim. His open blue-and-gray flannel shirt billowed as he knelt on the stone hearth. He plucked a log from the brass basket and laid it on the grate before surrounding it with kindling and striking a match to it. The dry wood sizzled and snapped, bright orange flames shooting upward in brilliant spears, permeating the air with the rustic smell of birch.

"This is so cozy," Tess said, luxuriating in the warmth and the view.

Mike stood up, wiping his hands on his jeans. Removing the poker from the brass ensemble, he stoked the fire, wood spitting, flames soaring. Whistling a tune, he winked. "All for you, darlin'."

Tess watched Mike, a warm glow spreading from her cheeks down to the most intimate part of her. A smile curled her lips. Yes indeed, Mike was the man who'd completely torn down the wall she'd built around her emotions…and her heart. She couldn't imagine being with anyone else. No one in this world could hold a candle to Sheriff Mike Andretti. He was a real keeper…he was hers.

"How's that for a little atmosphere?" Mike sank into the sofa, putting his arm around her.

He smelled like rain, soap and firewood. Tess moved a bit closer and kissed him. "Perfect, just like you."

Tess sipped her beer, eyeing Mike over the rim of her mug. Between the warm glow of the fire and the heat spreading through her body, memories of the night before flashed through her mind in living color. Their hands touched, causing her cheeks to flush with desire. She met his gaze.

Mike kissed her, running his thumbs under her shirt and up her torso. He nuzzled her ear, whispering, "Last night was a dream come true, darlin'. You're perfect; we're perfect together. This is just the beginning. Tonight will be even better. I want to take tonight slow and get to enjoy every aspect of it. First, though, I want to make sure you have plenty of energy, can't have ya' passin' out again. I pulled out a few steaks from the freezer and thought I'd throw them on the grill in a bit. After supper, how about we take a little stroll around the grounds?"

Tess ran her hands through his shaggy blonde hair, toying with the band of his ponytail. "It sounds like something I've been waiting a lifetime for."

Just then, Galahad flapped his wings and squawked, "Shitty weather, wipe your feet."

"He's restless," Mike said, walking across the carpet in his bare feet. The cage door clicked open and the parrot soared out whistling, perching himself in a corner bamboo tree.

****

Out on the patio, Mike flipped the sirloins, stepping back when the grease sputtered and spewed. Smoke billowed upward, filling the air with the tantalizing aroma of grilled onions, meat, peppers and mushrooms. It was a gorgeous night, stars glittering on a blanket of midnight blue. Mike poked a fork in the potatoes. “Hope you’re hungry. Food’s just about done.”

“I’m famished,” Tess said, dousing the fresh garden greens with creamy ranch dressing. “The animals are all fed, and I dare say Freddy is beginning to warm up to your crew. All three cats are snoozing on the sofa, and Sir Galahad must have finally called it a night. He’s in his cage, not uttering a peep.”

“Good,” Mike said, tossing a grilled hot dog to Hank. The big dog gulped it down in one bite, wagging his tail.

“You’ve had enough to eat.” Mike tossed a tennis ball out in the yard. “Go get some exercise so we can eat in peace.”

Watching Mike cook for her, the way he cared for his menagerie of pets, the way he went the extra mile for everyone in his life, squeezed Tess’s heart. Remembering the way he played his guitar with such finesse made her melt but thinking back to how those same fingers caressed her body made her wild for him.

But then her heart sank. Roberto Smith had murdered her dad, set it up to look like a suicide. And now the killer was stalking her, hunting her down. Why? Was she the reason her dad had been murdered in cold blood?

Enough. Not tonight. No more tonight.

“Dig in.” Mike plopped a sizzling steak smothered in onions and mushrooms on her plate. “Hot off the grill.”

Tess eyed the juicy sirloin and crisp baked potato on her plate. Even though the grilled food smelled delicious, she didn’t have much of an appetite. Not with all these unanswered questions swarming in her head. Roberto Smith and Bobby from her childhood were probably one and the same. Why would a kid from her past have such a vendetta on her and her dad? And where was he hiding? She scanned the woods surrounding Mike's ranch. Was he watching her now?

She wished she could stop these thoughts and focus on the evening. She cut a piece of the steak, forked it up and chewed. But she didn't taste a thing. She put her silverware down and stared at her uneaten meal.

"Tess." Mike reached across the picnic table for her hand. "I know today was rough on you, hearin' your dad was murdered. But we'll catch 'em. It's just a matter of time. You're safe with me. He won't get anywhere near us, I promise." He stopped and looked intently into her eyes. "I still want to teach you how to shoot a gun, how to defend yourself."

Tess nodded. "You're right, Mike. It's time I learned; otherwise, I'm a sitting duck. As much as I hate guns, I'll learn." She intertwined her fingers in his. *Because now that I've met you,* "I have something to live for, something I'm not willing to chance losing."

A chorus of crickets sang in the bushes, harmonizing with the hissing buzz of locusts. The air was sweetly scented with roses and clover after the cleansing rain. In the distance, the stallions snorted and whinnied, settling down for the night. Tess gazed out at the corral, drawing strength from the sounds of the wild. She thought of the sheer beauty of watching a horse give birth, but especially the tenderness in which Mike had eased Jezebel through her labor. He was a gift. Roberto Smith had killed her father, but he was not going to kill her. She had too much to live for. The pieces of the puzzle were starting to fit. If she could connect Will Gentry to it, another piece would snap into place.

"Come on, darlin'." Mike gathered up the plates, tossing a few bites of meat to Hank. "We'll wrap these up and have steak and eggs in the morning. Let's go inside and settle in for the night."

Once the meal was cleaned up and the dishes taken care of, he took her in his arms, pulling her close to his chest. The muscles in his arms quivered and bunched when he slid his hands under her sweatshirt, his warm fingers massaging little circles. His lips felt feather soft when they kissed the side of her neck, nuzzled her ear. The stubble on his jawline scratched her cheek, sending ripples of pleasure through her. His mouth was warm and wet, tasting of grilled onions and steak.

His voice was low and husky as he whispered, "Let's go inside and get cozy by the fire."

Chapter Twenty-Six

The following morning, Mike watched Tess sleep, her mahogany hair fanning all askew on the scarlet pillow.

She looks like an angel.

The last of the burning embers dwindled to a few smoldering ashes, the lingering scent of birch wood filtering through the room. Reaching for the patchwork quilt on the sofa, Mike tucked it over Tess, planting a feathery light kiss on her sweet, sweet lips.

Having her in his home felt right, he mused, his gaze sweeping the room for his family of critters. He smiled, a warm sensation coiling in the pit of his stomach. Hank lay cuddled on a gray velour robe he'd taken possession of one Christmas, Julio, Walter and Freddy snuggled next to him as snug as bugs in a rug.

With a sudden bolt, the peaceful serenity was broken. Tess thrashed wildly beneath the quilt, her arms and legs kicking, floundering, desperate to free herself from the entanglement of the comforter. Her arms shot out, hurling punches with tightly balled fists. Her eyes moved rapidly beneath her lids. She tossed her head from side-to-side, screaming, "Let me go, you big oaf. Put me down! Let go of me, you imbecile! I mean it, you're a freak. Everyone's laughing at you. Put me down!"

"Tess." Mike shook her shoulders, gently arousing her from slumber. "Come on, darlin'. It's just a dream. You're all right now. Come on, open those pretty green eyes."

Tess bolted upright, her eyes wild with shock. She looked right at Mike, dead center, tears streaming down her face. She pulled her fist back and hurled it into Mike's chest, her knuckles smacking into his bare skin with a resounding pop. "Take that."

"Holy hell." Mike shook her again. "You pack a powerful punch for a girl. Wake up, darlin'. It's me…Mike."

"Mike?" Tess blinked several times, trying to focus. She looked around, comprehension blooming. "I…ah…must have been dreaming."

"Damn straight. You were thrashing around, mad as a wet hen, kicking and screaming, fighting for your life. You were callin' someone a moron, an imbecile. Sure hope it wasn't me."

Tess's pupils dilated. "Oh my God, I remember." She threw herself into Mike's arms, her heart galloping at a wild rhythm. "I remember."

"What do you remember, darlin'?"

"You know the kids in the pictures? Well, sometimes we'd play damsel in distress in the bell tower, pretending it was a medieval castle. One day when it was my turn, I yelled and screamed for Bobby to come rescue me. He was real cute, all that red hair and freckles. He joked around, saying when we grew up we'd get married. He said he'd always watch over me, like a knight in shining armor." Tess paused for a moment as she seemed to try and collect her thoughts. "There was also this other boy, a kid who used to watch us from the woods, no one knew his name. He was creepy, had funny blue eyes, so bright they almost glowed. We were all afraid of him. Anyway, one day, we were playing the game and Bobby carried me down all those steep steps and I remember seeing him, standing behind one of the sugar maples, watching as Bobby carried me. When he put me down, the kid with the creepy eyes came charging out of the woods like some big burly bull and tossed me over his shoulders. He carted me across the courtyard to my front door where he deposited me. I was never so scared or so humiliated."

Tess massaged her forehead as the images kept coming. "I kicked and screamed like a woman possessed, beating my fists on his back. The creepy kid was chewing apple gum, so sickening sweet I wanted to gag. The whole time I was being humiliated, my friends were laughing which echoed across the courtyard. The kid with the strange eyes was Will Gentry. Something else came to me in this dream. Bobby always called me Princess Contessa. It's him, beyond a shadow of a doubt. Bobby is Roberto Smith."

"So whatever happened to this Bobby?" Mike asked, holding Tess in a tight embrace. "Do you remember?"

"That was the last time I ever saw him. At the end of summer, he told me his family was moving. He told me we'd be together some day, just the two of us and that we'd live in my sand castle on the sea. I blocked all that out until now."

"Anything else, Tess?"

Tess gazed out the window where the sun was rising to meet the horizon. "Remember the entry in my diary where I wrote I gave a silver hoop earring to Bobby? I gave it to him as a going away gift, along with a quick kiss. He said he'd wear it forever."

"This is good, Tess." Mike massaged her shoulders, easing out the knots. "We'll call homicide and add the silver earring to his profile. He wouldn't have been allowed to wear an earring in prison so it isn't listed. My guess is Roberto Smith romanticized his crush on you while servin' time. If he had it in his mind that the two of you would be together some day, what better way to get you back in the harbor than by murdering your father?"

Tess's lips quivered. She rubbed her temples. "My God!" She put her head on Mike's shoulder, heart-wrenching sobs keening from her very soul. "That was over twenty years ago. We were just kids, twelve-year-old kids! Why would he wait all these years to come after me, tell me he's my biggest fan? Why not just get in touch with me, tell me he'd like to get together? Why be so sneaky, so coy?"

"Don't forget he just got sprung for serving a ten-year murder sentence." Mike gently rubbed her back as her sobs lessened. "Bein' locked behind bars has a tendency to make a man think back, plan, give himself some hope—even if it is false. I'm guessin' that's what Roberto Smith did. Look at the facts, Tess. You're a New York Times best-selling author, heiress and sole beneficiary to a million-dollar estate. Add to that a twisted mind and you've got a damn good motive for killing your dad. Roberto Smith had it all planned out, get Daddy out of the way, lure you back and share the wealth. In his demented mind, he probably figured it was his right. Since he was one of the kids you hung out with, he'd know the layout of the manor. Now as far as his flair for theatrics, can you shed any light? Know of any reason he might wanna use the wax gargoyles as props? Set up the rooms like a staged performance?"

Tess stood up, rolled her head from shoulder-to-shoulder and moved over to sit down in a wingback chair. Hank lumbered over, placed his big head in her lap, doting brown eyes looking up at her. He whined softly. She patted his head, desperate to call up old memories. So many years had passed since then, so much had happened. She'd only known Bobby for one summer and had blocked him out of her mind until the dream last night. She closed her eyes, thinking back. Then it hit her. She looked at

Mike. "Like I said, he had an obsession for the home theater and the projector room, but Bobby used to ramble on and on about how he wanted to be a film major. He wanted to work with lights and cameras, behind the scenes. I invited the whole gang to one of Daddy's masquerade parties that summer, and no one was more fascinated with the wax gargoyles than Bobby. He kept touching them, talking to them like he was obsessed with them. I overheard him telling the winged beasts that one day he'd be the master of the theater."

"It's all adding up." Mike tore a sheet of paper from his notepad. "This is good, Tess. Damn good. Let me go put on some coffee. You can let Hank out if you want. You'll be safe with him. He might act like a dopey pup, but he'd go for the jugular if anyone tried to hurt you."

"Come on, boy." Tess barely had the door open when the big dog darted past, tail whipping her in the leg.

The big Irish setter scampered off through a patch of fallen leaves, straight for the woods. Tess watched him, breathing in the fresh air. From behind the stable, the sun peeked out, a fiery ball of gold rising to greet the day. Horses whinnied and neighed, followed by the call of blue and white herons from surrounding pines.

Walking around the grounds, Tess stopped to admire the Angel Face climbing roses meandering up the white wicker lattice. They looked pretty, fragrant mauve buds trimmed with lavender edging. She picked one, bringing it up to her nose to sniff. Hank darted toward her, lumbering through the foliage, twigs snapping, his white teeth forming a big doggy grin. He scooped up a birch chip and dropped it at her feet.

"So you wanna play fetch, big guy?" She tossed it out in the yard, the Irish setter giving chase, yipping and barking. A cool breeze swooshed through the towering pines as Tess walked the grounds, taking a stroll through a vintage grape arbor. Plump Concord grapes weaved in and out of the burnished copper patina.

Plucking one for tasting, Tess thought it might be nice to make home-made jellies from the fruit. She winced when a thorny vine nipped her cheek, ducking when it tangled through her long hair. The leafy canopy ceiling needed a pruning, a pang of guilt stabbing her heart for taking so much of Mike's time.

Looking down, she noticed she had an entourage at her feet, slinking in and out of her legs. Freddy and his two new buddies, Julio and Walter, had come out to rustle about in the leaves. Tess patted each of their heads. "Come on, guys, let's get out where it's warmer."

Feeling lazy, Tess sat on the old wooden swing, soaking up the sun. She rubbed her hands together, her mind wandering back to her dream. Had Bobby carried a torch for her all these years? Her gaze scraped the woods, goose bumps prickling her flesh. Was he out there, watching her? From deep in the clearing, a falcon soared into the thicket, its shrill call eerie and foreboding.

A scampering in the leaves behind her had her heart jumping. She whipped her head around as Walter shuffled toward her, rubbing her leg, meowing. His orange coloring blended in with the hues of the fall foliage. "You just want a little attention, don't you, Walter?"

Hank dashed over, licking the tabby's face, giving him his good morning kiss. A ruby red cardinal flapped its wings before taking flight across the yard, its fiery feathers a complete contrast to the jack-be-little miniature pumpkins in the patch below.

With a slight swoosh, the glass doors from the kitchen parted. Mike strutted out, two steaming mugs of coffee in hand. His hair was damp from a shower and pulled back in a ponytail. In the sunlight, his golden brown eyes gleamed like jewels. When he leaned down to kiss her, he smelled of clean soap, herbal shampoo...and just a hint of musk.

"Ready for a nice cup of java?" He handed it over with a smile, his dimple glinting in the glow of the sun. "Get it while it's hot, freshly brewed with the best gourmet beans."

"It smells heavenly," Tess said, inhaling the Swiss mocha blend, savoring her first sip of the day. "And it tastes as good as it smells."

Mike joined her on the swing, the rusty old hinges squeaking with age. He squeezed her knee. "Nothin' better than sharin' a cup of coffee with a beautiful woman the mornin' after a night of sweet love." He leaned over and kissed Tess, his lips warm, tasting of chocolate-laced coffee. He whispered in her ear, "Last night was simply perfect, just like you, darlin'."

Tess sucked in her breath. Just the sound of his low husky voice had her blood heating. She wanted nothing more than to bask in the aftermath of their lovemaking, let herself go, just give in and follow her heart. But she couldn't. Not until Roberto Smith was caught.

She gazed into Mike's warm eyes and smiled. "Last night was the kind of night dreams are made of. The only thing that would make it more perfect is finding Roberto Smith and having him locked up. We've gotta find him, Mike. This is tearing me up, cutting the life out of me."

"We'll catch him." Mike met her gaze, then he pitched a twig to Hank. "Now that you've pieced so much of the puzzle together through your dream, it won't be long." He patted his chest. "I'm thinkin' you know how to defend yourself pretty darn good. Where'd you learn to pack a punch like that, darlin'?"

"I've never punched anyone in my life…until you." A smile curled Tess's lips. "I knew there was something about Will Gentry, his eyes. I knew I'd seen him somewhere before. I wonder if he remembers me."

"Hard to say." Mike leaned over to pinch some dry foliage off some freshly planted mums. "His mind is only capable of absorbing so much."

"He must've thought he was protecting me from Bobby all those years ago, carting me across the courtyard over his shoulders," Tess said, gazing into the woods. "I guess he's still trying. He did say the man in the tower is watching me."

"I got a hold of homicide when I was in the house, filled them in on your dream. The department's short-handed right now, final vacations and all, so they can't provide a full-time cop to keep watch on you. But they'll have an unmarked patrol car doin' a check once an hour. Under no circumstances are you to go back to your place or anywhere near the bell tower. Homicide questioned Will Gentry, but all they got outta him was that the man in the tower was watchin' the pretty lady."

Tess's skin crawled. "So where is Roberto Smith? Where is he hiding and why?"

"The cops will find him." Mike took Tess's face in his hands, gazing into her eyes. "I'd better run down and check on the horses, see how Jezebel and her foal are comin' along. Wanna come with me, or stay here with the critters and finish your coffee?"

"I think I'll just sit here and think for awhile," Tess said, turning to plant a kiss on Mike's lips. "Then how about I make you breakfast? Fry up that leftover steak and eggs?"

"A woman after my own heart. My refrigerator is packed with whatever strikes your fancy. Knock yourself out, darlin'. Steak's on the bottom shelf, can't miss it."

Tess watched Mike strut down to the stable, his long legs eating up the land. He had the nicest ass; a low heat burned in her belly as she remembered the night before when she ran her hands across it, pulling him closer. Jezebel's whinny, as he opened the Dutch doors to the stable, broke her train of thought.

Tess heard a scuffing in the foliage behind her. Turning around, she expected to see one of the cats, or Hank. But there was no one. Icy chills skittered down her spine, making her aware of every sound, every sensation. Where were the animals? "Hank! Here boy. Come here!"

Panic bolted through her, adrenaline pumping. Why wasn't Hank coming? Did he follow Mike to the stable? Then she spied Freddy in the woods behind her where she'd heard the thrashing. It was just her cat, getting accustomed to his new surroundings, but when he hissed and snarled, her heartbeat accelerated. Something was wrong. His back was arched, the way it got when he spied something or someone he didn't like. "Freddy, here boy. What is it?"

Tess noticed he was circling something, digging beneath the leaves. Something inside her went ice cold. Every instinct in her screamed for her to go and get Mike. But she didn't listen. She moved toward it, scuffling through the leaves. Then she spotted it, a long white box.

Kicking the leaves off it, her heart skipped a beat. The name Contessa was scribbled in bold red ink. Not wanting to touch it and smudge any fingerprints, she gingerly kicked the lid off with the tip of her tennis shoe. Then she screamed loud enough to wake the dead. A headstone with her name on it was surrounded by dozens of withered up forget-me-nots.

Chapter Twenty-Seven

The homicide team gathered in Mike's yard, searching for clues. Badly shaken, Tess sat on the wooden swing, her green eyes hazy with shock and fear.

"Did you see or hear anything, Ms. Kincaid?" one of the detectives asked, his gaze sweeping the land. "Anything at all?"

"Just a crunching in the leaves. When I first looked, I saw nothing, but then my cat started digging around in the underbrush, his hair on edge. That's when I found the box. Roberto Smith's been here, no doubt about it. He was a kid I knew twenty years ago. I only knew him that one summer; in fact, all I knew him by was Bobby. I never even knew his last name. We were just kids, twelve-year-old kids. I can't imagine he killed Daddy…and has all intentions of killing me…"

"Hush now, darlin'." Mike sat down beside her, rubbing her back. "There's no way he'll get his hands on ya', except over my dead body."

"Ms. Kincaid." The detective stepped toward her, his boots scuffing up dirt and fallen leaves. "Do the blue flowers mean anything to you?"

"Forget-me-nots are my favorite flower, and Bobby knew it. That summer we all played together, everyone knew how much I loved them because I'd pick them in the meadows. One day when we were playing in the bell tower, I was the princess…and Bobby…ah, Roberto Smith picked them for me. He told me he'd never forget me because I was his first love."

"What else can you think of to help us in this investigation? A conversation that stood out, something he might have interpreted the wrong way?"

"Like I said, we were only twelve. At the end of that summer, I do recall him saying something about moving to Florida. Miami Beach, I think."

The detective made notes, nodding. "Anything else?"

"I gave him a silver hoop earring. I found it on the beach the last day we spent together. He stuck it in his left earlobe and swore he'd never take it out. Looking back now, I can't help but think that for a kid, he had a muscular frame. Wiry, but strong." Tess took a deep breath.

"Thank you, Ms. Kincaid. You've been very helpful."

Tess stared at the plastic headstone as it was bagged. She felt dizzy and her stomach was in knots. The coffee she'd had earlier churned in her gut, sour and acidic.

"We won't be able to trace that tombstone," the investigating officer said. "It's one of those cheap Halloween gimmicks that every dollar store sells. Your name is scribbled on it with the same writing that's on the lid of the box. We'll send it to the lab for prints."

Hank darted toward the group, plopping himself on Tess's feet. She ran her hand down his back, the gesture soothing her frayed nerves. But then something shiny caught her eye...her heartbeat tripled. "Oh my God, look."

A silver hoop earring glittered in the green grass like the evil eye of a serpent. Tess gasped, clasping her hand over her mouth. "That looks like the earring I gave Bobby."

"Bag it," the detective barked out orders. "He's

very close."

The detective heading the investigation crunched through the foliage, his mouth drawn in a thin, hard line. "Just got off the phone with Roberto Smith's parole officer. Smith suffers from schizophrenia. Without his anti-psychotic pills, he has delusions of grandeur. When he was released from jail, he was given sample packages, but his parole required him to keep his medical appointments as well as his parole meetings. Without his medication, Roberto Smith is completely unstable."

"Oh my God," Tess gasped, clutching her hands over her heart. "The sample package in my purse that day…that's how it got there. Roberto Smith went through my purse, stole my migraine medication and replaced it with his anti-psychotic pills to make it look like I was the one who was nuts. He also stole my cell phone."

"All right then," the detective said. "We'll take this box, along with the earring. We'll do another full search of these grounds as well as the Kincaid estate, including the bell tower. He's close. I can feel it in my bones."

Tess and Mike watched the detective and crime scene techs leave, pinecones and twigs snapping beneath tires. Mike looked at Tess. "More of a reason than ever to take you out to the range and teach you how to shoot." He put his arm around her, leading her toward the glass door. "Come on. We'll go get some breakfast and then head on out. I know it's not what you want, but this is the way it's gonna be—like it or not."

****

After the shock had registered, Tess sat in the kitchen, idly watching Mike man the stove. The muscle in his upper right arm flexed, stallion tattoo bucking as he whipped the eggs to a fluffy concoction. Unable to help herself, a little thrill shot through her. The steak and mushrooms sizzled in butter, making her mouth water. The animals hung close, hoping for a handout. Sir Galahad whistled from the brass curtain rod, quietly observing.

"What kind of cheese do you want on your omelet?" Mike turned to Tess, his T-shirt splattered with grease spots. "Got American, sharp cheddar or goat."

"Sharp cheddar," Tess said, putting the bread in the toaster. "Can I do anything else? After all, I did promise to cook for you."

"Brew us up a fresh pot of coffee," he said, giving her behind a playful swat with the spatula.

"Sure, it's the least I can do. What kind should I make?" She rustled through the bags lining the counter. "Let's see, you've got Swiss mocha, hazelnut, French vanilla, and Hawaiian. Can't settle on a favorite?"

"Love my mornin' java." He strutted over and planted a kiss on her lips. "How about some French vanilla? Unless you wanna surprise me?"

Just then the smoke alarm shrieked, the smell of charred meat filling the kitchen. The shrill scream of the fire alarm sent the cats running for cover, backs arched, hair on edge. Mike reached up and disconnected the alarm, bringing an abrupt halt to the piercing beep. He raced to the pan. "Ah, shit, burned the steak."

"Bad boy, Mike." Sir Galahad soared across the kitchen, perching himself on Mike's shoulder, peering into the frying pan. He flapped his wings and squawked, "Bad boy, Mike."

****

The smell of charred steak filled the house as Tess stepped out of the shower. Her heart felt heavy. She did not want to fire a weapon, a painful reminder of her dad's gruesome murder. She didn't even know, if push came to shove and she had to defend herself, if she could. What about the moral issue? Could she take the life of another human being, even one as low-down and dirty as Roberto Smith? She didn't know.

With a towel wrapped around her, she rummaged through her cosmetic bag for her aloe. Her skin felt tight from the sunburn. She massaged it on her arms and legs, loving its soothing effect. As the steam cleared, she studied her reflection in the mirror, noticing the dark circles beneath bloodshot eyes. She looked tired and drawn. Freddy watched her, cuddled in a heap on her sweatshirt.

"Time for some major repairs," she confided to her cat. "Before I scare someone."

The phone was ringing as Tess stepped into the hallway. *Probably Mike, calling from the barn.* She picked up and her blood ran cold. His dark laughter echoed through the phone.

"I'm coming for you. Just like the big bad wolf, I'm gonna getcha. And Princess, I promise to make you scream. Get ready."

She'd had enough. "Go to hell." She slammed the receiver back down.

****

Under Mike's tutelage, Tess learned how to handle and shoot a gun. The shocking phone call, on the heels of receiving a headstone, convinced her the time had come to take action. A deranged killer was hunting her down, and unless she learned how to defend herself, she'd be his next victim.

His chilling words vibrated in her ears, gnawing away at her last nerve. She wasn't about to be a sitting duck. The thought of the innocent kid she knew from so many years ago turning into such a demented psychopath chilled her to the bone, but knowing he was on the loose, without his medication, totally unnerved her.

Although Tess could shoot and hit the bull's eye like a skilled marksman, she hated every second of it. Gripping the metallic handle felt cold and heavy, just like her heart. Leaning forward and positioning her feet in proper pyramidal position, her hands tightly gripping the .22 revolver, Tess released the safety. The click ricocheted off the surrounding mountains. Her eyes narrowed, focusing on the mark. She raised her gun and was just about to shoot when a huge peregrine falcon soared across her line of vision.

Distracted, she dropped her gun hand to her side, her palms slick with sweat. Now her focus was off. But she'd get it back, because she was bound and determined to take charge of her life. His chilling words rang in her ears—he was coming for her. She'd be ready.

****

From the shadows, Mike watched her, his stomach tangled up in knots. Despite his pushing Tess to learn how to fire a weapon, his heart wept for her. Watching her pull the trigger left a sour taste in his mouth. It sickened him to watch her suffer.

The woman had spunk, he'd give her that. He knew how hard it was for her to shoot a weapon, a woman with high standards and moral ethics. He kicked the tip of his boot into the stump of a log and felt a little better. Scrubbing his hand over his chin, his jaw rigid, he watched Tess perfect her moves. Knowing she knew how to defend herself when he couldn't be there gave him a small sliver of comfort. Whipping his Stetson off his head, he swiped at the perspiration beading his forehead.

He couldn't take his eyes off her. She was a natural beauty, long hair rippling in the breeze, all those glossy mahogany tresses picking up a million sunbeams. It didn't matter if he was watching her or holding her close in his arms. He just needed to be near her. She was all he wanted and all he'd ever want.

His fingers itched to touch her. He longed to bury his face in her fragrant hair, lose himself in its sweet essence. The scent of her filled his senses, making him crazy. She was all he could think about at work, when exercising the horses, when he went to the store. He found himself buying things she'd like—those sugar cookies she could never get enough of. She was quickly becoming his number one addiction.

The thought of some nut harming her filled him with a primal instinct he had no idea he possessed. He had to find this psychopath, because as long as Roberto Smith stood between him and Tess, they couldn't have a future together.

He watched Tess hit the mark. She was good, but still, how good would she be if confronted by a demented psychopath hell-bent on killing her. Frustrated, he slapped his cowboy hat on his head and started toward her, his scuffed-up cowboy boots crunching through the gravel.

He watched her every move, his heart swelling with pride. Just as he'd trained her, she had a tight grip on the handgun, her eyes on the mark. Then with dogged determination, she raised the .22 and aimed it at the target. Pulling back the trigger, she unleashed the bullet. It zinged through the air with a splintering hiss that echoed through the forest. She hit the mark, bull's eye.

Chapter Twenty-Eight

As Tess and Mike descended the steep steps to the beach, the lull of the sea surrounded them. A buoy moaned softly in the distance, and over the crashing roar of the waves hitting the rocks, the clanking of the bell echoed through the harbor. Baked clams sizzled in the pit, the aroma wafting through the air.

Tess inhaled deeply. “Hmm. If that smell isn’t enough to tease the palate, I don’t know what is.” Her green eyes sparkled in the fading sun, her gaze sweeping every booth.

“Just the thing to mellow out the old soul,” Mike grinned, watching a robust man hurl seaweed into the pit. Butter and onions sauted on the grill, creating a sizzling symphony.

“Oh, Mike,” Tess yanked his arm, pointing excitedly. “Look out there, a whale.”

Mike looked just in time to see a fine mist sprout into the air. “That’s a humpback, passin’ through Frenchman Bay. Just another Bar Harbor attraction.”

A little girl of about six broke free of her dad’s hand, scampering off to a giant blueberry bush at the edge of the sea. Plucking the ripe berries as fast as her chubby fingers could twist them from the vine, she stuffed them into her mouth, giggling when the juice dribbled down her chin and pink hoodie. Just beyond, a trail led to Acadia National Park, where a lush forest of maturing red spruce trees reached up to the sky.

A seal paddled its way along the shore, splashing water, curiously eyeing the festivities. The seagulls scarfed the beach, squabbling and squawking, hunting for food.

"Oh, there's the stand for the Seaside Bakery," Tess said, drooling over the pastries. "Would you look at all those yummy treats just begging to be sampled? I might have to try a hunk of the Black Forest cake smothered in cherries. Hmm. Or maybe an ice cream cone."

"Lemon chiffon for me." Mike leaned over and whispered in her ear, "It's my secret passion."

"Really?" Tess yelled over the blast of the horn as a ferry docked in the bay. "I'll keep that in mind."

"Hey you two." Mandy waved, blonde curls bouncing in the breeze. "Isn't this great? We've been here for the past hour, making our rounds of all the booths." She batted her baby blues at Chip. "Isn't that right, honey?"

Chip patted his belly. "Already had two heapin' platters of clams. If I eat any more, won't have room for dessert."

"How about it, Tess?" Mandy beamed. "Is it any wonder I never left the harbor? I just love these beach parties, and this is always a real summer send-off."

"It doesn't seem to have changed much since I've been gone. This was always the high point of my summer vacation, even though I had to leave the next day."

Mandy's expression grew somber. "Chip filled me in on Bobby…Roberto Smith. That is so hard to believe, a sweet kid turning into such a hardened criminal. Who would ever think it, huh?"

"I know." Tess scanned the woods. "He has me on edge; it's downright frightening. Oh, Mandy. If you could have seen what he did in the ballroom and the den, using the waxed gargoyles as props, just like some bizarre theater production."

Mandy shook her head. "Well, you have the sheriff here to protect you, so I know you'll be safe. I heard on the news earlier that there's an all points bulletin out for his arrest. They'll get him, don't worry."

Mike stared into the thicket. "It's just a matter of time."

"Say," Chip broke in. "You two have to come sailin' with us some time real soon." He pointed to the dock. "There she is, right down there, *The Sea Urchin*. Nothin' like a day on a sailboat to sooth your blues away. So how about it, let's do that real soon, okay?"

"I'd love to." Tess smiled, staring out to sea. "I love the water and nothing is more relaxing than a day sailing."

"We'll do that," Mike said. "I wanna introduce Tess to some local folks, and my mouth's watering, so we've gotta sample some of those clams. We'll catch up with you two later."

"Let's plan a girls' night out real soon," Mandy said. "I know this place that makes the best Margaritas. We'll get a pitcher of those and some great Mexican food and catch up; okay, Tess?"

"Sounds great."

Mandy winked. "Maybe if Chip reads one of your thrillers, one with a scorching love scene, he'll get some ideas. Isn't that right, honey?"

Tess was still laughing when they left. The look on Chip's face had been priceless, like he'd just swallowed a sour lemon.

****

Basket after basket of jumbo clams came off the red-hot stones, grease spitting and spewing. Ears of corn smoked in the pit along with the fish, the silk retaining the flavor of the succulent kernels.

"Grab us a few ears of corn, and some tubs of

that country churned butter," Mike said, scooping a generous amount of clams into a small bucket. "And lots of napkins, darlin'. We'll go find us a place to chow down on the best meal you've sunk your teeth into all summer, guaranteed."

"I can't wait." Tess's mouth was watering from the tantalizing aroma drifting over the dock. "I haven't eaten a thing all day, just so I could gorge myself."

"What would a clambake be without a few brewskies," Mike asked, shoving clams into his mouth as they walked. "I'll go buy us some from the stand over there. It'll go down real easy, beer and clams, the perfect combo."

"Sounds good," Tess said, setting the plate of corn and butter on a patch of dry grass. "How's this?"

"Suits me just fine. Already sampled a few, and I gotta tell you, it's takin' all my willpower not to shove them all in my mouth. I swear they taste better every year. Come on, darlin'. Dig in."

Tess arched an eyebrow. "A few? Last time I looked, you had about ten of those slippery little devils in your mouth. Good thing you got a bucket full."

"Gotta ravenous appetite." His teeth grazed her earlobe. "One bite is never enough."

Tess took a lemon wedge between her thumb and forefinger, squirting juice over the clams. Then she licked her fingers, the tangy taste puckering her lips into a pout. She snatched one of the clams and popped it in her mouth, closing her eyes in ecstasy. "Mmm...ambrosia."

The breeze kicked up a notch, rippling through the waters, causing the waves to crest high in the air before crashing over the rugged rocks. The cool night air carried the smell of rain.

She gazed up at the mansion. It loomed in the

sky, presenting a daunting aura. When the bell in the tower rang out, her gaze settled on the massive dome, rocking back and forth like a pendulum.

"Hey, darlin'." Mike wiped his hand on a napkin, then he brushed his fingers along her arm. "Bite into a bad clam? Look a little green around the gills. Everything all right?"

Tess took a sip of beer, then smiled. "No, not a bad clam…just a bad thought. Knowing Roberto Smith is out there is like an anchor around me, pulling me deeper and deeper into the murky unknown. I'm afraid to let my guard down, even for a second. Every time I look up at the bell tower, I get the uncanny feeling he's spying on me."

She shuddered, the thought of him watching her sending icy chills racing down her arms. She peered into the woods, then to the bell tower. "I don't know where he is, but I feel his eyes on me, watching me. It's got me spooked. Then there's that eerie bird with the white face and black mustache keeping vigil on the steeple. I'm Irish, you know, and we're very superstitious. I keep thinking about the old legend about a banshee coming to predict one's death. I'm afraid that falcon came to predict mine."

"Come on now, darlin'," Mike said, pulling her close. "That's ridiculous. Legends are nothing more than silly superstitions, a bunch of malarky. You know better than to believe in such nonsense. Tess, think about what you're sayin'. Sounds like a best-selling paranormal to me; are you sure you're not considering that genre for your next novel?"

"Go on, make fun of me. But with Irish folk, superstitions aren't taken lightly. Didn't my dad ever mention any to you?"

Mike finished the last of his beer, crushing the cup between his fingers and setting it down on the clover. "Can't say as he did. Let's change the subject, talk about somethin' more pleasant. This is a clambake, so why don't we enjoy the Labor Day celebration. Look, they're setting things up for the fireworks. Let's just relax and forget about the superstitions and Roberto Smith for the next hour."

"You're right," Tess said, edging closer to Mike, feeling the heat from his body. She snuggled in a little closer, laying her head on his shoulder. She heard the steady beat of his heart and felt safe. She liked that feeling. Someone to watch over her. At least for tonight, she'd forget about her biggest fan.

Her gaze followed Mike's hand as he scooped up the last few clams, popping them into his mouth. His tongue darted out, licking up the butter dripping down his chin. Then he smacked his lips. How she wanted to taste those lips.

Sensing her thoughts, Mike moved even closer, his warm eyes heavy with desire. The next thing she knew, his mouth fused with hers in a smoldering kiss. Excitement soared through her, awakening every sensation in her body. His mouth was hungry, his lips demanding as he teased her with his tongue. He tasted of clams and butter, beer and lemon. His skin felt rough on hers, a face toughened by the outdoors and the sea. Through his sweatshirt, she felt his heartbeat, and a surge of liquid heat soared through her, the sky splintering into an explosive boom that echoed the wild beat of her heart.

Mike broke the kiss, glancing up at the sky. Then he winked. "Oh, darlin'. For a second, I thought those sparks and fireworks had to be my heart."

"Yeah," Tess whispered in his ear, touching his face, her voice low and throaty. "Me, too."

Sitting beneath a velvety blanket of midnight blue, fireworks crackled like boomerangs, singeing the night sky in a brilliant show of light. Snuggling closer to Mike, she let herself forget...if only for a little while.

Once the fireworks were over, Tess remembered she hadn't gotten her ice cream cone. She looked over, happy to see the vendor hadn't closed up shop for the night. She whispered in Mike's ear. "I'll be back in a flash. I'm gonna treat your lemon chiffon fetish."

"I could think of some real interesting things to do with that lemon ice cream." He winked, his eyes shimmering with desire. "But we'll save that for some other place and time."

Tess walked to the ice cream booth, her feet lighter than air. She felt her cheeks turn a fiery shade of crimson, thinking about the wicked wink Mike had given her, filled with enough sexual undertone to have her blood boiling. So lost in her fantasy, she passed the ice cream booth. Chiding herself for acting the fool, she turned on her heels, hoping Mike wasn't watching.

Chapter Twenty-Nine

From deep in the thicket, The Master spied, his night vision binoculars glued to his eyes. His heart jackhammered in his chest, every pulse throbbing beneath his skin. He watched the princess pass the ice cream stand, all hot and bothered after that smoldering kiss. The Master scoffed to himself.

Let the bitch have one more night of sweaty sex.

After tomorrow night, she wouldn't be doing any thrashing in the sheets with her lover. Indeed not. Her time had come. Very soon, with the elements of earth, wind and fire raging through the sky, pretty little princess would perform her final act. The Master drooled, watching Contessa lick her cherry ripple ice cream cone. He groaned, his blood heating with salacious intent. With Thunder and Lightning slashing their swords, crashing and colliding in the black of night, he'd make his princess pose for the camera in her black lace teddy, the one he'd liberated from her chest of drawers. The things he would do were oh so sinful.

The Master sniffed the air, his nose twitching. The wind hissing through the forest of red spruce and pines carried the electric scent of the coming storm. Lightning and Thunder wouldn't let him down. They'd give him what he demanded, a raging storm and a brilliant show of lights. He would reign in all his glory. He was master of the theater and he would have an all-star cast for closing night.

He visualized the grand ballroom, all set up with candlelight, tapers flickering in the dark. Dead forget-me-nots for the bride with the black heart. His waxy gargoyles were all set up, ready and willing, their lines well rehearsed. "Moonlight Sonata" playing low on the Victrola would add the perfect ambiance. Pretty little princess—queen for a day. Oh what a thrill. There would be no escaping her fate. Oh how frightful. Death of a princess.

****

The following morning, Tess sauntered into Mike's kitchen in a cherry red silk robe. The tiles on the floor chilled her bare feet, but when she saw Mike manning the stove in a pair of black silk boxers, her blood heated. When the smell of the bacon and potatoes sizzling on the grill filled her senses, she knew the sheriff was a definite keeper. He cracked eggs into a bowl and whisked them into a lathered frenzy that would make a gourmet chef weep.

Tess smiled, wrapping her arms around Mike's waist, sliding her fingers beneath the waistband, teasing him for a second before letting the elastic snap. The lilt of her throaty laughter rang through the room when he jumped, eggs splattering in mid air. Nuzzling her lips on his back, she purred. "Mmm. Smells delicious. I'm starved."

"Just put some chocolate almond coffee on." Mike turned and stooped to brush a light kiss on Tess's lips. Hank grumbled, hoping for a handout. When Mike backed up, almost tripping over the cats underfoot, he asked, "Before these guys attack me, how about feedin' them."

Tess jiggled food into the dishes, comforted by the domestic setting of Mike and the animals. It filled her with a sense of peace and harmony, one she could easily get used to. From his perch on the brass curtain rod, Sir Galahad whistled.

When Mike belted out a verse of the song playing on the radio, Tess knew it must be love, because she found his singing—shrill enough to shatter glass—endearing. Humming along to drown him out, she set the table. As the autumn breeze rustled the curtains, the air thick with rain, they chatted as if they'd been together for years.

"Wasn't last night great?" Tess said, putting on some toast. "I can't remember the last time I had so much fun. Those clams tasted every bit as good as I remember and the ice cream was the perfect treat."

"Made it to the stand just in the nick of time." Mike jumped back when grease spit out of the frying pan. "All right, hot off the griddle; it's all done."

"It smells delicious."

Mike chomped on a piece of bacon. "I was thinkin' maybe we could take a drive out to The Sea Harbor Inn. It's the bed and breakfast I was tellin' ya' about, my old homestead. You'll love my parents and they'll love you, too. Mama's gonna be over the moon. She keeps askin' me when I'm gonna bring a girl home for her to meet. Since I've been on my own, I haven't brought a girl home for Mama to fuss over...I was waitin' for the right woman to knock my socks off. You're that woman, Tess."

Tears clouded Tess's eyes. She went to Mike, her voice husky with emotion. She put her arms around his neck, settled herself on his lap, losing herself in his incredibly gorgeous eyes. "Remember when I told you that once you've had the best, nothing else will do? Well, I found the best in you, Mike. No one in this world could ever hold a candle to you. You're the one I want. You're the one I've been waiting for my whole life. I'd love to meet your parents. I can't wait."

"Oh, darlin'." He pulled her closer against his chest. "How'd I get so lucky?"

Kissing the tip of his nose, Tess returned to her seat to finish her breakfast. Warmth burrowed in the pit of her belly. She couldn't remember the last time a guy had invited her to meet mom and dad. It pleased her. With no parents of her own, she welcomed some down-home comfort. She brushed the crumbs from her lap and cleared the table. "Let me do up the dishes and go shower and dress." She turned to him. "Ah...should we take anything? Food? Flowers? A bottle of wine? We'll be passing through all those vineyards bordering the Maine coastline."

Mike's grin lit up his face, his dimple deepening. "Now that's real sweet, darlin', but Ma's always got more food, flowers, fruits and wine in her house than the Queen of England. Forget the dishes; go on and get ready. I wanna beat this rainstorm."

****

Tess came out of the bathroom, sauntering down the hallway to Mike's bedroom, cocooned in a thick terry towel. Humming the song stuck in her head, she took in Mike's bedroom at a glance.

It was definitely a room dominated by a male hand. Heavy brown curtains shrouded the room in bleakness, giving it a dreary atmosphere, but with the dark clouds hovering in murky skies, opening the drapes would do little to brighten the room. She flicked on the overhead light, cringing when the bedroom was showcased.

The room was swallowed whole by a huge four-poster bed, far too massive for the small boundaries. Lumpy pillows that had seen better days lined the headboard and a less than appealing brown and yellow plaid comforter with fringed edging covered the bed. Sitting on it, Tess sunk so low she felt the springs bounce. Barren beige walls had pictures of the horses and animals, the only decoration adding a spark of life. An old-fashioned wind up alarm clock sat on the night stand. That was it—no television, no computer.

How did the man survive?

Tess dropped her towel to the floor and

massaged lotion into her skin. Just as she snapped the front hook to her blue lace bra, Mike strolled in. His gaze took a slow sensual journey from head to toe, his eyes growing dark with desire. He watched her wiggle into a pair of jeans and a black turtleneck.

She smiled over her shoulder. "See something you like?"

He came close, biting her neck. "Yeah, but if we don't leave pretty soon, we won't be going for the next few hours. So...do you like your present? Seems to be a perfect fit."

Tess smiled. "What's not to like? I can't believe you actually took me shopping and paid for my entire ensemble of new underwear. You caused quite a stir in the boutique, you know. I think that silicone-enhanced clerk would have loved to model for you."

"Only got eyes for you, darlin'." The buzz of her hair dryer cut off what he was about to say.

Fifteen minutes later, hand in hand, they headed toward the Sea Harbor Inn, nestled deep in the hills of the rocky New England countryside. Tess couldn't wait to meet the couple who had spawned the one and only Mike Andretti.

Chapter Thirty

Passing gleaming white cottages overlooking Mount Desert Island and Frenchman Bay, Tess lost herself in the stunning landscape of sugar maples, pines and maturing red oaks. A drive along the Maine coastline in the fall was breathtaking. Diffused lighting enhanced the rich saturation of the foliage, scarlet, burnt orange and amber, merging into a vista of sheer beauty. A rumble of thunder snapped Tess out of her revelry. With the murky gray sky growing darker by the minute, she was glad when she spotted the sign for the Sea Harbor Inn. Just as the initial clap of thunder rolled, Mike made a left at the crest of the hill.

She turned her head. “How much farther?”

He squeezed her knee. “Sit tight, darlin’. Just up the road a piece; in fact, there she is…my childhood home.”

Pleasantly surprised by the eccentric appeal of the country inn, Tess checked it out. With its stone porch, natural pine and wicker furniture, and century-old evergreens, she thought it the perfect respite for a bed and breakfast.

Reaching across the truck, she placed her hand on Mike’s thigh. “I can’t wait to see where little Mikey grew up.” She rubbed his leg, daring to wander just a bit higher. “So…did you break every girl’s heart from the time you were old enough to dazzle them with your sexy little dimple?”

“You betcha.” He grinned as he grabbed and squeezed her hand. He parked his truck just as another clap of thunder exploded through the sky. "Looks like we got here just in time."

A meandering brook added to the peaceful ambiance of the country inn, along with fruit orchards and a garden gazebo. Undulating pines swooshed in the breeze as the wind kicked up a few notches. Behind the inn, rocky cliffs shrouded the harbor. Seagulls squawked over the clanking of bells and fishing boats bobbed at the dock.

Just as they leaped from the truck, scurrying to beat the storm, the sky opened, drenching them with pellets of rain.

Mike grabbed her hand. "Come on, darlin'. Let's make a run for it."

Damp from the rain they couldn't avoid, they got inside the double oak doors of the inn and stood in the foyer, wiping their feet before setting foot in the quaint Victorian parlor. Cream-colored sofas on clawed wooden legs surrounded a blazing fire in a wood-burning stove. Logs snapped and hissed, permeating the room with the rustic smell of birch. A middle-aged man with salt and pepper hair stood behind a heavy mahogany desk, puffing on a corn cob pipe.

He strutted toward them, a slight limp to his gait. He grinned, displaying a dimple—a carbon copy of Mike's. "Well now..." He grabbed his son in a tight bear hug, slapping him on the back. "Bout time ya' brought a girl home for your mom and me to meet." He beamed at Tess. "She's real pretty, too."

"Dad, I'd like you to meet Tess Kincaid. Tess, darlin', this is my dad, Harry Andretti."

Smiling, Tess extended her hand. "It's a pleasure, Mr. Andretti. Your home is lovely. I can see why it's such a charming bed and breakfast. Very cozy."

"Thanks, we like it just fine. Come on in and sit in front of the fire, get the chill out."

"That's some fire you got going," Tess said, taking in the home where Mike grew up.

Harry sucked on his pipe, taking a short, easy draw before tapping the ashes in a cast-iron ashtray. The room smelled of cherry tobacco, reminding Tess of her dad. The memory tugged at her heart strings. Listening to Mike's dad talk, Tess caught a lot of similar mannerisms.

"Yes, siree, got here in the nick of time. Surf's been high for days, and with this knee all gnarled up with arthritis, no city slicker weatherman needs to tell me a storm was brewin' on the high sea. Can feel it comin' like clockwork. Dampness crawls in the bones and burrows deep. Started back when I was a deep sea fisherman. Brought in some pretty good lobster, but believe you me, ya' don't wanna be out on the ocean when those waters rock the boat. No siree. Now would you just listen to me ramble on and on, another sign old age is settin' in. You're standing there soaked clean to the bone. Take off your jackets and go get comfortable. Your mother is millin' about here somewhere. Been all flushed with excitement ever since ya' called to tell us you were bringing your girlfriend."

"The pleasure's all mine, Mr. Andretti. I'm honored to meet Mike's parents and see where he grew up."

"Call me Harry," Mike's dad winked, a twinkle gleaming in his mischievous brown eyes

"Michael." A pleasantly plump woman in a pink checkered apron strolled toward them, her arms open in a wide embrace. Her smile lit up her entire face. "You're here. This must be your Tess," she cooed, folding Tess in her arms. "I'm Wilma. How nice to meet you. Welcome to our home. Michael, go get some dry sweatshirts from your old room before you two catch your death. Just whipped up some cider from our apple orchard, my dear mother's secret recipe. I sure hope you're hungry. Gotta pot of lobster bisque simmering on the stove, rich with cream and butter. My secret is adding chunks of apple wood bacon, gives it a nice kick."

"Smells heavenly," Tess said, inhaling the fresh herbs and seafood wafting from the kitchen. "This reminds me of my grandma's house. On cold winter days, you'd always find her in the kitchen, stirring chicken soup with a wooden spoon, tasting and adding a little more thyme or celery salt."

"Don't let Wilma here fool ya." Harry winked, nudging Tess with his boney elbow. "The secret ingredient in her soup is a generous dash of sherry, gives it an extra kick." He patted his belly, his red checkered flannel shirt not quite hiding his rolls. "Yes siree. Can't wait to dig into that chowder. Every spoonful's like a taste of heaven. So you go get out of those wet clothes and we'll have ourselves a nice visit."

Tess used one of the guest rooms to change into one of Mike's old sweatshirts. It smelled like him, the lingering scent of musk and aftershave. The guest room, an intimate setting with American antiques and a private bath, was very cozy. Wringing the rain from her sweater, Tess hung it in the bathroom. Anxious to learn more about Mike's family, she hustled back to the parlor.

"Go sit a spell." Wilma placed her hand over the receiver, pointing to her son snoring on the sofa. Her wire-rimmed glasses slid down her nose. "Wake up that boy of mine and tell him he's got bad manners. Help yourself to hot cider and fresh-baked pastries. Go on, don't be shy. I'll join you in a second."

A silver carafe graced a dark paneled sideboard, surrounded by Wedgwood teacups. Petite pink party cakes dowsed with powdered sugar were arranged on a mint green plate.

Tess poured a cup of cider, the spicy smell of

cinnamon and cloves teasing her palate. She inhaled, the steamy mist warming her nose. Gingerly removing one of the pretty confections, she popped it into her mouth.

Mike was sprawled out on the sofa, his snores muffled only by the crackling fire. She was surprised he didn't wake up the dead. Shaking her head, she traced her finger along the doily draped over the back of the settee. She caught Wilma's eye.

"Ah…I was just thinking about the time my grandma tried to teach me how to crochet. She had dainty doilies on all the furniture in her parlor. And just like you, Gram had fruit trees surrounding her home—apples, peaches and pears. I can still taste her homemade pies."

"Mom makes the best pies in Bar Harbor." Mike sat up, joining in the conversation without missing a beat. "Maybe the entire state of Maine."

"That's my aim, honey." Wilma shuffled over, snatching a party cake in her dish-pan hands. "I do so love making folks feel at home. Me and Harry, we work our tails off keeping this place up, but we love it. After Mike and the kids left, we sat around fiddling our thumbs. I was used to cooking big meals and doing for a family of six. We have two boys and two girls, but they're all scattered now and just come home for the holidays. So that's when me and Harry got the notion to open up a bed and breakfast; it keeps us hopping. Makes us old folks feel needed, guests to fuss over. But enough about me. God blessed me with the gift of gab and I could go on and on all day. So where are you from, dear?"

"I've been living in New York for the past twenty years, but I've inherited the Kincaid ancestral home, next door to your son, as a matter of fact. I lived there when I was a little girl, before my parents divorced. Mom and I moved to Manhattan, but every summer, I'd come home. Now that I'm back in the harbor, all the fresh country air should inspire my creative muse, help me start writing again."

"Thought you looked familiar." Harry straightened up, his knee popping. "So where do you get the ideas to write about all those nuts?"

"Ah..." Tess set her teacup on the coffee table, her hand trembling. "Writing about psychopaths and sociopaths used to be fun...until a demented fan began stalking me. Mike and the crime scene unit are investigating and it looks like the man stalking me is an old childhood friend with some sort of vendetta to settle. It seems he murdered my dad."

"Oh, honey," Wilma gasped, clasping her hand over her mouth. "I'm so sorry. You best be careful. Would you like to stay here until Mike catches the criminal? You're more than welcome, isn't she, Harry?"

Harry took a seat beside Tess, his hefty form sinking down low in the cushions. He patted her knee. "You betcha, honey. You just put your trust in my son here, the best sheriff Hancock County's seen in decades. He'll catch the stalker, damn straight he will."

After a delicious dinner, Tess hugged Mike's parents, feeling as if she'd known them forever. "As soon as all of this is settled with Roberto Smith, I'd love to have you both over for dinner. I want to start entertaining in the old manor again, bring some life back into the place, just like the parties Daddy used to host. I'd love you to be my first guests."

"Oh, honey," Wilma said, clasping her hands together, eyes twinkling. "We'd love to, just say when."

"Be careful, Tess," Harry said, stopping to light his pipe. He looked at his son, pride shining in his eyes. "Watch over her now, son. Don't let anything happen to this sweet young thing, hear?"

Chapter Thirty-One

"Gotta go transport a prisoner to court this morning," Mike said, nibbling on Tess's ear. "Hmm. You smell good. You sure won my parents over yesterday. You charmed them, same as you do me."

Tess draped her arms around Mike's neck, drawing him close, her fingers toying with the band of his ponytail. "Your parents are adorable. I enjoyed meeting them and can see a lot of them in you, especially your dad. You inherited his dimple, very sexy. Your mom's a great cook; that lobster bisque was delicious. I'll have to get her recipe. Want more coffee?"

His gaze settled on the coffee perking. "Glad to see you made some." He sniffed the air. "Toasted almond, suits me just fine on such a brisk mornin'. I'll have a cup and then I gotta get downtown. I'll be at the courthouse all morning, then I need to take care of the horses down at the barn."

Tess moved to the counter where the coffee maker spewed, fluffy slippers scuffing on the floor. Hot liquid sloshed as she poured, steam billowing. She handed it to Mike. "I'll join you later this afternoon. I think all this romance has inspired me to write a love scene." She winked, her eyes twinkling.

Mike strutted toward her, the air bristling with electricity. He set his mug down and leaned very close, grazing her lips with his teeth. "I'll be done at the courthouse at noon. Meet me down at the barn at half past for an afternoon delight, darlin'."

****

The phone was ringing just as Tess finished the chapter she was writing. Perfect timing, she mused, a slight thrill shooting through her. Probably Mike wondering where she was. She picked up, her voice throaty. "Ready, honey?"

"Well now, princess," his voice was low and salacious. "So long as you're asking, I'm always ready for you."

Tess slammed the phone down, her heart racing, pulse pounding. Her mind raced. Where was her gun? Then she remembered. In her purse. Was today the day he was coming for her? Her gaze scraped the windows, the surrounding woods in the thicket. He could be anywhere, spying on her.

Grabbing the pistol from her bag, Tess took off to the barn with the sprint of a marathon runner, tripping on slick pine needles. The dank smell of the earth clogged her sinuses. She couldn't breathe and her heart was pumping. Hank yipped and barked, dashing several feet ahead. The stallions in the corral trotted to the edge of the wooden fence to stare, snorting and neighing, their tails flapping. A hoot owl screeched from the woodland pines, the warbling cry echoing through the surrounding forest. By time Tess reached the barn, she had a stitch in her calf from running. Barging through the Dutch doors, she buckled over in pain, dropping her revolver.

"Tess!" Mike ran to her, bending down on his knees. "What's wrong, darlin'? Did you hurt yourself?"

"He called, he called on your phone…he made lurid suggestions. He…"

"Hold on, hold on. Slow down, take a breath. Come on now, start from the beginning."

By time Tess finished, her breathing had slowed to a normal rhythm. She stared into Mike's eyes, searching for answers. "Why is he doing this to me? What did I ever do to him?"

"Shh." Mike traced her lips with his finger. "First of all, settle down. You're safe with me. Roberto Smith's been livin' up in the woods or in your house. This is why I insisted you learn how to handle a gun. I can't be with you every second and knowin' you can defend yourself makes me feel a hell of a lot better. I'll put a call in downtown as soon as we head up to the house. Now as far as his motive, I dunno, but like I said, it's gotta be the money."

"Why?"

"Think about it. Roberto Smith's been in jail for the past decade, doin' hard time. He probably read some of your books and saw your name plastered all over the newspaper. Come on, Tess. You're a best-selling author; anyone can read about you on the Internet, read your reviews and blogs. He probably got to thinkin' about the old days, way back when you were kids and how you'd be together some day. Make sense? He gets sprung from the slammer, no job, no money, and here's his first love, Tess Kincaid, rollin' in the bucks. I can't say for certain what he wants or why he killed your dad, but it would be my guess he wants a cut of the pie. On top of all that, he's a schizophrenic on the loose without his medication. That would explain all his theatrics in the ballroom, his perverse sense of reality."

"I know you're right." Tess rested her head on Mike's shoulder, comforted by the steady beat of his heart. "As long as he's out there stalking the woods, none of us are safe. Roberto Smith is a deranged nut…and a dangerous felon."

"Tess…" He stared into her eyes, tiny lines crinkling the corners. "He's close. I can feel it in my bones. He's ready to make his move. There are unmarked patrol cars circling your estate and mine, and when he comes out in the open, they'll catch him."

Tess's stomach lurched. She walked over to the foal and ran her finger down her nose. The foal snorted and nuzzled her hand. Tess whispered the words so low they were barely audible. "I feel it, too; my senses are screaming to beware. I won't go anywhere without my gun. I know you can't be with me every minute and neither can the police."

She turned to him, her jaw rigid, her lips set in a hard line. "I'm ready. I know how to use a gun and won't think twice about using it if he tries to hurt me, because the things Roberto Smith's been warning me about are no idle threats. He's coming for me." She buried her face against the foal's ear, drawing comfort from her sweetness. "Aren't you pretty, Angel. You feel like silk."

"Tess," Mike said, pulling her toward his chest, whispering comforting words. "I know, darlin'. Shh…I know."

A bluesy instrumental of "Someone To Watch Over Me" played softly on the radio, the jazzy deliverance slow and easy. The sweet lilt of piano keys drifted through the air, counterpointing with the brassy sound of the trombone. A gentle breeze blew in from the open door, stirring the scent of hay, horses and clover with the heady smell of roses. The warbling wail of the sax vibrated, echoing the primal beat of Tess's heart.

Staring into her eyes, Mike drew her into his arms, expertly twirling her in a semi-circle before pulling her close for a tight embrace. Seduced by the music, they moved as one, gliding across the floor in a slow, sensual rhythm. Mike hummed the lyrics in Tess's ear, his bristly whiskers scratching her cheek. The smell of the barn clung to his skin—horses, hay and man. Tess inhaled, getting closer, feeling the beat of his heart. The song moved her and she sang the words.

Mike hummed along, the duet becoming a game of seduction, a mating ritual. He pulled her closer, his lips gently brushing hers. With a sharp intake of breath, Mike's grip around Tess's waist tightened, his muscles bunched and quivered. He yanked her against his chest, his mouth swooping down on hers, his teeth grazing her lips, hungry, demanding. He ran his hands through her hair, coiling his fingers through her long tresses, burying his head in it.

His erotic kisses made her tremble and quake, just on the verge of eruption. Her blood tingled from his kisses, every sensation, every pulse, charged with the electrical current that bolted through her from his touch. He ignited a flame in her. Her breath came out in a ragged sigh, the need to be his sweeping through her with a wildness she'd never known. She was so close she could feel him, hard and rigid and ready for her. She responded to his kisses, making his groans more primal, blatantly sexual.

Their hips swayed together in a sensual rhythm, rocking back and forth on the slippery edge of no return. Two silhouettes moving as one, their lips fused in a spontaneous kiss.

"You are so beautiful, darlin'," he whispered in her ear. "I want you." The breeze rippled through her hair, fanning it out in wild disarray. His hands tightened on her hips, pulling her closer still. "Do you have any idea how much I want you?"

She did. From the moment they'd met, she'd wanted him. Every pulse in her body throbbed, every nerve ending twitched. She wanted him with every beat of her heart. She stared into his eyes and met his gaze. "I do. I want you, too."

As the music softly played, Mike gently pushed Tess into a stall where fresh hay had been strewn. Reaching up on the ledge for a blanket, he spread it over the hay, cradling her head as he slid her down.

Chapter Thirty-Two

Toying with a strand of Tess's hair, Mike watched her sleep, her long eyelashes draping over her cheeks like fans. He loved her and wanted to be with her always. The thought of Roberto Smith laying a hand on his woman had his nerve endings snapping. It made him restless, wild, and just a little dangerous. She brought out the warrior in him, the need to protect and possess surging through his blood. She was so beautiful she stole his breath. From the first moment he'd looked into her bewitching green eyes, he'd been possessed. If anything were to happen to her, he couldn't live with himself.

His love for her would never be sated, the need to be close to her filling him with a desire he'd never known. She was the woman for him, the woman of his dreams, but nothing could blossom from their budding romance until Roberto Smith was caught. If he had to search every corner of the global world, he'd find him.

Low whimpers erupted from Jezebel's foal, cries of distress. Jezebel stomped her feet, shook her head, flared her nostrils and snorted, her huge eyes pleading as they met his. Hurriedly, he grabbed his jeans, climbed into them and scurried to the stall.

The foal was hunched in the corner, whimpering in pain. He'd seen this before, after the birth of a foal. Either she wasn't getting enough milk from her dam or she'd picked up an infection. She needed immediate attention—or she might die.

Tess stirred, sat up and stretched. “Mike? What is it? What’s wrong with the horses?”

“Angel’s in distress. I’m gonna have to call the vet for her. I’ll sit with her until he comes. Could you do me a favor, darlin’? I forgot my cell phone. Could you jog up to the house and give the vet a call? The number’s in the book by the phone. This could take a while. The animals need to be fed, and if you want, there’s some chicken if you feel like makin’ some dinner. As soon as I know Angel’s gonna be all right, I’ll head on up.”

“Of course,” Tess said, hoisting her hips to scoot into her jeans. With her hair all mussed and her lips swollen from his kisses, she never looked sexier as she strolled over to the stall. “It’s all right Jez. Your baby’s gonna be just fine. Mike will take good care of both of you. He’s real good at that.” She stood on her tip toes and kissed Mike’s lips. “I’ll go call the vet. Don’t worry about a thing.”

Mike watched her leave, his heart swelling with love for her. He waited until she reached the door. Night had fallen, and a storm was brewing. A bolt of lightning illuminated her hair, picking up shades of red, brown and burnished copper. His voice caught in his throat. “Tess.”

She turned around and smiled at him, her jade green eyes pools of liquid emerald. “What is it, honey?”

“Be careful. Stick close to Hank and be ready to draw your gun any second, just in case. You’ll be all right. If Roberto Smith was out there, the horses would be carryin’ on. Just be careful, don’t let your guard down for a second and you’ll be all right.” He walked across the barn and kissed her once more. “Once you’re inside, double bolt the door until I get there. I love ya, darlin’.”

****

“Good boy, Hank,” Tess yelled, pitching a twig to

the Irish setter as they jogged up to the house, crunching through the foliage. A loud clap of thunder rumbled across the horizon, warning of the coming storm. A bolt of lightning surged through the darkness, splintering black skies into forks of brilliant white light. Tess was filled with a peace and tranquility she'd never known. Watching Mike communicate with his horses touched her, struck her in a way words could never describe. She'd never spent much time around animals, with the exception of Freddy, but through Mike's eyes, a whole new world had opened up to her. She smiled, thinking of Sir Galahad. True to Mike's words, she'd finally found a bird she liked.

Tess inhaled the heady scent of roses as she passed the arbor. A drop of rain plopped on her head, and then several more. She'd reached the house just in time.

A rustling in the leaves interrupted the quiet. Tess felt a hard probing behind her knee that nearly knocked her down. Hank yipped and panted, scraping his big paw on the door. "All right, boy. Let's go see about supper. I know you're anxious. Hold your horses."

Tess set her pistol on the coffee table, thinking of Mike. She'd fallen hard for him and couldn't imagine life without him. Watching him take care of Angel showed what a wonderful and caring father he'd make one day. A smile teased her lips as she placed the call to the vet. The idea of a family pleased her.

Choosing some vintage jazz from Mike's huge collection, she put on several CDs, humming along as she sauteed vegetables for a stir fry. She thought about Angel, her heart going out to the foal, hoping she'd be all right. She was such a darling horse, so soft and sweet, the loving way she nuzzled. The vet said he was on his way and would be there soon. But until he arrived, Tess knew Mike would take good care of the equine family.

The green onions and peppers sizzled in the grease. She flipped them with the wooden spatula, reliving her afternoon delight down at the stable. Although she'd written love scenes taking place in a hay loft, she'd never had the pleasure of the real thing. Until now.

Sighing, she grilled the chicken to a crisp golden brown, the mixture of meats and vegetables making her stomach growl. Once the chicken had cooked, she turned off the heat. Totally content, she blended everything together, adding some wine and teriyaki sauce. Tasting it, she closed her eyes, licking her lips.

Julio and Walter rubbed her legs, meowing for their dinner. Hank lay at his dish, one paw crossed over the other, his big brown eyes following her every move, his tongue hanging out. From his cage, Sir Galahad squawked, "Bad boy, Mike."

Tess doled out the food, each pet having his own designated bowl. She shook some bird feed into Galahad's dish, noticing Freddy hadn't come when she'd called. She wished Mike had taught her his whistling technique. Just one more thing to add to the list.

Scanning the parlor, she called out, "Here, Freddy. Time to eat. Supper's ready."

Sir Galahad peered at her through his birdcage.

Just then, Tess caught sight of her cat outside the window, his green eyes glowing in the dark.

The little sneak, how had he slipped past me?

She could have sworn she'd seen him before, but then again, maybe it was Julio. They were both black and fast as lightning, given half a chance. She hoped Freddy cooperated. He had a mind of his own, and judging from his defiant stare, this was going to be one of those times resulting in a battle of wits.

Sighing, she opened the door a crack. “Come on in, Freddy. Time to come in and eat. Let’s go. Now, Freddy. I don’t have all day.”

The little demon came toward the open door, just close enough for Tess to grab him. Then, purring loudly, his ears slicked back, he dared her to take him on. Darting backward, he gave chase, his plump body amazingly agile.

“Dammit, Freddy. I’m in no mood for a game of cat and mouse. Come here this instant.”

With a gleam in his eye, the black cat came to the door, but just as Tess went to grab him, he backed off and got away. Tess pounced, but not quickly enough. The front door slammed shut behind her. The cat streaked past her into the foliage and into the night. “Freddy! Here boy, come back here!”

Tess heard footsteps stomping through the slick leaves. Relief stormed through her. Mike. He could whistle and Fred would come running.

Pellets of hard rain beat on her head and body, drenching her to the bone. With no jacket, shivers rattled her insides, raking her bones. Mike’s footsteps got closer. She spun on her heels, her eyes searching. “Mike, thank God. Freddy got away. Call him back, do that thing with your mouth, that whistle.”

“I’ll be glad to do things with my mouth, princess,” a gruff voice spoke from the darkness. “After all, I’m your biggest fan.”

“Bobby!” Tess’s heart jackhammered in her chest. Her feet froze, unable to move. She couldn’t think. She couldn’t see him. The sky had turned pitch black in a matter of seconds. Needles of rain beat down on her head. Her voice rang out just as a roar of thunder rolled across the sky. “Bobby? What do you want?”

His laughter chilled her to the bone. “Come on, Contessa. Figure it out. You write spine pricklers. I want you, princess. I've come to take you home, home to our medieval castle. You remember, princess, where we promised to live happily-ever-after."

"You're crazy." Tess backed up, slipping on the slick grass.

If only she could outsmart him and sneak back to the house, lock herself in where she'd be safe until she called for help. Her heart sank. Her gun was inside. She was out in the woods with a madman, unarmed. Her heart slammed against her chest. Panic surged through her. She was all alone with a schizophrenic killer. Beads of sweat trickled down her back. The wind swooshed through the pines, rustling leaves in all directions. The trudging of footsteps got closer, branches snapping and breaking. Dark laughter erupted from deep in his throat.

"You can run, princess, but you can't hide. Remember how I used to chase you when we were kids, down by the ocean. You could never get away from me. Don't you remember, Contessa? I promised I'd come back for you some day—and what do you know? It's your lucky day. I've come to take you home."

Tess tore through the thick underbrush, totally disoriented as she zig-zagged through the oaks and pines, acorns crunching in her wake. A quarter moon cast willowy shadows on the floor of the forest, huge branches swishing and swaying. The rain came down in sheets, stinging in her eyes, leaving her hair a saturated mop. Thunder exploded in the sky like cannon balls, shaking the entire forest. Her heart galloped a wild rhythm. Bobby Smith was crazy, nutty as a loon.

"I'm coming for you, princess." His warbling laughter rolled through the woods, his thundering footsteps wild as the storm raging through the night.

The faster she ran, the closer he got, his cackling causing every nerve in her body to twitch beneath her skin. He was coming for her, just like he promised.

"Don't be scared, Contessa. Think of it as a game of Hide and Seek."

Tess's legs pumped, her heart pounded. Her breathing was labored, her lungs on fire. She couldn't see through the foggy mist of rain, but she kept running, blocking out the hailstones needling her face, the blood thundering in her ears, the wild beat of her heart. She just kept right on running, muscles and tendons screaming, slipping and sliding in the sodden earth. She scrambled, trying to get her bearings. She had no idea where she was or which direction she was heading. Fog crept low over the underbrush. He'd kill her, just the way he'd killed her father. She prayed out loud. "Help me, Daddy; help me, God!"

""I'm close, princess. I see you, my pretty. Don't you remember how good my night vision is?" His chilling laughter rolled through the forest. "When I get you, I'll pounce on you like the big bad wolf. Ready or not, here I come."

Tess ran for all she was worth, adrenaline surging through her veins like wildfire. Hysteria pushing her to the edge of sanity, she tore through the forest, the pounding rain whipping her face. Her feet skidded in the slimy grass, thorny vines slashing out like bladed swords. The rotted smell of decay seeped from the underbrush, the dank air filling her senses. If she only could see, get her bearings. Then she spotted it, in the distance, the lighthouse in the harbor, standing out like a beacon in the fog-misted night. She was nearly in her courtyard. As her feet pounded familiar ground, she heard the waves cresting and falling, crashing over the rocks as they rolled into shore. She glanced over her shoulder. If she could just get to her house before the madman, she could get in and bolt the doors. She felt the pocket of her jeans, relief storming through her when she found her key.

"I'm coming, princess." His dark laughter echoed through the forest. "I see you, my pretty. The big bad wolf is close on your heels."

Tess raced until her legs cramped, tripping over a gnarled stump, going down on one knee, gaining her footing with the agility of an athlete. Her drenched jeans stuck to her skin, heavy and uncomfortable, sloshing in the mud. Saturated denim slapped together. Her running shoes squeaked on wet grass, laces untied, coated with grime.

The guiding light in the harbor lit the way. She was in her yard, just a few more feet. Tess reached her side door, jamming the key into the lock. Just as she was about to shove her way through, she looked up. A streak of lightning illuminated the sky, casting an eerie glow on the bell tower. In that split second, she caught a glimpse of him, shrouded in light. Roberto Smith waved at her, red hair and beard blowing wild in the wind. And then the sky turned black as the surrounding forest. Heart pumping, pulse racing, she shoved through the heavy mahogany door and bolted it, slumping to the floor. She was safe.

Chapter Thirty-Three

Tess sat on the marble floor of her foyer, her back against the wall, hugging her knees, shrouded in complete darkness. Her breathing was raspy and shallow. She gulped in air, willing wind back in her lungs. She was afraid to move for fear he'd be outside the window, peering in. The drapes were wide open, giving the madman full view. But he couldn't see if she didn't turn on any lights.

Heart thumping, she crawled to the phone, the closest a few feet away...on the mahogany end table. Her rain-saturated jeans dragged heavy on the wooden floors, puddling water as she snaked her way to the table. Reaching for the receiver, she brought it to her ear, heart in her throat. Hope sank. The line was dead. Either from the electrical storm raging through the sky...or because the wires had been cut.

But at least she was out of the clutches of Roberto Smith...for the moment. But for how long? Adrenaline pumped through her system, sweat dripping from every pore, mixing with her soaked skin and clothes.

Entombed in darkness, she acclimated herself to her surroundings. The Westminster clock ticked from the mantel, and outside, angry winds swooshed through the mighty pines, sheets of rain beating on the windows. A massive clap of thunder roared across the sky, followed by a streak of lightning, illuminating the night.

Sniffing the air, chills raced down her spine. The

lingering smell of butter wafted through the house. Then it hit her, a niggle of fear skittering along her backbone. Roberto Smith had been popping popcorn in the home theater…recently.

Then her world went even darker as reality struck. She'd been so busy locking him out, she'd forgotten he had access into the manor. Mike and the police had never figured out how he was getting in…but he was. Bobby Smith…no, Roberto Smith knew how to get in. She was what she'd promised herself she would never be. A sitting duck.

Her flesh prickled, as if millions of microscopic organisms were crawling on every inch of her body. Where was the hidden panel and why hadn't her dad ever discovered it? She tried to think of a place to hide, because like it or not, she had fallen into the spider's web. Roberto Smith had her right where he wanted her…under his thumb. Blood thundered in her ears. Was he in her house now, hiding, waiting to pounce?

Her mind raced, adrenaline gushing. She had to think, come up with a way to protect herself from the clutches of the madman. There had to be somewhere in this huge estate where she would be safe. And then it hit her: upstairs in the loft, a secret passageway behind the wall of butterfly masks. Her dad had shown it to her when she was a little girl, a sanctuary where she would be safe from the boogie man. And that's just what she'd do, hide from the big bad wolf until Mike came to her rescue.

Creeping up the stairway, silhouetted in shadows, she crept up the steps, her back against the wall. She sucked in her breath, not daring to breathe. Her heart pumped. She reached the landing, crawling on all fours to the loft. A floorboard creaked. The lighthouse in the harbor cast a glow in the window, painting willowy shadows on the wall.

When she got to the collection of face masks, she stopped and listened, straining for any sign of his presence. Satisfied she was alone, she eased up. With a trembling hand, she reached beneath the center face mask, an emerald butterfly with star-studded wings, and depressed a microchip; a secret panel parted with a slight hiss. Just as she was about to cross the threshold, the bell in the tower gonged, its piercing peels echoing the wild beat of her heart.

Entering the sanctuary, she walked straight into a spider web. Spitting and spewing, she swiped at the woven veil with her hands, flicking off the tangle enmeshing her face. She shuddered, imagining a hairy wolf spider crawling on her skin. She closed the door, the air thick and stuffy from too little ventilation. She coughed, her eyes watering from the dust, mildew and mold. The vault hummed with the deafening sound of silence. She wondered how long it would be before Bobby Smith came looking for her.

Then she heard footsteps, so quiet she thought she'd imagined them, but when she heard them again, closer, more pronounced, she bit her lip and prayed. Creak. He was in the house, on the landing. Then they stopped, started up again. Creak. He'd just entered the loft.

"Come out, come out wherever you are, princess." His laughter ricocheted off the vault. "Ready or not, here I come."

The door parted with a slight hiss and Bobby Smith stood there, holding a fresh bouquet of forget-me-nots. He grinned at her, his long red hair unruly, scruffy beard disguising the face of the man she knew as a boy. His front tooth was missing. He tossed back his head and howled. "Hello, princess. I've come for you."

Tess bolted past him, her heart pounding, but

his massive forearm coiled around her waist like a cobra, yanking her to his rock hard chest. He whispered in her ear. “Not so fast, my pretty. Is that any way to treat your beloved, the man you swore to love forever and ever? Give us a kiss.”

“Let me go, Bobby, please.” She closed her eyes, wincing as his hot breath fanned her ear, her neck. It smelled of stale tobacco, whiskey, and popcorn. Her back was wedged into his chest. She tried to think of all the self defense courses she’d taken, all the crime books she’d written, all the advice she’d given when she worked as a volunteer at the rape center. Her mind went blank. All she could focus on was the death grip he had on her, the sweet smell of the forget-me-nots from beneath her nose, the wild beat of her heart, and the unmistakable feel of the erection probing through his jeans.

“Cat got your tongue, princess?” He nuzzled her neck. “I’ve thought about you every day for the past twenty years, planned our happy little reunion down to the last detail. But when I get you back here in our medieval castle, the place where we swore we’d be together for all eternity, I find you’re no longer the princess I placed on such a high pedestal.”

“What are you talking about, Bobby? You’re not making any sense.”

His hot breath hissed in her ear. “No one calls me Bobby these days. I’m Thor, The Master, and that’s how you’ll address me. I’m the master director of the theater. Haven’t you heard of me, read my reviews? People come from near and far to see one of my thrillers on stage. Even the winged beasts hoot and whistle for an encore. Where do you think the theatrics came from for the greatest show on earth, your final performance? Allow me to clue you in, princess. I am Thor, king of Lightning and Thunder. Oh how grand, what we have planned. With a thrust of my hand, Lightning and Thunder will crash and collide into a brilliant show of lights. I've even popped fresh popcorn for the show. How's that for entertainment, Contessa?"

Tess couldn't believe what she was hearing. He was even more deranged than she had feared. His mind had completely snapped. A streak of lightning flashed. From the corner of her eye, she caught a glimpse of a gun on the desk. She tried to think, tried to wiggle away from him, from his erection. She had to do something, say something. She licked her parched lips. "Ah...Bobby..."

"Thor!" He yanked her closer, his body hot, wet and sweaty. "Call me Thor."

"Thor, listen to me. We were just kids, twelve-year-old kids. We never made any promises, you know we didn't."

"Sure we did, princess." His rough hand caressed her breast. "When we were kids, playing in the bell tower, and I came charging up those steep steps to rescue you, my damsel in distress. You wrapped your arms around my neck so tight and promised to never let go. Remember, princess?"

From the parlor, the Westminster chimes played. Tess tried to break free. She chose her words very carefully. One wrong move and he'd throttle her with his bare hands. "Ah...of course I remember, Bobby...Thor. But we were just kids, playing kids' games. All the girls took turns being the damsel, and that last summer when you said your family was moving to Florida, we said goodbye, remember? We didn't keep in touch. We were only twelve-years-old."

"Lying slut! You kissed me. You gave me a silver earring, a symbol of lasting love. I told you I'd come back for you some day. I loved you then and I love you now. Tell me you love me, and not that sheriff with the blonde ponytail, the guy you had sex with down in the stable, down at the old Wexler estate...tell me," he roared, shaking her.

Tess's face lost all color. Her skin was clammy, sweat drenching her skin. She gasped. "You saw me? You were spying on us?"

"Damn straight." He tugged a handful of her hair, so hard it whipped her head back. "I've been watching you and the White Knight for a long time, Contessa. Couldn't you feel my eyes on you, watching your every move? It was supposed to be us, you and me, Lord and Lady of the manor. I planned our sentimental reunion from behind bars, when I had nothing to do but think of you and dream of the old days. That's when I decided I was gonna fix it so you'd come back from New York to live here in your castle. Why do you think I got rid of your old man?" His cackling splintered the silence. "So you'd come home. I knew dear old Daddy left the estate to you in his will. I had to get him out of the way so we could be together, just you and me."

"You killed Daddy all because of some childhood fantasy?" She elbowed him hard in the chest, hurled the back of her heel into his balls.

"You bitch!" he roared, rolling in a heap on the floor, smashing the forget-me-nots. "You'll pay for this, Contessa."

Chapter Thirty-Four

Tess tore down the steps, past the second landing, whipping around the bend, heart pounding. The tip of her toe kicked a caged bell, a toy of Freddy's. It skidded across the hardwood floor, smacking into the wooden claw leg of the sofa. Hearing the madman's footsteps, she raced for the door. Just as she had her hand on the brass handle, palms slick with sweat, his steely arms snaked around her, jabbing the nose of the gun into her ribcage.

"Gotcha!" His laughter rang through the corridor.

"Bobby," she pleaded. "Please let me go."

"Thor!" His breath was hot in her ear. "Bobby's dead. Call me Thor. Don't make me tell you again, princess." The nose of the gun jarred deeper into her. He released the safety, the loud click ricocheting off the walls.

Heart in her throat, blood thundering in her ears, Tess was vaguely aware of a cool, damp breeze whistling through the corridor. The pouring rain seemed to be coming from inside of the manor. Then she caught it, the faint scent of burning candles…and reality dawned. No, not again. Perspiration seeped from her, drenching her skin. Even before he said it, she knew. The final scene had been staged in the ballroom. It was the grand finale. Tonight was the night Roberto Smith would kill her in the closing act.

"Let's go, Contessa." He turned her toward the

ballroom, nudging the gun between her ribs with jarring force. "The stage is all set for our wedding."

Tess gasped, her breath catching in her throat. Adrenaline surged through her, every pulse jumping. Their wedding? No, this could not be happening. The corridor was pitch dark, the haunting lyrics of "Moonlight Sonata" barely audible over the raging storm. A streak of lightning flashed through the stained glass window, casting an eerie glow on her dad's portraits, followed by a booming crash of thunder that exploded, shaking the walls. His unblinking stare locked with hers in that split second.

They got closer to the ballroom, music louder, the floating of piano keys crawling into her skin. The storm raged on, thunder and lightning crashing and colliding, willowy shadows painted on the wall. And then they reached the arched doorway to the massive hall. Tess's heart skipped a beat.

A female wax gargoyle stood at the entryway, long blonde hair billowing in the breeze. Her glass eyes shimmered with madness, an eerie smile on her bloodless lips. She was dressed in a flowing black gown, pleated bodice swooshing as the wind rippled through it from open terrace doors. In her hands was a bouquet of dead forget-me-nots.

Standing candelabras had been lit, flames flickering like medieval torches. The air carried their scent. Vases of dead forget-me-nots sat on the bar, surrounding a bucket of champagne on ice. Standing before the open terrace doors, a male wax gargoyle was costumed in a flowing black cloak and white collar, his smile so sinister Tess felt faint.

But what she saw on the walls left her stunned speechless. Photo after photo, old fashioned Polaroids of her were everywhere. At the awards ceremony the night she won the RITA, snapshots of her in a bra and thong, one of her leaning over the dresser. Her cheeks turned a bright crimson. There were even pictures of her and Mike making love in front of the fireplace in the parlor. She gaped at him. "How?"

"Princess in a centerfold," he sneered. "Snap, snap, princess. Took them with Daddy's old fashioned Polaroid camera, the one I found in his closet. Still had film in it with several rolls and bulbs to spare. You're very photogenic, might I add. Had myself some real arousing fantasies when I took those."

Tess couldn't believe what she was seeing. It was like some porn shop…with her as the star.

"How do you like it, Princess?" he whispered in her ear, gun pressing into her back. "It's your black wedding. Befitting, don't you agree? A black wedding for a black heart. Now get dressed in your costume, the one I personally picked the night I slept between your pink satin sheets." Dark manic laughter echoed through the grand ballroom. He turned her, whispered in her ear. "See, right there on the last bar stool."

Drenched to the bone, jeans heavy with mud and rain, Tess turned. She caught a glimpse of her reflection in the bar mirror, her green eyes wide with shock, hair sopping wet and stuck to her head, T-shirt clinging, nipples erect. Then she heard wretched sobs so loud she wanted to cover her ears to shut out the pitiful keening. Only when she saw her mouth stretched into a grimace—open so wide she could see clear back to her tonsils—did she realize the cries were spewing from her very soul.

"Get dressed, princess." He shoved her toward her wedding costume, her black lace teddy with petite rosebuds embroidered just where her nipples fit. Lying across the wicker high-back chair were her black thigh high silk stockings and a lace garter belt. To complete the ensemble, her black stiletto heels were upright beneath the chair.

"Tick tock goes the clock. Go on, Contessa, time's a wasting." Roberto Smith clucked his tongue. "To show you what a gentleman I am, I'll even turn around while you dress. You have three minutes. Strip down, the clock's ticking."

Tears streaming from her eyes, Tess shimmied out of her jeans, tugging the saturated denim down her legs. Hurriedly, she pulled the T-shirt over her head and then fumbled to remove the rest of her clothing.

Her hands trembled as she stepped into her black teddy, the one she'd intended to wear for Mike. She bit her lip, fresh tears pooling. Mike. It should be Mike she was dressing for, their wedding, a beautiful white wedding complete with family and roses.

"Thirty seconds, Contessa…or I'll blow your brains out all over the wall with your dad's Magnum…just the way I did to dear old dad."

Sitting on the bar stool, Tess slipped on her stockings, slid the garter belt up her leg and stepped into her heels. If only she could get the gun away from him, distract him somehow. In spite of what she once thought about using a gun, she had no doubt she could kill Bobby Smith without blinking an eye.

"Very nice, princess."

Snap, snap. He took her picture, then handed her the dead forget-me-nots. "Now let's go. The minister's waiting and we don't want to prolong our honeymoon any longer than necessary."

"Honeymoon?" A massive explosion of thunder crashed outdoors, the loud boom echoing the wild beat of her heart. No, she couldn't…wouldn't think about that.

****

Tess and Bobby stood before the gargoyle, its

waxy body in full masquerade as a minister. To Tess's horror, the words coming out of Bobby's mouth next were other worldly, a voice she had never heard him use.

"Dearly beloved," he rasped. "We are gathered this evening to wed these two in Holy Matrimony. Do you Thor, take this woman, Contessa, to be your wife, promising to love her until death?"

"I do."

"And do you, Contessa," he rasped. "Take Thor to be your husband, promising to love and honor him until death?"

Bobby pressed the gun to her temple. "Answer the minister, princess."

Closing her eyes, visualizing Mike, desperately hoping to save the words 'I do' for him, she whispered the words, "Yes."

"I now pronounce you, man and wife," he rasped. "You may kiss your bride."

Bobby grabbed Tess in his arms, brushing her lips with a chaste kiss. He whispered in her ear, his tone salacious. "We'll go consummate our wedding now where it all began, up in the bell tower. Afterward, because of your betrayal, all your lies, the way you cheated on me with the White Knight, I'll chop your head off in the guillotine. Let's go, princess. The final scene's all been written. When you're dead and gone, given I'll be your lawfully wedded husband, I'll inherit all dear old daddy's millions."

Tess's mind snapped, rage boiling in her. Not caring if he killed her, she slammed the pointed toe of her stiletto shoe into his balls and ran for her life.

"You bitch," he screeched, rolling to the floor in a heap, gun skidding on the cherry wood floor, the impact causing a bullet to fire. Gunfire exploded just as a loud clap of thunder roared through the sky. "I'll hurt you, make you pay..."

Tess kicked off her heels, grabbed the Magnum and ran for her life, huffing and puffing, legs pumping. She flew past the spooky gargoyle, out the door and down the corridor.

****

Tess skidded down the corridor in her stockings, desperate to escape the clutches of the madman. Her hands tightly gripped her dad's gun. She fled, her breathing ragged, but she kept right on running. She reached the door and flung it open, barging straight into Will Gentry, the very dead Will Gentry, his eerie blue eyes staring at her, cold as stone.

"Aaaahhhhh!" she screamed as his corpse fell with a thud. Trembling, every nerve jumping out of her skin, she fled, sheets of rain slapping her face. Lightning crashed and shattered the dark of night into the light of day; thunder roared across the sky. The waves rolled into shore, crashing over the rugged rocks with a mighty roar. Then she saw it, the ball of fire on the hill of the bell tower, the burning bush. Blinking, she looked again, expecting it to be gone. But there it was, a fiery ball of crimson and yellow, soaring flames lighting the night.

Somewhere in the cobwebs of her mind, it dawned on her there was no smoke singeing the air, no sizzling as the woodlands went up in flames, and no smell of fire. How could fire burn so bright in the pouring rain? It didn't make sense, but she kept running, no destination. Something was all wrong. Then she heard footsteps, hot on her heels. She turned, raised her gun, prepared to shoot.

"Got ya!" He yanked the gun out of her grasp, jabbed it into her ribcage, clutching the dead forget-me-nots in the other hand. Then he thrust her over his shoulders like a sack of potatoes. "Time to take you to the guillotine, princess, punishment for your betrayal."

"Nooooo!" she wailed. "Please, let me go, Bobby.

I'm begging you, let me go. I'll give you money, anything, the help you need, just let me go!!"

The ends of her soaked hair slapped her face. Pellets of cold, hard rain needled her body. Blood rushed to her head, being upside down made her dizzy. She visualized Will Gentry's face all those years ago, carting her across the courtyard to safety. And now he was dead.

He must have been coming to her rescue. Tears streamed from her eyes. She said a prayer for Will Gentry, the boy stuck inside a man's body. He'd been misjudged all his life and now he was dead. Bobby had killed him, shot him in the back of the head. And now he was going to kill her, just like he'd killed Daddy.

She thought of Mike, the short time they'd shared. She loved him and would never see him again, the gentle horse whisperer who she loved with all her heart.

Slick with rain, the staircase carved into the hill was treacherous. Bobby charged up the one hundred steep steps to the tower, his chilling laughter rolling through the forest.

"Bobby!" Tess closed her eyes, not wanting to look down. A boom of thunder shattered the sky, more rain clouds opened, sending hailstones crashing to earth. She felt like she was on one of those upside-down rides at a carnival. She was sick, her stomach churned. Pine branches swayed in the breeze, the bristly needles smacking her face.

She opened her eyes as they passed the burning bush, the ball of flame. It was staged, nothing but an illusion. Then she remembered something else as they got closer to the tower. She'd once told Bobby her biggest fear was that the woods would catch fire and burn her castle to the ground. He must have remembered that, wanting to scare her, making her as crazy as he was.

She opened her eyes and craned her neck just as they reached the top of the hill. A streak of lightning illuminated the bell tower, casting an eerie glow. There he was, hunched beneath the eaves, his beady black eyes boring into hers. The peregrine falcon, its sharp talons curled over the edge. With a flap of wings, it took flight into the thicket, its shrill cry foreboding. With no warning, the massive bell began rocking back and forth, its piercing gongs deafening.

Chapter Thirty-Five

Mike shielded his head in his arms as he jogged through the raging storm. Angel was going to be just fine, after some antibiotics to kill off the parasite she'd picked up. Tired as he was, his heart picked up a beat, thinking of Tess waiting for him in his house. His footsteps sped up, although he was careful not to slip on the slick grass.

Mud puddles dipped deep in the ground, rain smacking into the slimy pools. With each flash of lightning, he managed to dart between them. Rain slashed his face, piercing needles prickling his skin. Thunder boomed across the sky. He couldn't wait to get inside, shower and get into some dry clothes. The thought of Tess cooking dinner for him warmed the cockles of his heart.

Emotions lodged in Mike's chest, recalling the look of wonder and awe in her bewitching green eyes when the foal had nuzzled her ear. Her reaction had moved him, struck him. His animals were an important part of his life, his family, and if a woman couldn't accept his pet menagerie, she wasn't the right woman for him. But Tess had taken to his critters, and they'd taken to her, too. Even Sir Galahad, who usually was shy until he got to know a person, squawked and babbled in her presence.

As Mike trudged through the saturated earth, the hair on the back of his hair prickled. Something was wrong. Hank was barking, howling, working himself up into a full blown frenzy. Why wasn't Tess stopping him? Hank would never behave that way unless he was trying to get his attention. Mike knew the Irish setter was trying to tell him something. Breaking into a full run, his drenched ponytail whipping him in the face, he charged through the storm.

By time he reached the front door, every nerve ending buzzed with adrenaline. Hank was hurling himself at the door, desperate to get out, his sharp barking slicing through the night. Freddy scampered through the slippery leaves, sopping wet, meowing to go in. Tess would never let her precious cat out of her sight, out in the woods where he was unfamiliar, where a killer stalked. He jabbed his key into the door.

Hank pounced on him, licking his face, crying, yipping, before bolting through the open door like a streak of lightning into the night. The cats circled his legs, rubbing, meowing. Sir Galahad squawked from his cage, "Bad boy, Mike. Wipe your feet."

Mike spotted Tess's handgun on the table and his heart skipped a beat. He sped through the house, the smell of chicken, onions and peppers drifting from the kitchen. "Tess! Where are ya, Tess?"

He reached the kitchen, his boots skidding on the tiles as he fumbled for the switch. His pupils adjusted as the room illuminated in brightness. No sign of Tess, but she'd been cooking. He raced to the stove, shoved the lid aside, touched the stir fry. It was still warm. From the stereo, a warbling tune drifted, teasing and taunting, crawling under his skin. He spun on his heels, his hip hitting the edge of the lid on the granite counter, knocking it to the floor with a hollow clank.

His heart thundering, he took off through the house at a dead run, his mind racing. She was gone. Tess was gone. Every sensation was alert, every nerve wired tight as a garrotte. He nearly jumped out of his skin when the phone rang.

"Tess?" he barked into the receiver.

"Mike, this is Detective Jones. Listen very carefully. Under no circumstances let Tess out of your sight, not even for a second. Roberto Smith was spotted near your house earlier today. After a chase through the forest, he vanished into thin air."

"She's gone," Mike roared into the phone. "He has her; Smith's got her."

"I'm on my way," the detective said, "Stay put. I'll call for backup and we'll head up to the Kincaid estate. Stay where you are, Mike. This guy is extremely dangerous when not medicated."

Mike slammed the receiver on the cradle, raced for his Glock. Like hell he'd stay put. He could jog across the land to Tess's long before the cops arrived. Besides, Hank had torn off in that direction, obviously hot on her trail.

****

"Here we are, princess." Bobby flung her off his shoulder once inside the tower. "Home sweet home."

"Bobby, please," Tess begged, her mind racing, her eyes focused on the Magnum in his hand, the one pointed straight at her head. His muscular body was drenched. With jerky movements, he dropped the dead forget-me-nots to the floor, his long red hair slapping against his head as he stomped on the flowers, his unfocused eyes wild.

"Thor's the name. Don't make me tell you what happens to women who disobey their husbands." His bellowing voice boomed through the tower. "I wanted to plant gardens of forget-me-nots for you, because they were your favorite flower. I used to pick them for you in the meadows, tell you they were as pretty as your smile. Remember what you said to me, princess? Think back. I wanna hear you say it, just the way you used to when you looked into my eyes with such love. Say it!"

Tess licked her dry lips. She was cold, her flesh

prickled with goose bumps. She couldn't remember what she'd said twenty years ago.

"Tell me, Contessa. Look into my eyes and tell me, just the way you used to when you were the princess I placed so high on a pedestal. Tell me you love me and want to marry me."

Tess wondered how such a sweet kid had become so twisted, so delusional. She'd never promised him any such thing. At best, they were friends for three months, when they were twelve. When he left at the end of the summer, she'd forgotten all about him. Giving Bobby the silver hoop earring had meant nothing to her, certainly not a sign of fidelity or lasting love. It was all in his head, his very twisted mind. If he'd been taking his medication, none of this would be happening.

The rain pounded on the bell tower, waves crashed over the rugged rocks in the reef. In the distance, she heard the horses in Mike's corral whinny and neigh. A tear slid from her eye. How she longed to be safely tucked away in Mike's house. Her lip quivered. Would she ever see Mike again?

"I'm waiting, princess," he screamed, his raspy voice carrying in the wind. The gnarled branches of the red oaks reached upward, as if in prayer. Pine branches swooshed in the storm, swaying, undulating. The falcon cried from deep in the thicket, sending icy chills skittering up and down her spine.

"Tell me." He took a step closer. "Look into my eyes and tell me the words you used to say."

Tess whimpered, her back against the wall. Goose bumps broke out on her flesh, her very exposed flesh. She felt so vulnerable in her wedding *costume*...and so damn cold. She shivered, her teeth chattering. If she could stall him, keep him talking. She stared into his eyes. "I told you I'd carry a bouquet of forget-me-nots at our wedding."

"That's right, princess. Look what's become of your wedding bouquet. Dead as doornails, all black like your soul. But guess what, princess?"

"Bo…Thor, please. Let's talk about this. Why don't you tell me how you planned this reunion from prison? That was pretty clever of you. Tell me how you did all these things. You had us all fooled, pulling all these tricks with your theatrics. I remember how fascinated you were with Daddy's theater, his gargoyles, his music. You said you wanted to major in theater, behind the scenes with lights, camera and action."

"That's right, princess." He grinned, puffing out his chest. "I had it all figured out. Damn clever of me pulling one over on the cops, your white knight lover, none other than the sheriff himself. But especially you, princess, the best-selling author of thrillers. I got a few ideas from you, truth be told. I read every single one of your books when I did time. Thinking of you and planning our reunion kept me sane."

Tess cringed, her gaze fixed on his missing front tooth. All those years in prison had made him hard core. She wondered what had happened in his life to make it all go so wrong. He'd been a nice kid twenty years ago, and now he was over the deep end. She offered him a faint smile. "Thanks, Thor. I just love talking to my fans."

"I'm your biggest fan," he preened, taking a step closer. His brown eyes were hugely dilated. "No one believed me when I told them you and me were gonna be married when I got sprung from the slammer. Damn inmates kicked the crap out of me, knocked out my front tooth. They laughed in my face, spit on me, said I was crazy. But I told them, let them know how we were gonna live happily ever after in our medieval castle, just you and me, Lord and Lady of the manor. And you wanna know something funny, a real ball breaker?"

Tess thought she heard Hank in the distance, barking. Could help be on the way? Her heart pounded, hope soared. Mike was coming. If she could just keep Bobby talking about himself, she'd be all right. But he had that magnum, and his hands were trembling. He'd killed her dad and Will Gentry. Would he kill her, too?

"They made me go on meds down at the prison, said I was delusional when I told them my name was Thor. Not only did I read all your books, princess, but I read everything about the ancient theater when Thor reigned as master of the stage. We had so damn much in common; it finally hit me. I was The Master, Thor, reincarnated. They wouldn't believe me, none of them. They put me on anti-psychotics. If that doesn't beat all, huh, princess?"

All the pieces clicked. She cleared her throat, adrenaline pumping as Hank's yips got closer. In the distance, she heard a siren squealing over the roar of the ocean. They were coming, help was on the way.

"So I quit taking the damn pills once I was released from prison, just kept the sample pack, the one I put in your purse when I stole your cell phone. How'd you like that one, Contessa, the old switch-a-roo."

"That was ingenious. How did you manage to get into the mansion? How did you discover the hidden panel?"

"Ah…shoot, ma'am." He took a bow. "That was easy and leads me to the best part of my performance tonight. I have been living in your house ever since I got released from prison, hitched a ride straight from the Broward County jail. Flipped the parole officer the bird and never looked back. I knew they couldn't track me down, I'm too smart."

Bobby puffed his chest just a bit more as Tess nervously listened for more signs of help. "With your old man being drunk all the time, he never locked the doors. So one night I slipped in and blew his brains out, made it look like suicide. With his unsavory track record of being the old cripple turned drunk, no one doubted he blew his brains to kingdom come. After that I lived here, eating his food, drinking the aged wine from his private collection, smoking cigars from his humidor. Do you have any idea how much money your old man left lying around the manor, cash in every room, all twenty-four of them. That's how I arrived at your New York condo, used your old man's money, his ID, and no one was the wiser."

He cleared his throat and continued. "But I'm getting off track. You want to know how I got in and out of your mansion when all the doors were locked up. Tsk tsk, princess, the things you find out on a person's computer. Dear old Daddy had a very detailed map of the entire mansion on his desktop, highlighting all the hidden panels and the secret tunnel. That's right, princess. There's a trap door in the pantry floor that opens up to a freight elevator. And guess where that leads? To an underground tunnel leading straight to the bell tower. That's how I've been spying on you, Contessa. From up here in the tower or the woods, using dear old Daddy's night-vision binoculars."

Tess's skin prickled. She had to play her hand very carefully. One wrong move and it was all over. Hank's barks were close now and the sirens were louder. She had to keep Bobby talking, keep him preoccupied. "What do you mean, Thor? Show me the trap door up here. I'm curious and very impressed; you pulled a fast one on all the cops. Show me."

Bobby grinned, displaying the gaping hole where he'd lost his front tooth. His unruly red hair blew wild in the wind. "Say the magic password, the one that granted us the key to the castle."

"Pretty please."

"Permission granted, princess." He shoved her out of the way, stomping to the east wall of the tower. "Can't see it in the dark, but there's a pine knob in the oak paneling shaped like a cowboy boot. Right about here." He pressed it and the wall opened to a steep staircase. "See, there she is, big as day."

Tess couldn't believe her eyes. There was a trap door leading to an underground tunnel and straight to the pantry in the mansion. She stared in disbelief.

"How do you like that, princess?" His eyes darted from her to the door, pointing the muzzle of the gun to the steep steps. "That tunnel leads straight to the butler's pantry. So I've been appearing and disappearing like the Great Houdini, performing the greatest show on earth."

Tess remembered all those creaks in the floorboards, creaks she'd written off to the age of the estate, and all the while, it had been Bobby, prowling around her house.

"If you coulda seen your face the day I snatched your cookies from you, princess. You were such a natural you could have won an Academy award. Then the night I stuck my mug in your window, my face all disguised in Daddy's ski mask, you were so scared you pulled the curtains down right on top of yourself, pretty little princess tangled up in blue. But the best show was when I deposited the corpse of the falcon on your stoop. You looked so sexy jiggling around, doing the Hokey Pokey, got myself a hell of a boner, let me tell you."

Tess went ice cold. He'd been watching her, getting aroused? Her skin crawled.

"Well now, princess." He ran the tip of his gun over her breasts, using his other hand to press the door closed. "Speaking of a boner, it's about time we consummate our wedding vows, don't you think, princess?"

She turned, leaned out the open window of the bell tower and screamed at the top of her lungs. "Help me!"

Bobby cackled like a wild hyena. "Nobody can hear you over the raging storm, princess." He shot his hands upward and screamed. "Let there be fire for the greatest show on earth."

Right on cue, thunder and lightning raged through the sky, fierce warriors slashing swords, crashing and colliding in a magnificent show of lights. The Master reigned. The elements of earth, wind and fire were in all their glory.

Bobby took a sweeping bow. "Ladies and gentlemen! Welcome to closing night. Beheaded in the guillotine."

Tess stared in disbelief as he once more shoved her aside and opened the trap door. It had been so dark when he'd opened the door the first time, she'd missed it. He stooped down and snatched up a big tub of popcorn, popped fresh from her home theater. Her mouth fell open when she watched him pitch the popcorn out the open window, bucket and all. Then he turned to her. "Take your clothes off, princess. It's time."

"Ah…there is something I'd like to know first, Thor. It's about the fire on the hillside out there." She gestured with her chin to where the burning bush lit up the entire mountain. "Where'd you get it, tell me how it works."

He howled, his dark laughter chilling her to the bone. "The things you can purchase over the Internet. I did a search for a blazing fire lamp, and wouldn't ya' just know it, princess? Found one on eBay. I bought it from your old man's computer, even used his charge card. Then I had it delivered here and hid it in the tunnel, set it up for your eyes only at the midnight hour, when I knew you were sure to see it from where you worked up there in the loft. Go on, princess. Take a gander. Gotta a bird's eye from up here, right into your loft. I watched you, saw the great Contessa Kincaid, hard at work on her next thriller, up close and personal. Doesn't that beat all?"

"So tell me how the burning bush works, Thor?" Tess asked, hearing Hank barking, his yips close. "Explain it to me...please."

"Sure, princess, I'll grant you your last wish. It's called a blazing flame lamp, uses two high intensity quartz halogen tinted bulbs, has an embedded fan and silk fabrics to create the illusion of flames when the fan blows them upward. Dude on eBay said they look so real, no one can tell they're fake unless they're real close. Said he uses them at his barbecues, a real crowd pleaser. It sure had you going, didn't it, princess? All I had to do to put out the fire was click a freakin' switch. Then when the fire department got there, poof...no fire on the mountainside, no burning bush, no ball of flame rolling down the hill. They thought you were plum nuts. Gotta tell ya', it was a hell of a show from up here in the watch tower."

"Why did you do it?"

"On account of what you told me years ago, princess. You said your biggest fear was the mountainside catching fire and burning down your castle. Oops, time's up. Strip."

Chapter Thirty-Six

The minute Mike reached the Kincaid property, he spotted it, a flaming ball of fire on the hillside of the bell tower. Even through the pouring rain, the burning bush lit up the entire mountainside. Guilt overwhelmed him, thinking how he'd doubted Tess when she'd reported it. He reached for his cell phone. He needed to call the fire department, tell the guys down at the hall to get to the Kincaid manor before the whole forest went up like wildfire.

But something was wrong. The closer he got, the stranger it seemed. There was no sizzling of flames, no smoke curling upward in billowy clouds, no movement. Why? That's when he heard them, blood-curdling screams that pierced his heart. It was Tess, his sweet Tess. The sounds were coming from the tower. Hank was already halfway up the steep cement steps—yipping, barking, snarling.

Mike took off running, his gun cocked, ready to fire. Roberto Smith had her up there. His heart jackhammered, rivaling the booming claps of thunder. Hailstones pounded his head, angry winds furiously blowing through the sea. Waves slammed against the rocks. Just then, a streak of lightning illuminated the night, splintering the sky into forks of brilliant white light. Thunder exploded like cannonballs a split second before more lightning crackled across the sky.

Tess had her head out the window, her eyes wide with shock. She spotted him, hysterical screams erupting from her mouth. Her eyes locked into his—begging, pleading. He couldn't see Smith, but he had to be behind her, doing God knew what. Adrenaline and testosterone surged through his veins, pushing him to the brink of madness, urging him to move.

Drenched with rain and perspiration, he was hot on the heels of his Irish setter. The dog was on the attack, fiercely determined, on a mission, growling and snarling. Mike flew through the door just as Hank leaped on Roberto Smith and sunk his canines into his shoulder, his jaw clamping down on him.

In one fluid move, Smith spun around, flinging the dog off, the barrel of his gun aimed at the setter. Mike raised his Glock and squeezed out a bullet. Gunfire exploded from two guns, their bullets crossing, ricocheting through the tower. Hank winced, blood saturating his fur as he slumped over in a heap. Mike's bullet struck Roberto Smith in the chest. Dark blood bloomed on his white T-shirt, spurting out in thick blobs.

Stunned and shocked, he staggered backward, never losing his grip on the Magnum. He grabbed Tess around the waist, yanked her against his chest and pointed the gun to her temple. His breath ragged, his eyes unfocused, he slurred his words. "Put your gun down, Sheriff, or I'll blow your lover's brains out, just like I did her old man's."

Mike's heart hammered, his nerve endings jumping. From the corner of his eye, he spotted Detective Jones and two policemen sneaking in, weapons drawn. He had to proceed with caution, one wrong move and it would be all over for Tess. He wouldn't look at her, couldn't look into her frightened green eyes. If he did, he'd lose it, blow it, and her death would be on his conscience, something he couldn't live with.

"Drop it, lover boy." Roberto Smith fingered the trigger, his hand badly shaking. "Do it."

With the moves of a warrior, Hank bolted upright, lunged in the air, knocking Roberto Smith's gun out of his hand. It hit the tower floor with a resounding thud. Roberto pounced on it, shoving Tess out of the way, blood gushing from his wound as he retrieved it and pointed it at Tess.

Mike didn't hesitate. He shot Smith in the head, the sound of his bullet deafening. Roberto Smith fell back, sprawled out and bleeding from the gaping wound in his forehead, his lifeless eyes staring upward.

The police rushed in, followed by the paramedics. Hank's breathing was shallow, ragged, but his eyes were alert.

"Are you all right, darlin'?" Mike ran to Tess, his hands touching her face, her hair, her shoulders. "Did he hurt ya'?"

"I was never so scared." Tess wrapped her arms around his neck and placed her head on his shoulder. "He made me dress in this teddy and stockings...made me marry him in the grand ballroom where he..."

"Hush now, darlin'," Mike whispered soothing words. "We'll worry about that later. We'll get you warmed up." He turned to the paramedics.

A woman handed her a blanket. "Here, honey."

Tess allowed them to cover her. Then she kissed Mike and fell to her knees where the paramedics examined the setter. "Thanks, Hank," she said, tears streaming down her face. She leaned over, stroking the fur on the top of his head. Her eyes were wide with fear. "He's gonna be all right, isn't he?"

"He's a trooper," the paramedic said, his gloved hand moving over the dog's body. "Just a superficial wound. The bullet barely grazed him. I've stopped the bleeding, but we're gonna wanna take him to the vet, get him checked out."

Mike knelt down. "Good boy, Hank. Hear that?

You're gonna be just fine. And you're a hero."

Detective Jones stepped forward. "We could use ten Irish setters like him on the force."

Tess watched them place Bobby Smith in a body bag and zip it. It was over; the stalker was dead. Now she could put it all behind her and focus on her life with Mike. She bit her lip, realizing how close she'd come to losing it all. A few more seconds and…

"We'll need a full statement from you when you're up to it, Ms. Kincaid," the detective said. "Could you come down to the station first thing in the morning?"

"Yeah." Tess nodded, suddenly so exhausted she could hardly think, but the image of Will Gentry's corpse flashed through her mind. "Ah…there's something else. Will Gentry is dead; his corpse is in the courtyard. I'm sure Roberto Smith killed him."

"My men found him. Do you have any idea what he was doing on your property?"

"I think he was trying to warn me, help me. He must have seen Bobby chasing me through the woods and wanted to help. I've misjudged Will Gentry. I thought he was creepy, dangerous even, and here all along, he was every bit as harmless as Mike believed he was."

Tess watched the paramedics place the dog on a stretcher, slowly making their way down the rain-slick steps. The strings around her heart tightened. She'd be eternally grateful and knew she had a buddy for life. "Be careful with him. He's one of my two leading heroes."

Tess and Mike stayed behind; the only sound was the rain that had finally tapered off to a drizzle. Words weren't necessary as she nested deeper into the warm embrace of Mike's arms. She clung to him, taking in his scent, the feel of his unshaven face scratching her forehead. This was all she wanted, all she needed in this world. After a moment of silence,

Mike broke the quiet.

"Ready to go home, darlin'?"

Tess liked the sound of that. Her sand castle on the sea was no longer where her heart was. Her home was with Mike, at his ranch, with him and the pets.

"I'm ready," she said, turning off the switch on the wall. The blazing lantern went dark. She looked into Mike's eyes. "It was all an illusion, all something to make me go out of my mind. Bobby staged it so it would look like the hillside was on fire from afar, and then before anyone else could see it, he'd disconnect it and store it in the trap door. He was sick, mentally disturbed."

"We don't have to get into any of that now, Tess. You're exhausted and need to get into some warm clothes. And before ya' go getting' yourself all riled up, Freddy's snug as a bug in the rug, found him waitin' by the door."

"The little demon." Tess shook her head, too tired to think how her beloved feline's cat and mouse prank had turned into a deadly game of the big bad wolf. Right now, she just wanted to be with Mike and their family of pets.

"I was thinking," she said, as they slowly descended the slick steps. "There is no way I want to live here, too many bad memories. I haven't even cleared out Daddy's room yet, but I will."

"All in good time, darlin'," Mike said, as they reached the bottom. "Whenever you're feelin' up to it."

"I have an idea." Her gaze scanned the courtyard. The image of Will Gentry's corpse would be forever burned in her brain. She looked at her blue garden where her forget-me-nots had been dug up. Her stomach went into knots, remembering. She sighed. "This place will never be my sand castle on the sea again, far from it. But with all the land so beautifully manicured, all the clipping, pruning and planting, an idea is blossoming in my head."

"Oh yeah? What's that, darlin'?"

"I think I'd like to turn this estate into a Western-style bed and breakfast, a tribute to Daddy. It might be nice if I showed the old films Daddy starred in. It would take some work, but not all that much, really. I'd hire a full staff—someone to operate the theater, a souvenir shop, cooks, maids, etc. What do you think?"

"I think your dad would like that. It would make him real proud. I can't blame ya' for not wantin' to live here with all of the bad memories. It's over now, and we have our future to plan…together."

"It's funny." Tess stopped as they walked through the forest, the chickadees starting to chirp as the sun came up to greet the day. "I think of your house as home, being tucked in all safe and sound with you and the animals. I've become real attached to them…and to you, too, Mike Andretti."

"Oh, yeah? Tell me about it, darlin'. We have the rest of our lives."

****

The sun was coming up as Mike and Tess walked through the door. The cats slinked around their ankles and from his cage, Sir Galahad squawked. Tess sighed. "It's good to be home."

She stared into Mike's warm eyes. "I never thought I'd see you or our animals again. We've got a lot to be thankful for, don't we?"

Mike kissed her. "We sure do, darlin'. Now go on upstairs and get into some warm clothes. I'll make some hot tea and get a fire started. Go on before you catch cold."

Tess kissed him before turning. "You sound like your mother, but that's okay. It's sound advice and I'll take it."

Before starting the fire, Mike turned on the

radio. Static screeched, causing Sir Galahad to squawk. Just as Mike was about to hurl a birch log into the hearth, the news stopped him cold.

"Breaking news, fire and rescue squads are on the scene of a four-alarm fire at the Sea Harbor Inn at the foot of Cadillac Mountain. The bed and breakfast appears to be completely destroyed. The fire was started when a propane heater was knocked over in one of the rooms."

"Oh my God!" Tess flew down the steps. "That's your parents' bed and breakfast. Let's go."

Epilogue

Tess kneeled at her father's grave, planting forget-me-nots at the base of his headstone. The warm summer breeze stirred through the surrounding pines, mingling the sweet scent of honeysuckle and clover. In the distance, the sawing hiss of a lawn mower harmonized with the serenity of Tess's heart.

She stood up and stretched, her back aching, her belly swollen with child. A slight coating of perspiration beaded her forehead. She swiped at it with the back of her hand, then reached down for her bottled water. Taking a hearty gulp, she turned around. Her husband stood at the crest of the grassy hill, his sheriff's badge shimmering, his gun tucked in its holster. Their eyes locked for a second before he strutted toward her, causing the pulse in the hollow of her throat to flutter. His golden brown eyes gleamed in the late morning sun, his streaked blonde ponytail swaying in the breeze. When he reached her, he rubbed her back, his fingers massaging little circles on her shoulders.

"That feels like heaven," she purred, closing her eyes as pleasure soared through her body. "Never stop. Did I ever tell you the reason I married you is because of your magic fingers?"

"I love working my magic on you, darlin'," he said, his warm breath fanning her neck. "But as pretty as those flowers are, all fresh and lovely, you look a little tired. Feel okay?"

"Just a bit overheated." She brushed the freshly

dug soil from her hands and turned to face him. Reaching up on tiptoes, she planted a kiss on his lips. “I brought some extra forget-me-nots. I wanna plant them at Will Gentry’s grave.”

Mike picked up the flowers and gardening tools. “That’s a real nice idea, darlin’, but I’ll dig. My son is not gonna be born in a cemetery.”

Tess took Mike’s hand and placed it on her belly. “Feel that? He’s kicking in there, just letting us know he’s ready to come out and meet his parents. But it won’t be for another month or so. Are you glad it’s a boy? Or deep down were you hoping for a little girl, someone to spoil?”

“Come on now, darlin’. How can you ask me such a question? It doesn’t matter to me, either way. I’ll love any child we have.”

“Here we are.” Tess gestured to a gravestone where weeds and tall blades of grass grew wild. “Doesn’t look like Will’s uncle’s been out to see him, does it? I’ve been thinking of something, and I’d like to run it by you.”

“What’s that darlin’?”

“We’ve been kicking names back and forth like a football, and if we don’t settle on one pretty soon, our son’s gonna be called ‘Hey, you’.”

Mike’s hand went to her belly again. “We’ll settle on one, sooner or later.”

“When I was planting this morning, it came to me. How about Jake William? We could even call him JW.”

“Jake William.” Mike tipped his sheriff’s hat to the sky. “After your dad and Will Gentry. I like it. Jake William Andretti has a nice ring to it, and so does JW.”

“Good, cause I’m already kind of attached to it. I was talking to him when I was planting flowers at Daddy’s grave. It seemed so natural, calling him little Jake. But JW has a unique ring to it, something all his own. If only Daddy were here to meet his first grandson, his namesake."

Misty-eyed, Tess gazed up at her seaside estate. Then she smiled. "The bed & breakfast has really taken off, hasn't it? It still takes some getting used to, calling it The Rodeo Bed & Breakfast. The memorial to Jake Kincaid is quite a hit, and with your parents running it, knowing the ins and outs of the business so well, it's bound to be a smashing success. Isn't it funny how things work out? Your parents lose their bed & breakfast just when I'm looking for good help with mine. God really does work in mysterious ways. Your parents are such naturals at the business. I think the biggest attraction is the theater, with the old projector. Guests love watching Jake Kincaid in his glory days. And that popcorn vendor still cranks out the best buttered popcorn on the Maine coastline. It brings back some real nice memories of the way things used to be."

"Turning your estate into a bed & breakfast and memorial was a great idea, darlin', and the joy it brings my parents is a Godsend."

The sweet scent of grass and freshly dug earth filled the air, a pungent reminder of the circle of life.

"Ready to head back?" Mike took her hand in his as they walked. "I'm hungry. How about I make us some lunch before I go back on duty?"

Tess patted her belly. "What's a few more calories?"

They walked along in silence, quietly observing the hillsides dotted with grapes in the vineyards. Vivid shades of crimson, amber and purple peppered the rural setting. In the distance, their house sat on a hill surrounded by hayfields, horses and forests rich in birds and wildlife.

"Oh, look." Tess grabbed Mike's arm, pressing her finger to her lip. "Shh. Over there," she whispered.

Twin fawns trampled through a meadow of creamy white pom poms. Scarlet and salmon wild flowers peppered the hillside, the spicy orange fragrance as sweet as the baby deer, trotting alongside their mother, totally unconcerned with anything but the trails of nature.

"One of life's simple pleasures," Mike said, as the family of white tail deer stopped to feed on some blueberries. A cardinal flew overhead, flapping its wings as it soared into the glossy green thicket.

As they got closer to their house, Tess stopped. "Let's go over to The Rodeo B&B for a minute. I wanna make a wish in the fountain."

****

"Well hello." Wilma walked toward them, beaming. "Just in time for some freshly squeezed lemonade and chocolate chip cookies, oven fresh."

"Hi, Mom." Mike kissed her. "How's business?"

"Business is booming, honey. But first I wanna hear all about my little grandson." Wilma patted Tess's belly. "How is he, dear?"

Tess glowed. "Kicking like a trooper. A glass of lemonade would go down real easy, but first, I'd like to take a look around."

"We'll sit on the veranda where it's nice and cool."

Tess waved to Harry, clad in his chef's hat as he grilled burgers in the courtyard. Guests sat around beneath umbrella tables, sipping mint tea and lemonade. The melodious sound of laughter echoed above the crashing waves as kids rode the mechanical bucking bronco.

Tess smiled as she walked into the house, the buttery smell of popcorn filling her senses. From the home theater, an explosion of gunfire erupted, the zing of bullets ricocheting off the cavernous walls. Tess scurried down the corridor, tears filling her eyes when she saw the full house. Guests filled several rows, eyes glued to the screen, munching on popcorn and sipping cherry cokes. Tess touched her belly. "That's your granddaddy, an icon in his day."

Just then, Jake Kincaid turned full face, his penetrating brown eyes searing into Tess's. His indomitable presence filled the entire theater. The baby kicked. Emotions got the best of Tess. "Oh, Daddy."

As Tess walked through, it pleased her that every bedroom carried out a theme of one of Jake Kincaid's movies. She knew it would please her dad to know folks were in his den, now The Outlaw Saloon, drinking and shooting the breeze. The living room served as a souvenir shop on one end and a Victorian parlor on the other, a gathering place for guests to sit before a roaring fire.

A young couple stopped to read the menu Wilma had written on a chalkboard in front of the dining room. The luncheon special was lobster pasta salad.

Standing in the entrance to the grand ballroom, Tess stared, emotions swirling. Tonight was the masquerade, reminiscent of the ones her dad used to host. The hardwood floor gleamed as the sun poured in through open terrace doors. The crystal chandelier sparkled from the mirrored ceiling, and in front of the polished mahogany bar, the wax gargoyles were costumed and ready to carry on with the tradition that had made the parties legendary. Tess swore she could hear her dad's robust laughter echo across the ballroom.

A tear slid from Tess's eye as she walked to the fountain where the bell tower used to stand. A huge horse head was at the top of the gushing waterfall.

The blue shadows from the distant woods tinted the water with a hazy shade of cobalt, her dad's favorite color. Emotions wedged in her throat as she reached into her pocket, retrieving a shiny new penny. Rubbing it between her finger and thumb, she made a wish and turned around, pitching the copper penny over her right shoulder.

Tess gazed up at the azure blue sky where billowy white clouds aimlessly drifted.

"To the Elysian Fields," she said in barely more than a whisper. "An abode to the blessed after death."

****

Hand in hand with Mike as they entered their yard, Tess took in the beauty of nature. With a gentle flutter of wings, a butterfly floated past, landing in the rose arbor to feed on nectar. From the corral, the stallions snorted and neighed, trotting along with their heads held high, their tails gently flapping in the breeze. The fresh smell of hay and clover mingled with the perfume of the roses and wildflowers. Hank tore down the hill—yipping and grinning his doggy grin.

"Easy there, big guy," Mike said, patting the dog's head. "No jumping." Tess bent down and picked up a birch chip, pitching it. He dashed off, panting and barking, eager for some play time.

The cats circled their feet, competing for attention.

"I guess it's lunchtime." Tess opened the door. "Come on, let's go eat."

"Pretty girl, Tess," Sir Galahad whistled from his cage.

Tess walked ahead of her family of pets, feeling like the Pied Piper as they followed her to the kitchen. Turning around, she embraced life to the fullest. She had everything she could ever want, right here in this house. It was where her heart was. Tess was finally home.

A word about the author...

Sharon Donovan lives in Pittsburgh, Pennsylvania with her family. Prior to the loss of her vision, she was a legal secretary for the Court of Common Pleas, where she prepared cases for judges in Domestic Relations. Painting was her passion. When she could no longer paint, she began attending creative writing classes and memoir workshops. After a long and winding road, a new dream arose. Today, instead of painting her pictures on canvas, Sharon paints her pictures with words.

Sharon writes stories of inspiration and suspense. She has certificates in business and medical transcription and is a published author with The Wild Rose Press, White Rose Publishing, Whimsical Publications and Chicken Soup for the Soul. *Echo of a Raven* is a Recommended Read from the reviewers of Coffee Time Romance, and *The Claddagh Ring* is a CAPA nominee.

To read excerpts and reviews of Sharon's books and to sign up for her newsletter, visit her website: www.sharonadonovan.com.

She loves to hear from readers!

Breinigsville, PA USA
25 September 2010
246079BV00005B/9/P

9 781601 548139